A SPY AT EVENING

'An exceptionally promising debut from a
writer who knows how to make your hands
tense and your spine shiver . . . Taut
writing, interesting characters, and lots of James
Bond-style fights and action make this a winner'
Annabel

'Good on action and character, with a nicely
drawn Russian agent who uses the cover
name Pushkin.' *Times Literary Supplement*

'A readable, believable, rich book written with
understanding of people and love for places.'
Eastern Daily Press

A Spy at Evening

Donald James

CORONET BOOKS
Hodder and Stoughton

Copyright © Donald James 1977

First published in Great Britain 1977
by William Collins Sons & Co Ltd

Coronet edition 1980
Reprinted 1980

British Library C.I.P.

James, Donald
    A spy at evening.
    I. Title
    823'.9'1F   PR6060.A453S/

    ISBN 0 340 25390 8

Printed and bound in Great Britain for
Hodder and Stoughton Paperbacks, a
division of Hodder and Stoughton Ltd.,
Mill Road, Dunton Green, Sevenoaks,
Kent (Editorial Office: 47 Bedford
Square, London, WC1 3DP) by
©ollins, Glasgow

Chapter 1

The old stones wept water. It trickled between the cobbles and splashed into steep gutters. When the wind rose rain blasted ancient archways and drove through the thin arrow slits. It was a hell of a day to visit the Tower of London.

Within the cobbled courtyards small groups of tourists clung together for protection against the hostile elements and hurried through a thousand years of English history with the stony-faced indifference much of it deserved. Proofed against the streaming rain the guides retailed their daily quota of recorded history and improbable myth. As the sky darkened most of the tourists looked as though the whole show might better have been reconstructed somewhere under cover in Des Moines or Haute Terre, Indiana.

I affected interest in the Traitors' Gate, read the inscription at the base of the Byward Tower, listened to the tugs on the river and registered that my man was ten minutes late. If, of course, they really intended him to come. When the still fashionable melancholia lifts Russians tend towards a lusty, primitive sense of humour. As the chill penetrated my top-coat I began to wonder if I wasn't the current butt.

In any other circumstances I would have given up long before this – but it was not every day that Russian Military Intelligence asked us for a meeting. Waiting under the cover of Traitors' Gate I decided to give it another ten minutes before phoning no-go to Mansfield, but the thought of his reaction made me in no hurry to put through the call.

The rain appeared to be letting up a little now and the yellow tinge in the sky seemed to have shifted off over Shadwell and points east. I had thrown away my second damp Gauloise and was searching in my pockets for a two-pence piece to call Mansfield when the crunch of gravel behind me made me turn. The two men were Russians by any standard of dress, or at least the taller one was. The short man with him might have been German, or Dutch, somewhere half-way to sartorial salvation.

They stood.

'The whole panoply of English history.' I waved my arm

5

around until the rain trickled down my sleeve.

The shorter man smiled amiably.

'Mr Hart?'

I nodded.

'You will tell us your authority,' the taller, more lugubrious character put in.

'Pushkin,' I told him.

'For our purpose,' the short man said, 'I am Pushkin.'

'And your friend?'

'Tchaikovsky.'

A gifted pair.

'English history,' Pushkin continued, 'has long interested me.'

Tchaikovsky seemed impatient.

'You were very lucky I think with your monarchs,' Pushkin went on. 'Other countries passed through the feudal period with less sense of national identity.'

It seemed a reasonable enough remark. I began to like the affable Mr Pushkin.

'I didn't know there was a great deal of interest in English history in the Soviet Union, Mr Pushkin.' I used the name self-consciously.

'But indeed. Do you know the work of Kosminsky?'

I shook my head.

'Vlerdaev?'

'I'm afraid not.'

He was about to lighten my darkness when he was interrupted by a deep-throated Russian mutter from Tchaikovsky.

'I am reminded by my friend that we have a task.' He smiled apologetically. 'It is to give you this.'

I took the large buff envelope he produced from under his coat.

'Royal Hotel, Mr Hart, Paddington. A call will reach us.' He began to turn away.

'Just a moment.' I struggled to extend the interview.

Tchaikovsky sniffed hard but Pushkin silenced him with a minute movement of the hand. He had a round, open face, friendly, but tough as nails.

'Is there any message,' I asked, 'to accompany this?'

He looked at the envelope and smiled gently.

'No,' he said. 'I think, unfortunately, it is self-explanatory.'

'You speak English well,' I told him.

'And our data bank tells me that your Russian is syntactically faultless, though accented.' He patted his pocket as if my file

6

were kept in there. 'I'm happy to have had the opportunity to meet you, Mr Hart. Our records indicate that our paths have very nearly crossed on a number of occasions in the past.'

He put out a square hand and shook mine. Hard.

I released my hand and waved it in the direction of Tchaikovsky, but he showed no inclination to be civil.

'In Kiev, Mr Hart,' Pushkin said as he turned away, 'I have two children who would love to see your Tower. They are very much interested in your history.'

I smiled goodbye and watched his broad back as they strolled across the cobbles and through the archway. I had shot at Russian backs like that. Some I had hit. I wondered if they too had had children in Kiev or Minsk interested in English history. Well, there were parts of it that would never be told.

Chapter 2

I walked back to the office to give myself a little thinking time. I suppose I should have taken some sort of evasive action but, as far as you can ever tell, I seemed clear enough of any sort of tail. In any case I guessed that the sub-offices at Wardrobe Place and the Art Ceramics cover were well enough known to the GRU. Maybe not. Contrary to popular belief our main fault is that we usually over-estimate the opposition.

I don't think I saw the accident. I heard the sharp burn of tyres on the greasy road surface, the thin clatter of a crashing car and I sensed rather than saw the wild movement of a last desperate attempt to control the skid. When I really looked it seemed incredible that all that glass could come from one windscreen, that the crumple of vicious tin had once been a marvel of maroon cellulose finish. It seemed incredible that a man should be on the point of death.

I watched the black bundle grunt his life out on to the wet kerbstone, then turned off Ludgate Hill before the crowd gathered. The other car was already out of sight.

I had been part of so much deliberate killing I was shocked at the effect an accident could have upon me. My legs trembled and involuntarily added an unsteadying inch or two to my stride. I felt sick. It did no good to tell myself I should have felt different. Death, like sex, has that capacity to hurl surprises from a totally familiar framework.

I took it slowly that last few hundred yards to the section office, stopping at the bomb site to light myself a cigarette and push my mind into thinking about Mansfield. My dislike of Mansfield was so pervasive an emotion that I had even used it on occasion to obliterate hunger. Today it conveniently drowned the memory of the dying man on Ludgate Hill.

I had long thought that the only genuine medieval barons left in this tradition-loving land were the giftless amateurs of the Intelligence services. The senior department officers like Mansfield – a big red-necked naval hero with more guts than sense who played the game to schoolboy rules. And, damn him, seemed to get a fair amount of success.

But I had to believe that part was luck. Six tours out had left me with nothing but puzzled contempt for the George Mansfields of the Service. At one time I'd hoped to be the first who was going to do something about it. But the money spent, the good and bad men dead, the bizarre or downright looney basis of the reasoning behind the waste, these were all for someone else to worry about. Since the first day in June I had been fighting for my offical life.

It had been altogether a bad year: strikes, lockouts, recessions, political unrest in most of the major Western countries, bombings, vigilante movements, crop failures, bankruptcies, redundancies . . . and among them, *me*.

Three months ago, on a soft early summer morning, I had got the call I was waiting for to go up to control centre in Northumberland Avenue to see Mansfield. He himself had just made deputy director level, and as he had been my mentor and Svengali since I joined the Service fifteen years ago I was looking forward to promotion to my next assignment. Like a child I never guessed it might have been the bullet.

He'd been polite and friendly, that I give him. He'd gestured to the most comfortable armchair, accepted with a smile of pride and pleasure my compliments on his new enlarged office and offered me scotch and water. He'd then sat down behind his leather-topped desk and slowly read over to me my fifteen-year record with the Service.

We covered Vienna, Berlin, Turkey, my stint in the Far East and my year in the United States (oh yes, we do it there too – in a friendly way). True enough, that last year in New York and Chicago hadn't been my most successful and the Service had had to pull me out of a little trouble, but as a field-agent I'd had a record second to none in every single one of my other appointments.

I'd stood in response to his gesture of invitation to refill my glass as he concluded his review. It looked good – so that when he said those words – when he said 'We're going to have to let you go, Tom' – I just stared at him dumbly. My eyes filled with water and I stood there, a thirty-eight-year-old man, glass slopping whisky across the tops of his decanters and my lower lip quivering like a two-year-old's.

'You're spilling your drink.' Mansfield nodded at my sagging right hand, then went on briskly, 'I've got you a special payment from the termination fund . . . of course you'll have your pension, and I'll see what I can find you in the way of the odd courier job from time to time.'

I blinked hard, took a pull at the whisky and mastered the trembling of my lower lip. But it still took all I had to get the one-word question out. 'Why?' I waved the glass in my hand and again spilt whisky across the drinks table, 'Why?'

Mansfield frowned.

'You know why, Tom,' he said. 'The world's changed. The sort of field-men we needed in the sixties don't have a rôle any longer. We have to put a chain on the blood-and-thunder boys.'

'All right,' my voice rose. 'All right, put a chain on me. And attach it to a desk.'

'You're not a desk man, Tom.'

'Are you? You came in from the outside; bring me in too.'

He stood up shaking his head judiciously – or what passed as judiciously. 'No,' he said slowly, 'I'm sorry, Tom. The decision's been taken. It's not reversible.'

Suddenly, I understood – understood exactly what he was doing. He was proving to *his* boss, the Director, that he was not wedded to the rough and tumble of espionage work. By firing me he was demonstrating, in dramatic form, that he had closed the door on his own past, that he now appreciated the importance of desk work, assessment and evaluation, in the new climate of the mid-'70s.

I wanted to hurl the whisky in his face, to kick his elegant drinks table across the room, to throw myself at him and drag him out of his big armchair. But he would probably have broken my back. At fifty-five he still had the strength and skill that had made him one of the most dangerous agents we had ever fielded. And in any case it wouldn't help me back into the Service.

'I'm sorry you decided this way, sir.' I put down my glass and carefully picked up my briefcase. 'Of course I'd welcome anything that kept me in touch with the Department.' I forced a grin. 'I'm certainly not above any courier job that comes along – and if you have anything more demanding perhaps I can show you that I can still play a part, however much things have changed.'

I took his proffered hand and shook it firmly.

He smiled. 'Glad you've taken it this way, Tom,' he said amiably. 'Spend a couple of weeks chasing crumpet in the South of France. Forget all about us here.'

'Forget all about us here'! Forget your friends, forget the pubs you've used, forget the secret warmth of knowing, at a party, that you're not what you say, forget the flush of excitement of the odd girl who guesses, forget the privy thrill of knowing months before the world knows! Forget the way you've lived your whole adult life!

Throughout that summer my strategy was based on the hope that, while doing an occasional courier job for Mansfield, I could bring myself to the notice of one of the other department heads. But so far nothing had worked that way. I had taken packages to Rekjavik and Copenhagen. And I had once met a man on the Austrian/Hungarian border and passed him a line of figures which I had been required to memorise. Then finally this morning's job to pick up the envelope from the affable Mr Pushkin at the Tower. But here at least I was going to get a chance to find out a little more about it.

Chapter 3

The offices of Art Ceramics could never be called luxurious. On the site of the old Royal Wardrobe, they were the top floor of a converted eighteenth-century house, entered by a dog-stained doorway, reached by a winding stair. But then they did have a doorman, a dead give-away, ex of Scotland Yard, a man with kindly eyes and a .38 bulging like a malignant tumour under his left arm. Unaware of my changed circumstances he scrambled to his feet. 'See anything of the crash, sir?' It was a dull day sitting there in his horse-box. I shook my head.

'Heard it.' I told him, 'Probably sounded worse than it actually was.' He agreed reluctantly and I escaped upstairs.

Stevens, the head of the Art Ceramics section office, the job I'd hoped to get, was waiting for me as I entered his room. Fat, fifty and queer as a three-pound note, he had come up through A & E, the assessment and evaluation department of the Service, specialising in smuggling prices on the Russian-Chinese border where the world's riskiest smuggling business depended on China's lack of sophisticated engineering equipment. To someone like Stevens price fluctuations in smuggled machine tool cutting heads could tell a lot about China's own ability to produce the engineering equipment it needed. But as Mansfield had tried to point out, it was the sort of evaluation that had passed me by. I'm not quite sure why but Stevens and I had always got along well in the fifteen years I had been with the Service. Alone with me he would mince and camp it up and show that irreverent and iconoclastic self that was entirely kept from Mansfield. I suppose he trusted me. Perhaps, when I first joined the Service, he had even fancied me. But that was all past now. As far as it was ever possible to penetrate the flighty veneer, we were old friends. And I relied on him to a fair extent to keep me informed of the changing patterns of alliances among the department heads. If ever I was to get back on the inside it would be through information and gossip supplied by Stevens.

'So, Thomas,' he said, throwing a short fat leg over the arm of his desk chair to indicate I was receiving his full attention, 'what did our squat friends want? Not just a guided tour of the Tower of London, I take it?'

'They gave me this.' I threw the envelope Pushkin had given me on his desk.

He picked it up, weighed it in his hand and sniffed it as if for perfume.

'Mansfield will be here to collect it in fifteen minutes,' he said, pursing his lips.

'Which just about gives us time to take a look at it for ourselves.' He nodded and rummaged in his desk drawer, bringing out a handful of ordinary brown envelopes which he spread across the desk.

'This one, I think. Yes.' He selected one of the envelopes similar in size and quality and replaced the others in the drawer. Then he handed me Pushkin's envelope.

I tore it open.

Inside was a single sheet of paper on which, under the heading 'Red Banner', were typed about a dozen names with addresses in London, Paris, Hamburg, Amsterdam and Milan.

Stevens and I looked at each other. Neither of us had any doubt that this was a document of first-class importance – and the fact that it came from the Soviet Embassy indicated a change of policy on their part of at least equal importance. It was exactly the sort of 'prime work', as the Department calls it, that I had been anxious to become involved in since the day Mansfield let me go.

'If this is the Red Banner leadership,' Stevens said thoughtfully, 'this is the finest piece of raw information that's come our way since Red Banner arrived on the scene.'

I was excited. This last year had seen a proliferation of social anarchist groups throughout Western Europe. Better organised, numerically stronger than early-seventies terrorists like Baader-Meinhoff and under names reminiscent of pop groups – 'The Changing Face', 'Galloping Hooves' and even 'When?' – the new social anarchists employed all the weapons of the urban guerilla – kidnapping, bombing, hi-jack and doorstep murder. As a result security had become Europe's biggest growth service industry and strange uniforms had begun to make every European capital look like war-time London.

Among the different social anarchist groups internecine warfare was vicious and wide-spread and the body in the side-street or the canal or car park was now a commonplace worth no more than a line or two in the press reports.

The precise aims of these groups were not vouchsafed to the European publics. Like the early Nazis they contented themselves with the claim that the new society would be 'as different from the present as possible'. Between themselves they struggled bitterly over concepts of de-urbanisation, de-schooling and de-industrialisation, and killed to prove their point.

Besieged by threats and ransom demands daily, the democracies of Western Europe had struggled to maintain former values. Some, like Switzerland and Italy, had already introduced the equivalent of internment or a 90-day detention law. France and Germany were using 'remand during police enquiry' procedures which had the force of internment. Britain was under heavy pressure from other European governments and its own people to do the same.

Red Banner had appeared on this scene about a year ago and had rapidly established for itself a reputation for ruthlessness even among the psychopaths of the social anarchist groups.

Their bombings tended to be recognisably more damaging to

life and property than their rivals' and their threats had a way of being carried out. They had been the first to introduce the terrifying subway train bomb which left hundreds of people screaming and clawing among the dead and wounded in the darkness below ground. They had been the first, too, to develop the sinister rocket truck which stalked landing aircraft from the perimeters of airports. And at two airports, Schiphol in Holland and Leonardo da Vinci outside Rome, they had succeeded – with horrifying results.

And yet, as many people like myself saw it, the greatest danger in all these developments was the lurch to the Right in public attitudes. While no one imagined that Red Banner, even if it succeeded in its attempts to impose its own leadership on the other groups, would ever achieve control in any European country, yet daily, it now seemed, we were hearing of the formation of local vigilante groups in Milan, in Amsterdam, in Manchester, Hamburg or Grenoble all demanding police recognition, the power to stop and search and the right to carry arms.

Stevens held the list of addresses between finger and thumb and wrinkled his nose in distaste. 'Do you want a copy of this, Thomas?'

I told him I did. I planned to keep as close to this new development as possible. In it I saw the vague shape of a way back into the Department.

Stevens led the way into his secretary's office. 'Be a darling, Sandra,' he said to the girl typing at the IBM golf-ball machine, 'go and get yourself some coffee.'

She looked up in surprise and only slowly registered he didn't want her around for a few moments.

'Yes, of course, sir.' She quickly gathered up the familiar red information files which Grosvenor Square CIA send daily marked 'For sight of our British and Canadian allies only', and left the room.

Stevens sat down at the typewriter and slipped a sheet of paper into the machine. With surprising agility his fat fingers flew across the keyboard. As he ripped out the finished list he caught my look. 'My first ambition was to be a very private secretary,' he said. 'After I'd realised nature had cheated me of the chance to be a stewardess, that is.'

I took the list of names from him and shoved it into my pocket. We returned to his office and he slipped the original of the list into the selected brown envelope and passed it to me. With a gross eye-rolling parody of oral sex he indicated I should seal it.

As I did so his phone rang to say that Mansfield was on his way up.

'Did they make any attempt to explain the list?' Stevens asked, putting his head round the door to check Sandra was back in place for Mansfield's visit.

'No. But they did give me a contact point. A hotel in Paddington. But I think at this stage I'll keep that to myself.'

'You won't tell Mansfield?'

'No. So that if he needs to follow this up he'll have to come to me. I intend to keep my fingers in this particular pie, Steve.'

He frowned. 'A dangerous game, Thomas. And please, do not call me "Steve". It sounds so fearfully butch.'

As the sound of an outer door opening and Mansfield's gruff naval charm being exercised on Sandra came through the partition wall, Stevens's manner changed abruptly.

He got up and opened his own office door, his face composed, severe even. 'Good morning, sir,' he said crisply. 'Hart's waiting for you in my office.'

Then Mansfield stepped past him into the room. He was wearing a dark blue pin-striped suit, white shirt and Navy tie. His immaculate bowler hat was held in one hand and his umbrella, like a rifle at the trail, in the other. He had perfectly even small white teeth of which he was inordinately proud, but his lips were not shaped to fall naturally into the configuration of a smile. The result was therefore an impression of a forced, wolfish charm.

'How do you like being back in harness, Hart?' he said, shaking my hand in his iron grip, another asset he felt a generous nature had bestowed upon him.

'Love it,' I said, extricating my hand. 'Can't get enough of it.'

He took the point.

'Well, what was it they wanted?'

'They gave me this.' I produced the brown envelope and handed it to him, while Stevens poured a scotch and water and set it on the desk.

Mansfield tore open the envelope and read rapidly down the list, nodding to himself.

'Anything else?' He fixed his eyes on me as he put the paper back into the envelope and pocketed it.

I had a moment's hesitation. Bucking Mansfield was indeed a dangerous game as Stevens had pointed out. But if it was the only way of getting back on the team . . .

'No, sir,' I said firmly.

'What did they have to say, sir?' Stevens asked, his face expressionless.

' Not your department, Stevens,' Mansfield said brusquely. He turned back to me. 'Did you recognise the courier?'

'There were two of them,' I said.' They must have been fairly new to the Embassy. I didn't know either of them. Do you want me to go through the photographs?'

'Maybe later,' Mansfield said. 'Not important at the moment.' He turned to Stevens.

'Right, while I'm here I'd like to have a look round.'

'Of course, sir.' Stevens was on his feet immediately.

Mansfield inclined his head in my direction. 'That's all, Hart. Collect a cheque from Accounts. I've already authorised payment.'

And he was out of the office, followed by Stevens – whose left eye closed in an outrageously languid wink as he passed me.

Chapter 4

It was just gone eleven-thirty when I collected my car from the Art Ceramics car park and headed north towards the Cambridge road. I was grateful to have something to keep me out of the pub – eleven-thirty had been my first drink most days since Mansfield fired me. Which was all right, I suppose, except that eleven-thirty, twelve hours later, had seen me still in a bar or club with a couple of seedy journalists for company or a no more than ordinarily prepossessing girl that I planned to take home for the night. Booze and sex is a round that tends to raise the guilt-edged Puritan in me far quicker than mugging some Yugoslav courier in the echoing colonnades of Trieste at night.

At Stevenage I stopped for a cup of coffee, parked the car and headed for the local Lyons. A left-over habit from more penurious days, I still made for Lyons when I wanted coffee rather than a drink. Which was usually when I had thinking to do.

I sat among the clatter of cups being collected and the smiling, only part-comprehensible chatter of the West Indian waitresses, and wondered why Major-General Sir Richard Deedes, VC (retired) should have telephoned me last night. A 'proposal', he said, that might well interest me. But Major-General Deedes's activities since retirement were not such as to interest me very much. He was head of one of those slightly crackpot, mostly innocuous organisations that had sprung up in the West recently to reaffirm the old values, offer their services in the case of a nationwide strike and generally to keep the clock turned back as far as they decently, non-violently, could. And of course they did represent the worries and fears of a great many ordinary Englishmen and Dutchmen, French and Germans.

There had been groups before with apparently similar aims. General Walker's Civil Assistance had gained adherents in the early '70s. Colonel Stirling of the Long Range Desert Group had also entered the field. Strange how many Support for the Civil Power groupings are led by military men. But then of course I realised it wasn't strange at all. The military cult of action, corporate action, made a senior officer the most likely leader of such a movement. In banana republics the only difference was they didn't bother to retire first.

On the phone Deedes had sounded crisply urgent. I told him I couldn't make an early morning meeting, making myself sound as busy as I could, and promised him I'd be there for a late lunch. He settled for that, gave me a few superfluous directions about getting to his house, and said how much he looked forward to our meeting. I was telling him I was similarly atremble with anticipation when I realised he had already hung up on me.

Driving through Cambridge flooded me with nostalgia. I circled the familiar streets – King's Parade, the Market Place – crossed Magdalene Bridge and came back down Trinity Street, to let the feeling seep in. To be twenty-two on a summer afternoon, unhooking her bra in an oak-panelled room in Trinity, never having killed a man.

I parked the car off the Market Place and wandered back down St Edward's Passage towards King's. Undergraduates flowed before me carrying books, gowns, bottles, squash racquets: the impedimenta of university life. Friends met with studied English casualness, drifting past each other before turning to enquire and reply about tonight's party or tomorrow's game, securely wrapped in arrogant innocence.

I killed my first man with enjoyment. Garrotted him with piano wire in a homosexual brothel in Vienna. From that day on I was Mansfield's boy, given limelight jobs, promoted, pushed ahead.

Before I was twenty-six I headed up a group operating in Berlin. And there I killed another man, a salesman for both sides, a bald, sleazy husk of a man who had survived the *Einsatzgruppe*, the Ghetto, Auschwitz and the SS Dobermans and succumbed to me, pushed gently into the sub-zero river when he refused my price. A job like any other job, Mansfield always said. The old man's huge overcoat billowed round him in the black water, the cold tightened his sparrow's chest, constricted his larynx and he disappeared without a sound. I had counted on it.

In Turkey two years later it was a James Bond folly. A private war with a light machine gun kicking chips of rock around my head. It was the day Mansfield stood up with a .45 in each hand and blasted away at them like an Indian fighter as if the crack and whine around him were no more lethal than the products of a sound effects unit. As we approached their huddled bodies one jumped up and ran leaping across the rocks. Mansfield passed judgment with a nod of the head and I obediently took up their l.m.g. and gunned him down like a mountain goat. When I looked for some sign of approbation, for a job well done, Mansfield had already turned casually away. I was struck with admiration.

But then I was young in blood.

The Deedeses' house was one of a terrace of university properties off Queen's Road. I approached the white Georgian door and admired the tracery of the fanlight above. I rang the circular brass bell-push and began to rub with an exploratory index finger at the black-grey brickwork framing the door. I was meditating in maudlin fashion on a lost world of craftsmanship, a world that cared, when the door swung open.

The woman smiling at me was about fifty-five, grey and dressed with that genteel sloppiness that only English ladies still believe they can afford. The husband of this one never introduced a nubile Ghanaian au pair into the nest, I was betting myself as I gave my name.

'The General has been slightly delayed.' She stepped back to allow me in. 'On a day like this perhaps you'd like to wait in the garden.'

I thanked her and followed down the narrow hallway, descended three steps, and as she opened the glass door stepped into an oven-hot conservatory.

She smiled: 'Will you excuse me? I have some work to finish.

You'll find Lady Deedes out in the garden.'

'Lady Deedes?'

Again she smiled. 'I'm Miss Cavendish. The General's private secretary.'

I passed through a fair simulacrum of the Indonesian jungle and opened the conservatory door on to an expanse of cool green lawn edged by an ancient brick wall. There was no sign of Lady Deedes.

Lighting a cigarette I seated myself on one of the white-painted wrought-iron chairs that ringed a small table and noticed for the first time an iron gate in the middle of the far section of the garden wall.

After a moment or two a crackle of flame and a drifting plume of sweet-smelling grey smoke indicated someone at work on a garden fire on the far side of the gate.

The minutes passed. I finished my cigarette and was wondering whether devoted gardeners would object if I crushed it into the lawn when the iron gate opened and a woman in her early thirties came through. Seeing me, she stopped.

She wore jeans tucked into cut-down wellington boots, a green round-necked sweater and a pair of grimy canvas gardening gloves. Her face was smudged from fire-lighting and strands of dark brown hair, escaping from a makeshift pony-tail, fell across her forehead.

She came forward in a graceful, high-stepping walk, brushing the hair from her eyes with the back of the absurd canvas gloves.

It was a Mediterranean face, tanned and full-lipped but from somewhere, under Mendel's incomprehensible laws, she had received light-brown eyes.

Her smile was brief but startling. Undisguised by smoke smudges, rubber boots and a shapeless sweater, she was a very beautiful woman.

'I do apologise, Mr Hart . . . it *is* Mr Hart, isn't it?' Her voice had a very faint New England accent.

'Tom Hart.' I extended my hand and forced her to remove the clumsy canvas gloves.

Perhaps she knew something from my handshake. Or perhaps a certain hauteur was her bag, but whatever it was she stood before me refusing intimacy. Her physiognomy may have been Mediterranean, her nationality American, but her manner was crushingly English.

18

'Do sit down, Mr Hart. My husband won't be a moment.'

'Don't let me interrupt the fire-lighting,' I said, hoping to hear her protestations.

Her mouth moved in the direction of a smile she didn't mean.

'Let me tell Albert to get you a drink – what shall you have?'

I asked for gin and tonic and watched her move away towards the house with her marvellous, high-stepping gait. It was painful.

The promised drink was brought by a short, balding man in white mess-waiter's jacket. His friendly formality could only have been learnt in the army. He was pouring the tonic and commenting on the weather for this time of year when Major-General Deedes emerged from the conservatory door and began covering the lawn in enormous, raking strides.

About six feet two, with huge hands and red, boney wrists; the moustache, grey hair, ruddy face and affable military manner compounded the cliché of a retired British general. He assigned me a rank somewhere around captain, ordered a gin and tonic for himself and dropped his heavy frame on to one of the garden chairs. I watched the chair legs sink half an inch into the lawn and waited, lighting myself a cigarette.

'You know our organisation?' he said, looking far over my head.

I nodded. 'You've done very well for yourself in the press this last year.'

He shook his head quickly. 'Scallywags,' he said. 'Every last one of them. Determined to make me out a neo-Fascist. If we're going to work together, Hart' – he leaned forward and held me with his pale eyes – 'you should know something about me and about Action England.' He stopped and again fixed on some point on the garden wall high behind my head.

'I'm damn proud of this country,' he said quietly. 'I serve the Queen and I'm a fervent believer in the democratic process. Action England is an organisation at the service of the community – and at the orders of the legally constituted government. That's all there is to it.'

'All right, General,' I said. 'I accept that.'

He nodded crisply and took his gin and tonic from the tray proffered by Albert.

'Lunch ready yet?' he asked him.

'When you are, sir.'

'Let's have it now, then.'

As Albert moved away he turned his attention back to me.

'We have money,' he said, 'resources donated by over a

million well-wishers. These resources are to be used in any way that myself and the Action England committee see fit. This brings us to you.'

By what particular thought processes I knew not. But the General was not a man to waste words.

'One of our major resources is an informal information service. Nothing organised, you understand. But effective. Our committee have received through it a report that a French freighter out of Le Havre for Rotterdam has disappeared at sea. Skipper's name – Lucien Morel. Got that?'

I nodded and remained silent. He'd tell me in his own good time what the freighter was carrying.

'Gelignite,' he said. 'Two hundred tons of gelignite.'

I pursed my lips – it was the least I could do.

'When did this happen?'

'Two, three nights ago.'

'How about a simple radio failure?'

He shook his head. 'The British Government obviously doesn't think so. It's done its best to keep the news from the press.'

'Not easy.'

'But not impossible, as I'm sure you know. We're dealing with a cover-up, Mr Hart. Or at least my committee is virtually sure we are.'

'Why would the British Government need to do that?'

'Simple, isn't it? Over fifty major bombing incidents in the United Kingdom alone last month. The government under pressure to introduce internment here and to bring back the death penalty. In party political terms they daren't do either without receiving a lashing from the Left Wing. Admit that a vast new quantity of gelignite has fallen into the wrong hands, and they'll be forced to act by public opinion.'

'Yes,' I said, 'I can see it would be difficult for them.'

'Understand it clearly, Mr Hart. This is a European problem. The issue of mounting violence in every European country is being evaded by one government after another. That freighter-load of gelignite could be on its way to London, Hamburg, Paris or Rome.'

I surreptitiously crushed my cigarette under the sole of my shoe.

'What made you get in touch with me?'

'Our information service suggested you might have the right background and indeed adequate leisure . . .' he smiled, 'to take the job.'

Some information service.

'The job being to find out what happened to the gelignite?'

'My goodness, no!' He laughed for the first time. 'Much simpler. We plan to release the news to the press. But first we want our information confirmed. Establish that a freighter-load of gelignite *was* hi-jacked – that's what we want from you, Mr Hart.'

I didn't need to give it thought. I liked the job. I accepted.

'A *per diem* of fifty pounds – travel expenses in addition. Fee: five hundred pounds.'

There was no room for argument. But then at those rates I wasn't disposed to.

We both rose as an Admirable Crichton procession carrying lunch trays approached from the house. Albert, the mess waiter, was followed by two older men – perhaps gardeners or odd-job men. As they set the places and arranged dishes and wine glasses I glanced up to see a shape distorted by the glass of the conservatory door. It opened and Lady Deedes began to cross the lawn towards us.

She had changed. The jeans were replaced by flared white trousers, the old green sweater by a crisp yellow shirt. Her dark brown hair, released from the pony-tail, fell thick around her face. The General rose.

'Ah, you haven't met my wife, Virginia.' He turned to her: 'Virginia, Mr Hart.'

I was about to speak, to say we had already met, when she stretched out her hand towards me.

'How do you do, Mr Hart.'

I took her hand and shook it, looking into her eyes. They were as beautiful as before – and as blank.

Of course you can never play games with too many beautiful women, but I've played enough in my time to know what to do when the spinning bottle points my way. Yet this time I was baffled. Throughout lunch while the General described the aims and activities of Action England Virginia sat silently, eating little between sips of white wine. Then on two occasions, when the General rose to go into the house for a book and then again when he went in search of an explanatory pamphlet, she turned immediately towards me.

'Will you take the job?' she asked me on his first trip indoors.

'Yes.'

'Why?'

'I need the money.'

21

She gave a small nod of gentle contempt. 'Will you do anything for money?'

I thought for a moment. 'Yes,' I said, 'but that's probably because I'm more honest now.'

She leaned forward and took up her wine glass. Lifting it to her lips she sipped her wine, watching me over the rim of the glass.

'You're very beautiful,' I said.

Still she watched me. Then very slowly she smiled.

The conservatory door slammed closed and I looked up to see the General, black book in hand, devouring the lawn with his stride, like a low church preacher sighting souls.

As he reached us her smile faded into careful composure. For a further twenty minutes I asked polite questions about Action England and received in return in the General's heartily concise answers a picture of an organisation of patriots, run from the house. 'No complicated infrastructure', in the General's words, an organisation not short of money, comprised mostly I supposed of people like the General – 'people who feel old England is fast disappearing, the things we knew, a special way of doing things. Don't you agree, Mr Hart?'

Do you mourn the passing of the Music Halls?

As I prepared to go he left us for the second time, insisting I should take with me some Action England literature, 'to read in the bath.' I watched him across the lawn, then turned back to Virginia. She waved her hand, encompassing the garden with the gesture. 'So much time spent,' she said, 'taming nature. I'd like to think it's all worth it.' Her New England accent seemed stronger now.

'You're an American,' I said.

'Only sometimes.' She lifted her wine glass to me.

'What are we toasting?' I asked her.

'Freedom.' She fixed me with her hazel eyes.

'Whose?'

'Yours,' she said. 'Or don't you have any?'

'I have it regularly.' It was an attempt to shock her. She shrugged.

'But does the little woman know – or care?'

'There is no little woman,' I said, realising for the first time that she was slightly loaded.

'I'm sorry, I'm asking indiscreet questions, Mr Hart.'

'Tom.'

She burst out laughing. 'Do you like my garden, Tom? It's all mine. Every leaf, every flower, every blade of grass.'

For answer I poured her some more wine. I liked her garden very much.

She stood up. 'Come,' she said, 'let me show you my garden.'

She reached out and took my hand and pulled me gently from the chair.

Her hand dropped away as I came up next to her.

I turned and saw the General emerging from the conservatory.

'Hart!' he called across the lawn.

I waved to indicate I'd heard and turned back to Virginia. Her face was cold. Again the 'My last Duchess' trick.

'Goodbye,' I said.

'Goodbye, Mr Hart.' She shook my hand without warmth.

'You won't mind me saying that you're a lady of puzzlingly variable mood.'

She looked at me. 'I hope it doesn't upset you, Mr Hart – it's just so much less bother than contemplating adultery.'

She stepped back to allow me clear passage across the lawn. At the conservatory door the General handed me the Action England literature. Then, bidding me goodbye and good luck, he pressed discreetly into my hand a pleasingly bulky envelope.

Chapter 5

I suppose it's only when I'm troubled that I go and see Jazz. At least, that's what she tells me.

Pulling back into London against the flow of commuter traffic I let the car direct me down through Hampstead, across the park and through Kensington and Chelsea towards the river. At Oakley Street I turned right and parked the Lancia outside The King's Head and Eight Bells. Popping my head inside I was lucky enough to catch the eye of a barman I knew.

'Jazz?' I asked him.

'She hasn't been in all week,' he said. 'Try the flat. I think she's got a commission on.'

I knew what that meant even though he obviously didn't. Jazz was one of London's part-timers. Six years ago she was a totally respectable, though somewhat frustrated Surrey housewife whose husband suddenly upped and left her, taking their two small children to, she believed, America. Local report and the condolences of good friends quickly revealed that he had been knocking around with a maturely rich American lady for the last six months. Then again other reports made her Australian. With two continents to choose from and the bills to pay Jazz had given up the ghost.

I had met her in a Soho club shortly after she had sold up in Surrey, hired herself out in London, tried to kill herself with a barbiturate overdose and gained entrance to St Martin's School of Art. I'm not absolutely sure that that is the precise order of events – but it's close enough. What by now she had become was a talented painter who still made rather more from her assignations than her assignments.

She was not, I freely admit, fashionably slender. Nor was she trendily dressed. Four years at art school had failed to eradicate the Surrey housewife. But then I rather liked that.

Only by sleeping with the landlord could she possibly have afforded an apartment like the one she occupied. I mounted the steps, rang the bell a couple of times and let myself in.

She was always good on the greetings, was Jazz. This time she flung her arms round my neck, kissed me in a less than sisterly way, laughed and giggled while I made free with my hands and broke off to pour me a drink.

'I hear you've got a commission,' I said.

'They'll do anything to blacken a girl's character down at that pub. I'm back on the game.'

'A new source?'

'I have a contact who sends me a stream of visiting Japanese businessmen.' She shrugged. 'What the hell – they pay well and they're all so little you hardly know they're there. Another month and I'll be able to take off to Florence for the winter.'

'I'll miss you,' I told her, lolling back on the sofa, drink in hand.

She came over and sat on the arm of the Chesterfield and tickled the back of my neck.

'How are things, Tom?'

I shrugged. I had planned to tell her about the accident I had seen that morning, but I found it strangely difficult to get the words out.

'Been drinking a lot?'

I denied it. Then conceded I was drinking more than I should be.

'And the job – no more news?'

Jazz was great. Jasmine Mary Oliver, deserted by her husband, her children snatched, her talent disregarded and her body for rent, she still had the sort of warmth and ordinary human sympathy that brought tears to your eyes. I'd Dutch Uncled her, of course, through her times of the troubles, but she'd done that and more for me, especially when I returned from New York trying to work out whether I really was in the middle of a mental breakdown or not. Truth was she knew me well – warts and all.

'I think,' she said after my third drink, 'that you'd better stay here tonight.'

I was pleased to accept. I might even get to tell her about the accident on Ludgate Hill.

'What about the Japanese delegation?'

She smiled: 'Forget about them. If they turn up tonight, I'll tell them the Emperor just kicked the bucket. They've a fantastic sense of decorum.'

Next morning I lay in bed beside the warm body of Jazz Oliver and phoned the French Embassy in Knightsbridge while she played me into suitable shape.

'Directory of the Merchant Marine? Yes . . . Morel, Lucien, born 1919, resident Honfleur. Master's Certificate, 1946. Decorations: Merchant Marine Medal, 1945.'

I pulled Jazz upwards by her hair and she settled astride me and began to sing low: 'Ride a cock horse to Banbury Cross . . . see a fine lady on a fine horse . . .'

'Publications: L. Morel, *Sea birds of the Le Havre Estuary*, 1951. You're welcome, monsieur.'

Chapter 6

I drove off the Southampton-Le Havre Sealink ferry ramp down past a smart police salute to the side of a *képi* and headed the Lancia to the southern exit of Le Havre. A dreary roadway led the convoy of cars from the ferry past institution-green corrugated iron huts above which rose the tips of loading derricks, ships' radio masts and the occasional black and red funnel of an ocean-going freighter. France's premier port didn't exactly sparkle in the sunlight.

Even with my imagination under the whip I could make nothing of the Antonioni landscape of Le Havre's petrochemical suburbs. When the graceful trajectory of the Toncarville Bridge disgorged me into the Norman countryside I felt I'd put some evil vision of the future far behind.

I took it slowly to Honfleur, moving back through a century as I passed villages through which Model's panzer divisions had rattled to meet Montgomery's advancing tanks; copses and woods where ground-sheeted Tommies had struggled with horse-drawn gun limbers as they broke bivouac in the streaming rain to head north towards the rumbling gunfire of the Somme; or village memorials to imperial guardsmen who fell at Waterloo.

But then in Normandy the English imagination is constantly under siege.

I reached Honfleur just after six and took an attic room in the Hôtel Cheval Blanc. A few minutes with the telephone directory revealed that Captain Lucien Morel of the Merchant Marine lived on the Rue Haute, a street of picturesque houses where sea captains and navigators had lived for over three hundred years.

No. 96 was one of the smaller houses leaning heavily on its sturdier neighbour. I must have been already under observation as I stopped in the steeply angled street outside, because I had hardly knocked once when the door was opened. She was grey-haired, drably dressed and the possessor of a remarkably disconcerting squint. And she put me on to something right away with her first question. 'You've found Lucien?'

I must have looked like a man from the Le Havre Merchant Marine, or maybe anybody did, she was that worried about her missing husband. I took advantage of her anxieties, introduced myself as Captain Thomas Hart of the British Merchant Service, and told her I was investigating the question from the other side of the Channel.

She insisted I came in and I sat in the small, seldom used salon among the yellowing Navy photographs and the brass sextants and bottled ships, exploiting her misery and telling myself I had gone soft. A few years ago I would only have been concerned if she'd been young and bedworthy.

She 'recapped', as they used to say on the quiz shows, and it soon became clear that General Deedes's informal information service was so far on course. Her husband had left three days ago to sail the freighter *François Villon* from Le Havre to Rotterdam. She didn't know its cargo but she did know the owners were paying captain and crew a special increment. Gelignite fitted (from the petrochemical complex at Le Havre) and the special increment pointed to danger money. I gave Madame Morel a story about radio failure and a freak storm which we believed may have carried the *François Villon* off course, and she was worried enough to half-believe it. In unwitting return she gave me details of the *Villon*'s owners and chartering company from her husband's land log, and I left her suggesting sleeping pills and a few stiff brandies to take her through the night.

I myself threaded my way back through the late medieval streets past the ancient Lieutenance fortress built and rebuilt over the centuries, to come to rest in the Gars Normand, a small, unpretentious and spectacularly good restaurant overlooking the quayside.

I was almost through my *moules marinières* and most way through a bottle of reasonable Aligoté when I first became aware of the excitement out on the quayside.

Information filtered back from the waiters who took time off from popping corks and flaring sauces to run outside and ask a quick question or two before my fellow diners got restive. A fishing boat had returned. This was something of a mystery in itself, since the boats normally fished all night. A further foray out on to the quayside revealed that the problem was not broken nets or engine troubles – indeed the skipper, who was known as 'grand Charles', didn't appear to have a problem at all. Far from it, the third waiter informed the whole restaurant, le grand Charles was driving immediately into Rouen to register a big salvage claim.

My stomach lurched at the words. I got up scattering francs to any waiter who extended his hand and ran for the small group of people gathered round a battered Citroën into which a tall man in fishing sweater was climbing. I broke through the crowd and pushed my head through the open window on the driver's side. I was no more than two inches from his face.

'It's the *François Villon*, right?'

He reeled back under the twin assault of garlic and the prescience of foreigners. Catching him momentarily off balance I pressed on.

'I'm a journalist,' I told him. 'I'll pay you five hundred francs to get your crew to take me out to it.'

A bird in the hand, he was thinking, as his pale blue eyes

27

weighed me up. Five hundred francs now – it would be a long squabble through the salvage courts before this night's work paid hard cash. He nodded briskly and pushed my head away to allow him to call to a young fisherman on the edge of the group.

Some whispered instructions and an exchange of fifty ten-franc notes later, I was following the young fisherman's seaboots across the cobbles to the edge of the jetty.

I have never in my life suffered from seasickness. But then I had never in my life ventured into the Seine estuary in a 30-foot-long fishing boat, its function proclaimed by a half-inch of fish scales underfoot and an embracing aroma of rotting fish that came out of the woodwork. While the lights of Le Havre petrol refinery still winked on our right the waves were already coming off the Channel in twenty-foot-high walls of black water, shattering on the bow and wheelhouse and bouncing our small craft helplessly from crest to trough. In vehement support of the sea's ugly intentions the wind tore at oilskins and sou'westers and drove pipe smoke and tobacco cinder in a horizontal line from our young skipper's pipe bowl as he leaned nonchalantly against the wheelhouse peering into the blackness in a stout Cortes act which I felt must be for my benefit.

Inside the three-sided wheelhouse I gripped the edge of the chart table and tried not to think about the mussels and Aligoté I had enjoyed at the Gars Normand.

At the wheel a short, fat Frenchman exuded the inevitable smell of fish and grinned fiendishly in my direction as the sea increased its efforts to capsize us.

We had been pushing through the waves for at least an hour when the young Frenchman in the sou'wester appeared in the open side of the wheelhouse and jerked his thumb at the blackness ahead.

I swayed and stumbled out with him and was blasted by the tail end of a wave that rattled across the deck like driven hailstones. As the fishing boat rose from the trough I saw before us the black hulk of the *François Villon*.

At six thousand tons it wasn't much as freighters go, but from the trawler it rose above us with the mass and bulk of an abandoned supertanker.

The young man with the pipe took over the wheel, and with much shouting and gesture (a sudden and alarming abandonment of what I took to be his habitual cool) began to manoeuvre

the fishing boat as best he could towards the iron side of the
François Villon.

A rope ladder hung down the riveted flank of the freighter,
and it was against this that the young man at the helm was trying
to position the boat. But waves which would raise the freighter
no more than a few feet seemed to hurl us high against the ship's
side with a deafening clangor, then equally suddenly fall away
to drop us into a trough twelve feet below the bottom of the
rope ladder.

'Vas-y, mon vieux,' the sadistic fat man yelled each time we
were swept towards the freighter's side, and I crouched trembling
with cold and indecision ready for the leap.

At our third or maybe fourth pass the helmsman cut the
engines while we were angled at the crest of a wave, and like a
midnight surfer I felt the trawler sliding under me down the deep,
black-green scoop of water then up past the level of the bottom
rung of the rope ladder. For a second we were poised not four
feet from the freighter's side.

I jumped. Into the black spray, clawing wildly for the rope
ladder, conscious of the trawler moving faster than myself
towards the freighter, threatening to crush me between them. As
my outstretched fingers touched the stiff, wet roping I gripped
hard and jerked my legs up from the deck level of the trawler,
as again it crashed against the freighter's side and fell away,
leaving me kicking for a foothold on the ladder's wooden slats.

Trembling with effort I climbed the last seven or eight feet
through the flying spray and was hauled over the hand-rail to
lie panting on the deck like an expiring plaice.

I dragged myself to my feet and focused unsteadily on the two
fishermen before me. Taking me for a salvage officer they conducted me into the galley and had poured the second large
brandy and lit my cigarette before I was able to explain my
journalistic deal with le grand Charles.

It was clear this was the biggest thing that had happened to
them in a lifetime. The salvage payment for a freighter like the
François Villon would be more for each man on le grand Charles's
boat than ten years of fishing could provide. While I sipped my
third brandy they told me the story.

They were about an hour out from Honfleur moving past the
Seine estuary for a mid-Channel position when Charles had first
spotted the freighter. At first they had not clearly realised that it
was moving only with the running tide. More striking was its
lack of navigation lights and the immediate danger as it loomed

over them. Catastrophe had only been averted by Charles's handling of his boat.

The realisation that the freighter was abandoned had been slow. At first they had taken her for a smuggler nosing her way at half speed and lights out to a rendezvous in the estuary, but her heavy yawing motion had soon disposed of the idea she was under steam. They had hailed her, then boarded her while Charles took the fishing boat back to Honfleur to establish their salvage claim.

I was feeling better. The brandies had settled my stomach and I had peeled off the oilskins to find I was relatively dry underneath. I told the two fishermen I'd like to take a look over the ship, and when neither of them seemed inclined to follow me I set out down the breezeway to look first for the hatches to the hold.

The motion of the freighter was relatively gentle compared with the wild bucking of the fishing boat, and the sea reached me now only as a slap and thump against the iron flanks and a spume of spray above the hand-rail.

The *François Villon* proclaimed its building in Brest in 1953 in peeling white paint on its blackened smoke stack, and the bubbling eruptions of rust around the entrance to the companionways suggested it hadn't received a paint job since its commissioning.

I located the forward hatches without difficulty. There were four – each with the tarpaulins peeled back and the hatch itself thrown clear of the opening to the hold. Cautiously negotiating the slippery deck I approached the edge of one of the openings and peered into the black chasm. Let into the deck beside me, in a heavy waterproof housing, were two electric switches. I pushed both down and flooded the hold with light. Apart from neatly stowed piles of deck tarpaulins and a line of red fire extinguishers clipped to the bulwark the hold was empty. That 'informal information service' of General Deedes looked more professional by the hour.

I stumbled around in my landlubber fashion for another ten minutes before I located the captain's cabin, and was forced to prise open the mahogany desk to find what I wanted. The ship's manifest set it out in triplicate – the *François Villon* out of Le Havre for Rotterdam was carrying 200 tons of nitrocellulose and glyceryl-nitrate – known and loved by us all under the name 'gelignite'. Well, it wasn't any longer.

I detached one of the manifest copies, slipped it into my pocket and had started back along the companionway to the galley where my nose told me the two fishermen were brewing coffee when I first heard the noise. It was an eerie hollow knocking from somewhere down in the bowels of the ship. Something about the rhythm of the sounds made the hair on the back of my neck stand on end. It was no door moved by wind or wave, or bucket rolling to the motion of the ship; rather a beating of iron on iron to a rhythm determined by human muscles. I began to run.

Sliding down steep companion ladders, following the sharp twists of rough, welded passageways, I moved towards the hollow metallic sounds. It was not difficult to see that I was being led down towards the engine room. I turned a final corner and in front of me a heavy steel door prevented any further advance. The sounds now filled the narrow confines of the passage and the impact of heavy blows shook even the solidity of the steel door. The operating wheel to open it had been secured by a massive length of padlocked chain. And the key had been tossed casually to the floor.

I undid the padlock and let the heavy chain rattle through the steel locking wheel. Inside the sounds had stopped. I spun the wheel and swung open the steel door. The dozen or so seamen inside pressed back against the mass of tubing and pipes which was all I could see of the engine room. Hollow-eyed and unshaven they reminded me of pictures from war-time boys' comics of the Altmark rescue. Standing slightly to the fore was a man in his late fifties. I stepped into the fetid atmosphere of the engine room.

'Captain Morel?'

He reacted warily to my accent. Even as he nodded I realised the intensity of strain and exhaustion he was suffering.

'The French authorities will be out here in a matter of hours. I suggest you take your men up and get them fed.'

The tension flowed from the men behind him. They broke forward with a ragged and pathetic cheer and surged around me all trying to shake my hand at once.

Morel detailed his first mate to take the crew to the galley and ordered an omelette and coffee to be brought to his cabin. I didn't try to explain who the two disappointed fishermen were who would be drinking coffee and cognac in the galley, and was not sorry to accompany the captain and miss that particular confrontation.

Still in my journalist's persona I pieced together the events of three days ago as the captain swallowed his omelette and drank coffee and brandy. The *François Villon* had emerged from a late-summer storm in the Seine estuary and had set course north for Rotterdam sixteen miles off the Le Havre light when Morel on the bridge had seen the navigation lights of a motor yacht appearing out of the mist. He had taken standard action and given the yacht a few blasts on his horn when he became aware that, far from moving clear, it was sailing on a collision course with the *François Villon*. As he told it, Morel was much too concerned about avoiding a collision to speculate on the motives of the yacht's captain, and as the yacht passed close on the port side Morel felt only relief and a mounting anger at the drunken amateurs who risked the lives of inexperienced crews in these busy waters. For his log he noted the name – *Jamaica Storm* – and the fact that it was an 'X' class motor yacht registered in Great Britain. He was still discussing the near-miss with his mate when a shout from one of the crewmen on the deck below made him look to their starboard rear. The motor yacht had crept through the mist on their other side and, all lights out, was sailing a parallel course a matter of ten or fifteen feet away. A final adjustment to the yacht's wheel brought her close alongside the freighter and what followed, still after three days, left the captain shaking his head in disbelief. Grappling hooks and nets had been hurled at the freighter hand-rail and a hooded and totally silent boarding party had leapt for the freighter's side.

Heavily armed with automatic weapons they had corralled the captain and his crew in a matter of minutes. Then, still in total silence, they had led them below and locked them in the engine room. Thinking to forestall the hi-jackers the captain had ordered the engines cut. As two hours passed and the captain gradually realised they were alone on the freighter he was afraid to restart the engines for fear of collision with the Normandy coast. Thus, drifting blind, they had passed three days of tension with only sporadic work on the remote possibility of forcing the steel door to maintain their morale.

By now, under the captain's orders and after radio signals had been sent to Le Havre and Honfleur, the *François Villon* was under way again.

I stood on the bridge while the captain agonised and speculated about the loss of his cargo. But my mind was on something else. The total silence of the raiding party was impressive. It was also, unless working with the very best of professionals, almost impossible to achieve. Tension mounts in any operation to a point at which the inexperienced yawn, laugh and finally suffer an overwhelming need to curse. Anything can then cause the outburst – a comrade under foot, a box or hawser brushing the leg. And the amateur curses to release his tension.

I checked carefully with the crew as we sailed into the estuary. Nobody had heard one single word from the six men who had boarded them. That to me meant that the leader at least had been trained by one of the principal government agencies in the field – Russia's GRU, the CIA, MI6 or France's SDEC.

I drove back from Le Havre with Morel as dawn was beginning to lift the night from the warm countryside to landward. In the lightening haze the petrochemical complex looked even more aggressively 21st century – its squat round tubs of petrol with their giant numbered sides, the flaring outlet chimneys of the natural gas plants and the swooping lines of light bulbs that lit the area like some abandoned and desolate fairground.

The captain drove silently beside me, worried about his career, his wife, his 200 tons of gelignite – and quite unworried by the desecration of the most beautiful country in Europe. Leave that, I thought, to us *Observer* readers. And after the petrol companies have moved out we'll buy up our own bijou petrol tanks and paint them white and make them look quaint. But by that time of course we shall all be looking back on the twentieth century as a magic period when even the merest steel erector had concern and taste and faith in his job.

The Honfleur quayside was buzzing as we drove past the wooden church and parked outside the Gars Normand. I spotted the tall figure of Charles and the young skipper who had taken me out to the *François Villon*, and I was looking around for my fat sadistic friend to disappoint with the news that I had suffered not so much as a severed limb when the group of men began to bend and haul on what I took to be a net.

I crossed the quayside a few paces behind the weary captain, watching the cork floats at the edge of the net appear over the rim of the stone wall. Then suddenly with a final heave by the fishermen it appeared to jump from the water, enclosing what appeared to be a section of white superstructure, streaming water.

Even the exhausted Morel showed interest as we both read clearly on the side of the false plywood superstructure the words: *Jamaica Storm.*

It had been a heavy night. I dropped off Morel and parked the car outside the curious little wooden church of Ste Catherine, its nave and tower separated by a cobbled roadway, and stumbled down to the quayside where the Hôtel Cheval Blanc overlooked the bassin.

It was seven-thirty when I rattled on the glass door for a young chambermaid to let me in. I headed for the stairs with a muttered good morning and reached my room on the first floor. The bed was turned down – the mattress looked two feet deep. I undressed, climbed in and only just awoke in time to make it back to Le Havre for the overnight Southampton ferry.

Morel and Madame Morel came to see me off. She was touchingly grateful, squinting at me with tear-filled eyes. He was very proper, very restrained, but as I prepared to drive on to the Southampton ferry he grabbed me and kissed me on both cheeks. I don't often meet nice, ordinary people in this line of business. When I do, I remember them.

Chapter 7

England greeted me with a white sea mist and a red ball of sun rising through it. For the beginning of autumn it was going to be a warm day.

As the Sealink ferry moved under half-steam along the Southampton dock front I obeyed the Tannoy call and clattered down the companionway with a few dozen other drivers into the iron belly of the ship. The enormous container trucks were having their restraining chocks removed. Drivers mounted high cabs and sat waiting for the word like a military convoy ready to move off. The private cars, cringing beside the juggernauts, were signalled to pull away first towards the square of light, and I was soon guiding the Lancia down the ramps on to the Southampton quayside.

I drove for the green, nothing-to-declare customs area, but a man alone, of course, is always stopped. The customs officer was round-faced, friendly and liked to talk as he worked.

'How long have you been out of the country, sir?'

'A couple of days. On business.'

He finished with my bag, scrawled on it in chalk, and began to walk round the car.

'I see, sir. Then perhaps you don't know about the Alert?'

For a moment it only rang a very uncertain bell.

'Alert?' I said. 'You don't mean General Deedes's organisation?'

'That's it, sir. Action England. My colleagues tell me they've been out in force since first thing this morning. They're hoping to cover the whole of Hampshire.'

'Doing what?'

'Quite a bit it seems, sir.' He got into the car and opened the glove compartment. 'Stopping cars, asking for identification. Playing soldiers generally, I gather.'

He climbed out of the car.

'Just thought you'd like to know, in case you get stopped.'

'Well, what the hell are the police doing? I mean, they're not just letting this happen, are they?'

He sniffed. 'The Home Secretary announced last night that the police would only intervene in the case of an actual breach of the peace. You know what that means – it's as good as telling any Chief Constable: keep your nose clean, turn a blind eye.'

I got into the Lancia and slammed the door.

'What would you do in his place?' I asked through the open window.

'Me,' he said, waving me on, 'I'd shove the whole bloody lot of them in jail.'

I drove out through a quiet, early Sunday morning Southampton, heading north for Cambridge, and hit the first road block a mile or two after the suburbs had given way to the rolling Hampshire hills.

Wooden poles had been placed across the road, forcing cars to slow to negotiate the gap in the barrier. The line of cars and trucks were being signalled through by four men in dark-blue peaked baseball caps, dark roll-neck sweaters and dark trousers tucked into black army gaiters. A similarly dressed figure, whom I took to be their commander, stood at the side of the road with a mill-board, recording the number of each vehicle that passed. They appeared to be stopping about every tenth car for a few moments, one of the Action England men coming forward to talk to the driver while the others opened the boot and poked around in the contents.

I was furious. In the last year we had all of us, in Western Europe, come to accept the necessity of police and regular army road blocks as a means of restricting the movement of gelignite and plastic 808 explosive by the terrorist groups. But this was too much. I wheeled down the window and yelled at the nearest dark blue baseball cap:

'What bloody right do you think you have to stop private citizens like this?'

He signalled the officer who stepped quickly across.

'Can I help you?' he asked with what seemed to me a sinister combination of politeness and suspicion. He was about fifty, fattening and with a military brush moustache.

'I want to know by what right you're stopping cars. You're a private army, aren't you? And they happen to be illegal in this country.'

'We are the Hampshire South association of Action England,' he said calmly. 'We are engaged in a communications and traffic control exercise in support of the Civil Power.'

Drivers behind were already beginning to sound their horns. He stepped back and waved me grandly on.

'The Civil Power doesn't need your support,' I said.

'Pass on, please,' he said stolidly, making it clear to the other drivers that *I* was the cause of the hold-up.

The build-up of car horns behind me was too much. I glared at him and let in the clutch, turning the Lancia on squealing tyres through the slalom of poles and out on to the clear road beyond. I was determined to have a word with General Deedes about this when I reported to him later in the day.

As I drove on through Hampshire there was plenty of evidence of the numerical strength of Action England but no further road blocks to raise my ire. Small groups of men, in the para-military dress I now realised was characteristic of the movement, were to be seen in the fields laying telephone landlines, erecting first aid tents or queuing for food at emergency field kitchens. Dark blue trucks with Union Jack and Cross of St George emblems were parked at intersections and youngsters on motorcycles wearing dark blue crash helmets and flying Union Jack pennants sped with messages from what I guessed was one mobile headquarters to another.

I had to admit it was all pretty impressive in its way and certainly indicated a considerable popular support for the General's movement. Of course I wasn't surprised at that – the fears and anxieties of the last few months of mindless bomb incidents in British cities had made that almost certain. I wondered what response the other European groups had obtained – Aktion Deutschland, Actione Italia, Action France . . .

I hit my next road-block a few miles later. Again it was constructed to form a slalom of poles through which the vehicles were being waved and spot-checked. But this time I noticed two of the Action England men by the side of the road were carrying shotguns.

I had decided after my last experience to submit to the delay and make my protests later to the General himself, so I edged forward in the line of cars and was ready to pass through peaceably when I was waved down.

A boy of about eighteen stepped forward and bent low so that the peak of his blue baseball cap was level with the Lancia's window.

'Do you mind emptying your inside pockets, sir?' he asked with great politeness.

'You're damn right I mind.'

He blushed, perplexed.

'I'm sorry to have to ask you, sir. But those are my orders – every tenth car.'

'They may be *your* orders but they are certainly not mine. Now kindly unhand this car because I propose to drive on.'

'All right, Simon. We'll deal with this gent,' a powerful voice said from behind the boy.

I looked up to see the two men with shotguns.

'Let's stop play-acting,' I said. 'You don't intend to use those, whatever I do.'

The driver's door flew open and I was grabbed by the shoulder of my jacket and with impressive strength hauled out of the car to find myself scrambling on all fours in the roadway.

'We're not play-acting, mister,' one of the men said from somewhere above me.

I got slowly to my feet. The two men were broad-shouldered and about my height. Both were around forty and both were handling their shotguns as if they appreciated the weapon value of the butt. Somewhere close behind me there were three or four other bluecaps. I glanced at the line of drivers waiting behind my car. The only thing I could read on their faces was an intense but docile curiosity. No, I wasn't going to get any help from them. I decided this was not the time to stand and fight.

'Inside pockets, please,' one of the men said.

I turned out the inside pockets of my jacket. Nothing very significant – money, used Sealink ticket folder, passport.

The young boy had already driven my car across to the side of the road and two other bluecaps were giving it a fairly thorough examination. It didn't take them very long to find my reserve passport – in the name of Synian – tucked under the back-seat carpeting.

One of the big men gestured to the farm gates opposite.

'Over here,' he said, pursing his lips at the two passports he had been given.

'Just listen to me,' I said, furious that I was going to be forced to explain to them. 'I'm on my way to see General Deedes now. I've been on an assignment for him.'

'We'll look into that at the farm.' One of the men pushed me in the direction of the low cluster of buildings. The other moved into position with his shotgun butt ready.

I glanced over at the line of cars, but the drivers immediately behind me were no longer looking in my direction. They were eagerly threading their cars through the gap in the poles, glad, even grateful, to be on their way again.

I passed through the farmyard gate, flanked by my escort, and came into an enclosed courtyard where nine or ten men were standing around with that disconsolate air of prisoners of war. The guards here were half a dozen well-built men in their early thirties, each carrying a white baton and wearing white gaiters in imitation of regular military police. Again I couldn't help being impressed by the attention to detail.

I was taken into a bare farmhouse room, whitewashed and oak-beamed, and invited to sit on a bench which, apart from a trestle desk and chair, was the only furniture. The one window was covered with a blanket and an office reading lamp on the trestle provided the room with its only illumination. I had seen enough interrogation centres in my time, from the well-appointed and ritzy to the crude and functional, to have no difficulty in recognising the genre.

After a few moments in which I sat smoking, the door opened and a tall, almost clerical figure entered. He wore no cap, but his allegiance was indicated by the dark roll-neck sweater and dark trousers.

He smiled pleasantly but said nothing until he had seated himself behind the desk and arranged his papers in front of him and balanced a pair of rimless spectacles on the tip of his nose. Then he leaned forward.

'Mr Hart,' he said. 'Or' – a thin smile – 'is it Mr Synian?'

'I think we should get something clear before we begin, Head-master,' I said. By the way his head jerked up I felt I may have achieved a shot in the dark. 'I do not in any sense accept your right to ask me questions. If I answer it is under duress, influenced as I am in my craven human fashion by half a dozen bully boys out there with white sticks . . .'

'Mr Hart,' he interjected severely, 'this is a communications and traffic control exercise – '

'I know – in unasked support of the Civil Power. You're all damn well rehearsed, I give you that. Now what I want you to do is to get on to General Deedes immediately and tell him you have Tom Hart here. Then we'll talk.'

'You claim to be on an assignment for the General, I understand,' he said doubtfully. 'Is that true?'

'I'm saying nothing more until you've phoned.'

He was obviously hesitating, pen poised, anxious to get down to the details of my *curriculum vitae*. After a second or two of silence he stood up, scraping the chair back on the stone floor.

'Please wait outside, Mr Hart,' he said primly.

I walked out into the farm courtyard and the Headmaster followed a moment or so later. His papers tucked neatly under his arm, he hurried across to the main building.

My fellow detainees looked at me curiously. I drew on my cigarette and stared back until a little fellow in green tweeds detached himself from the group and came across.

'No trouble, I hope,' he said. He was thin-faced with black hair brushed back in a 1930s widow's peak. There was nothing trendy and Red Banner about him.

'What are they holding you for?' I asked him.

'My own fault, really,' he said, 'I'm in the jewellery business.'

I told him that didn't seem particularly reprehensible *per se*.

'No, I mean, I carry a gun, you see. Perfectly legal under the new personal arms law, of course. But like a fool I wasn't carrying the licence with me. They're just getting clearance for me now.'

'Clearance?'

' Just checking with the wife that I'm who I say I am.'

I looked at him. I found it difficult to believe he was accepting it so easily.

'And doesn't it stick in your throat – these self-appointed watchdogs?'

'Somebody's got to do it if the Government won't. Look what the country's come to in the last year. Bombings all over the place, political strikes – Scotland going Communist. Doesn't it make you think?'

'It makes me wonder what good a private army like this'll do us.'

'I don't know. I was in Switzerland when Action Suisse held an Alert. Went like clockwork.' He laughed. 'Then I suppose it's bound to in Switzerland, isn't it? Anyway, point is they pulled in over a thousand pounds of gelignite and detonators in one day. And handed over about fifty suspects to the police.'

I nodded gloomily. Yes, I'd heard about the success of some of the Continental alerts. I suppose that was what was making it all so depressing. But I'd genuinely thought someone like General Deedes would handle things differently.

The Headmaster came out into the courtyard and hurried importantly across to where I was standing.

'Our apologies, Mr Hart,' he smiled. 'The General has given you complete clearance.'

'I'm touched,' I said.

The smile faded. He handed me a piece of paper. 'This will take you through any further road blocks between here and Cambridge.'

I didn't want to take the paper, but the thought of going through all this again every twenty or thirty miles made me relent. I took it and shoved it crumpled into my inside pocket.

He frowned. I believe he really expected me to be grateful.

After a stop for lunch (and three or four road blocks easily negotiated with the aid of my pass) I arrived in Cambridge in the late afternoon. I soon parked my car, and made my way down Trinity Street to the Blue Boar.

The Blue Boar has been one of my favourite Cambridge hostelries from a long way back. In my first term as an undergraduate I had met Joan Burtle, my tutor's wife there. She had something of a reputation, which for the best part of that year I found was entirely deserved. Dodging up and down college staircases with Rabelaisian zest she would arrive at my set of rooms overlooking Trinity Great Court, let herself in and close my oak. The 'oak' or outer door of a Cambridge undergraduate's room is supposedly only closed when he is working. No one may knock and disturb him when the oak is sported. What medieval freedoms the system originally protected I know not, but many thousands of undergraduates before my time and since have found it the near perfect way of achieving privacy on those most private of occasions.

Sexual guilt I suppose is tolerable because it's so rewarding. In what other circumstances could I have retained for a whole year my ardour for a somewhat overweight, not particularly innovative, 43-year-old mistress? Later, much later, I began to feel the weight of other guilts. Guilts not to be savoured in the same delicious fashion, guilts that destroy sleep and appetite, guilts that can only be salved by drink.

It was in the Blue Boar too that I had met Mansfield for that crucial meeting in my last term when he had posed as an export director of an engineering company and discussed the prospect of my joining his firm. I had read Slavonic languages for the tripos and had achieved a fair degree of skill in Russian and Polish. That had interested him. My national service with the SAS had also interested him. I didn't think to wonder why at the time. In the next few weeks I took a battery of incomprehensible tests and wrote several papers on 'Anglo-Polish trade prospects', commercial rubbish of course but politically self-revealing, and all this without having the faintest idea I was being recruited. Indeed I spent over a month on a training scheme for Anglo-Polish Electronics before the penny dropped. I was delighted.

I registered at the desk, and my bags were taken up to my room while I headed for the bar. It was nearing eight o'clock and I bought myself a double whisky and carried it to the phone.

Virginia Deedes answered. 'Lady Deedes,' I said, 'this is Tom Hart here. We met a couple of days ago . . .'

'Indeed, Mr Hart.'

'I was hoping to speak to the General,' I lied. 'Is he back from his exercise yet?'

'I'm afraid not,' she said. 'I'm not expecting him back tonight.'

How sad. 'I have some rather important information for him. What time will he be back tomorrow?'

'I'm not absolutely sure,' she said. 'But I imagine during the morning.'

'Then I'll call round then if I may.'

'Please do.'

'If the General does come back tonight I'm staying at the Blue Boar. Perhaps you could get him to phone me here.'

'Yes, I'll ask him to do that if he returns in time. But I don't really expect him back.'

'In that case I'll have dinner here and an early night. Unless . . .' this was the moment . . . 'you'd like to join me for dinner. Since we both seem to be on our own this evening.'

It seemed a long pause. 'As a matter of fact I've just had some

41

sandwiches on a tray,' she said. 'I don't think I could really manage dinner.'

'That's a shame. I was looking forward to meeting you again.'

'Mr Hart,' she said after a moment or two. 'I behaved rather badly the other day. Perhaps I'd had a little too much white wine.'

'You were very charming,' I said. 'And if that's the effect of white wine I've no possible objection.'

'Please,' she said. 'I was trying to apologise.'

'Do it over lunch tomorrow.'

'No,' she said quickly. On the phone it was difficult to judge. But it didn't seem a very determined refusal.

'I'll be at the house to see the General tomorrow morning. Perhaps I'll get an opportunity to ask you again then.'

Again there was a long pause. 'No, Mr Hart, I'm sorry. I have a lunch appointment tomorrow.'

There seemed no point in pushing it further at that time. I said goodnight and took my whisky back to the bar.

Again the autumn weather appeared to be holding. I left the Blue Boar at about eleven o'clock and walked slowly down King's Parade in warm sunshine, then turned into Silver Street and bought a pint of bitter at the Mill. Carrying it out to the stone bridge I sat above the spurting mill race and sipped my beer in the sun.

At just before twelve I mounted the stone steps of the Deedeses' house, leaned against the elegant cast-iron flambeau holders and was about to press the bell-push when the door opened. Virginia Deedes was wearing a skirt. This, at least, was the first thing that struck me as she stood surprised on the doorstep. For the rest it was a dark brown shirt and a yellow silk scarf tucked in at the open neck.

'I was hoping to see your husband,' I lied.

She recovered. And smiled formally.

'Mr Hart. I'm afraid the General has a visitor with him at the moment. But let me tell him you're here. I'm sure he'll want to see you.'

She led me along the narrow hall and invited me to wait in a small room facing on to the garden. As the door closed after her I looked around to register two or three cane chairs, relics of the Raj, and a small monochrome television set in the corner. If this was the television room it certainly wasn't the hub of social life in the house. I wandered to the window. And was rewarded by the sight of Virginia crossing the lawn. Again that strange, appealing, high-stepping gait. She stopped at the table at which the General sat with a tall bronzed guest of about his own age. Bending over her husband's chair she said enough to make him look sharply towards the house. Major-General Sir Richard Deedes didn't seem entirely delighted that I had arrived.

I watched her return across the lawn and listened to her heels across the stone conservatory floor.

'Were you ever a model?' I asked her as she opened the door.

'Good Lord, no,' she said. Then smiled.

'He'd like me to come back in an hour or two. Right?'

'No, Mr Hart, wrong. If you don't mind waiting my husband will be ten minutes at the most.'

'And you?' I asked. 'You're one of the Syndics of the Fitzwilliam Museum? You have an honorary fellowship at King's College and you're off to lunch at the Senior Combination room to discuss dry rot and its effect on old master drawings?'

'A very good guess,' she moved her lips together.

'But in fact . . . ?'

'In fact I'm going to take a walk along the backs.'

'Over Newton's bridge, through Queen's?'

'I'll come back that way. I usually do.'

'Back home?'

'Usually.'

'Will you have lunch with me?'

'Yes.'

'The Blue Boar at one o'clock?'

'Yes.'

There was no more to say. She closed the door behind her and I stood alone in the room, elated.

If he wasn't ten minutes, he was not much longer. That I give him. I stood at the window watching the parting rites performed . . . the moving back of chairs, the slow winding-up of conversation.

The General's guest was almost the same height as he was, almost the same age and clearly out of a very similar mould. Yet there was a difference. Mostly, I suppose, in dress. The General wore cavalry-twill trousers, a sports jacket of generous check and a Viyella shirt and tie. His guest was more formally dressed in a light grey suit, pale blue shirt and English club tie. But he wasn't English. The suit was a give-away. French? German? South American-Spanish? I wasn't sure. And yet as he turned full face towards me and then paced slowly towards the house

43

his face seemed familiar. But then this is a minor psychological hang-up I have. Many strangers' faces seem familiar. Perhaps it's my need to be loved, or recognised . . . or if I can't be recognised at least *to* recognise. But still he seemed familiar.

Their heels didn't have the same erotic quality across the conservatory floor. I calculated (right this time) their entry into the narrow hall and threw open the door.

'Good morning, General.'

He turned, raising an eyebrow.

'Ah, Hart,' he said. Then a shade more easily, I thought, turning to his guest, 'Hans, this is Thomas Hart who has been doing some investigatory work for our organisation. Hart – General Freiherr von Arnitz.'

I knew the name, Hans von Arnitz, divisional commander at 29, the youngest senior general the German army had produced in the Second World War. The last-ditch defender of Smolensk, Lvov and of the faith. Of course I knew General Freiherr von Arnitz.

He bowed from the neck, smiled perfunctorily and turned to the General.

'Sir Richard. We must fight that battle again some day. But across a real war game table next time.' He sounded like a screen German general trying to cover up what they had really been talking about.

General Deedes winced.

'Hans,' he said quietly, 'there's no reason why Hart shouldn't know what we were discussing.' He turned to me. 'Freiherr von Arnitz is the new Senior Organising Officer of Aktion Deutschland, a group, as you know, very similar to our own. Same principles, appealing essentially to the same sort of people. People who are not prepared to sit back and be taken over by subversive forces without an extra effort to support the elected government. Right, Hans – in a nutshell?'

The German nodded. 'Yes, in a nutshell.' He stretched out a hand to the General. 'Sir Richard, I value your advice. I'll think about it.'

The General turned back from the door as his guest departed.

'If you don't mind me saying so, Sir Richard,' I said, 'that's fairly surprising company you're keeping.'

He looked at me, and his mouth turned down. Then hard: 'They were soldiers like us, Hart. And in any case it was a long time ago.'

'General, I accept that most Germans were soldiers like any

other, no better, no worse, just a bit more effective at the game than most. But not von Arnitz – he was SS.'

'You're revealing a civilian ignorance, Hart. Hans von Arnitz was *Waffen SS*. He and men like him were simply soldiers; they had nothing to do with concentration camps.'

'Theodore Eicke was a man like von Arnitz, General,' I reminded him. 'Shorter, fatter, not so polished, but a *Waffen SS* divisional commander like your friend. He commanded The Death's Head, Totenkopf division. Before that he was Himmler's inspector of concentration camps. He *founded* Dachau. Don't tell me the SS weren't more often than not all the same sort of men.'

The General stood his ground. 'I only know that Hans von Arnitz is an honourable and compassionate man. I don't propose to discuss the matter further.'

I clearly hadn't done a lot to increase my job prospects with Major-General Sir Richard Deedes. But the truth was I had some liking for the man, and I could see how the press would tear him to pieces if they heard he was associating with people like von Arnitz.

I was willing to try again.

'General Deedes,' I said, as he led me through the conservatory and out into the bright sunlight of the garden, 'in my line of business the political smear is as destructive a weapon as the tank is in yours.'

'I don't follow you, Hart,' he said crisply as we walked on the lawn while Albert cleared the table.

'I mean that Aktion Deutschland run by an ex-SS general is not going to do the image of Action England that much good.'

'I thought I'd made it clear I had no wish to discuss the subject,' he said as we sat down again.

'All right, General – if you only want to hear good news . . .'

'News, in fact is what I'm interested in, Hart. Not speculation.'

'How long have you known him?'

'Von Arnitz?'

I nodded.

'Many years.' He seemed to have decided to say no more, then suddenly he changed his mind and added: 'I was a member of the de-Nazification court in Hamburg the year the war ended. I know a great deal about von Arnitz as a man and as a soldier. He was one of the few SS officers actually to oppose Hitler in 1945.'

I laughed. 'General, Heinrich Himmler was another. But what

does it prove? Only that by that time the game was up – and they realised it. Listen, General. There were basically two types of anti-Hitler movement – those who opposed from 1939 or earlier – and there were many of them – generals like Beck, civilians like Goerdeler, younger colonels like von Stauffenberg, pastors like Bonhoeffer. Even students like members of the White Rose. Then there was the second group – the SS opposition – Himmler and Schellenburg. But their opposition begins at what you might think is a significant point in time, General. Their opposition begins when every village idiot could see that the war was lost. So don't talk to me about civilian ignorance, or I'll start talking about military naïveté.'

He sat stiff-backed and shocked at my outburst. I felt pretty foolish myself.

'I appreciate the history lesson,' he said slowly. 'Now perhaps you'll give me your report on the freighter.'

'Yes, I'll give you the report, General. But I'll tell you this much – if I knew then what I know now about Action England, broke as I am, I would have turned the job down flat.'

'I don't follow you,' he said angrily.

'I'm talking about the whitewash you gave me in this garden a couple of days ago.'

'Whitewash?'

'You carefully didn't mention anything about barricading roads and searching private cars . . .'

'You're talking about the Alert yesterday?'

'Of course I'm talking about the Alert. You sat me here and went on about democratic processes and support for the Civil Power and all the time you had a uniformed army preparing to take over from the police.'

He gestured impatiently. 'A simple problem of timing. Part of the object was to see how quickly we could mobilise our organisation. It would have defeated the purpose to announce ten days earlier that a mobilisation exercise was to take place.'

'And this way you also jumped the gun on any left-wing opposition to the Alert?'

'That was a further consideration – yes.'

'General, I don't know where you were yesterday . . .'

'I was in my tactical headquarters.'

'I was driving from Hampshire to Cambridge. I was stopped a number of times – once by men with shotguns. I was also detained by uniformed men with batons. Is this what Action England is about?'

He leaned his elbows on the table and looked at me hard.

'Have you ever been involved in trying to cross a factory picket line, Hart?'

'No.'

'Well, since a craven government gave pickets almost equal rights with the police, it isn't much fun.'

'Perhaps. But I don't see how it's relevant either.'

'Were you physically harmed in any way yesterday? Or do you know anybody who was?'

'I was detained, General.'

'Inconvenienced. Aren't you prepared to put up with a little inconvenience?'

'From the police or army, yes. But not from self-appointed para-military forces.'

'You exaggerate, Hart. Do you appreciate the success of yesterday's Alert?'

'I appreciate the extent of it.'

'No, the success, Hart. We proved that in a matter of hours we were able to establish emergency communications and monitor civilian movement throughout an important section of Southern England. And . . .' he lifted a hand to silence me . . . '*and* we were successful to the extent of delivering a number of terrorist suspects, with evidence, to the police. Isn't *that* worth a little inconvenience, Hart?'

I looked at his long jaw-line and earnest blue eyes. 'I think you're playing with fire, General,' I said.

'Nonsense. The Action England organisation has been offered to the Government. At any time it can decide to take it over as a regular arm of the Civil Power. My belief is that they *will* take it over as they become increasingly aware of its effectiveness and following. That's my ambition, Hart.'

I nodded, tight-lipped. 'When do you plan your next Alert, General?'

'For early November. And this one will be announced in advance.'

'As an open challenge to the government?'

'Yes – as a challenge to take us over and use our organisation as it should be used.' He raked me with his blue eyes. 'I'm sorry you feel you can't agree with our aims, Hart.'

'Oh, I agree with your aims,' I assured him. 'It's your methods I'm less certain of.'

'Either way I feel it's unlikely we shall have you as a supporter . . .'

I shrugged.

'. . . So perhaps you'll deliver your report on the freighter.'

I recounted my story and put special emphasis on the plywood superstructure that had been fished up near the sea area where the *François Villon* was hi-jacked. But the General was really only interested in my confirmation of the gelignite theft. Already while I was in France there had been three large explosions in Liverpool, and two in Manchester. The newspapers at least were baffled as to the source of the quantities of gelignite used. Based on my information the General no doubt planned to give them the answer – and once again to hammer home the effectiveness of Action England.

We didn't part on good terms. He was cold and distant as he thanked me for the work I'd done, and he paid out my expenses disdainfully in one-pound notes from a battered cash box. I'd already dropped from captain to corporal in his eyes.

He stood up as Albert arrived to see me out. 'I thought I'd found a good man in you, Hart. I don't mind telling you I'm disappointed.'

I shrugged. 'I don't mind telling you, General, I feel the same way.'

We sat at the table in the restaurant of the Blue Boar and talked about Action England. It was clear that she shared the General's basic worries about the way things had developed in the last year here at home and throughout Europe. The Italian situation was becoming desperate, with rail communications often paralysed for days with hoax and real bombs placed at vital junctions the length of the peninsula. In Germany and Holland things were somewhat better but the monthly casualty toll of letter bombs, car bombs, shop bombs and aircraft bombs had mounted rapidly in the last few months, since Red Banner had apparently imposed some sort of organisation on the previously idiosyncratic killers.

France and Britain, with security forces experienced in Algeria and Northern Ireland, had so far kept the bombings to manageable proportions. But it was difficult not to agree that as economic conditions worsened things were deteriorating rapidly.

She asked me what I guessed would happen in the next year or so, and I told her what I honestly thought – that in the last year the crystal ball had lost its value. Come to think of it, you couldn't get a price on the scales of justice either. Put it down to television or the lack of vitamin E in the bread, but the fact was that too many people who should have known better had chosen in the early '70s to *understand* why the IRA did what they did, to *understand* the desperate murders of the Palestinian terrorists. Everybody fell for it – including the Catholic Church in Ireland and the United Nations' Third World block . . . and now the hands fly to the mouth in shocked surprise if it's suggested they *condoned* the murder of innocents. They simply *understood.*

'And in that, at least,' I said, 'I admire your husband. Not for him the *traison des clercs.* He believes that some things are worth fighting for.'

'Don't you?'

'It's what I've done all my adult life.'

'And were you wrong to do it?'

'No, I don't think so. But what's important, just as important, is the way it's done. People like your husband perhaps don't always keep sight of that fact. People like your husband – and like me as I used to be, perhaps.'

'What changed your mind?'

'A Polish girl. Named Theresa. Just a very ordinary, homely little thing. But she worked as a secretary in a chemical plant outside Warsaw – and the chemical plant had Polish military contracts. So I was assigned to get to know her.'

She looked at me without speaking. I drank some more wine.

'I took her out to all the student dives that are the rage in Warsaw, went for long walks along the Dnieper, yawned our way through an opera or two. Three months later I had the contract details in my pocket. The big important contract that London desperately wanted information on was for the supply of a barrack latrine cleaning fluid. The closest it got to bacterio-logical warfare was that it was classed as a germicide. That night Theresa was picked up by the State police.'

'What happened to her?' Virginia asked.

'Nothing dramatic. She wasn't shot. Or tortured. She just lost six years of her life. In a labour camp.'

'If it really had been a germ warfare contract, would that have made a difference?'

I shrugged. 'I don't know. I don't know, I just haven't worked that out.'

I suppose I'm in something of a confessional frame of mind these days, and the problem is my stories don't really offer much chance for more than sympathetic listening. Even Jazz, I knew, found it hard going at times. With Virginia I managed to produce

49

ten minutes of false starts and awkward silences.

Then gradually as we began our second bottle of wine we began to talk about her. She had grown up in the impeccably preserved, white-painted colonial town of Lexington, Massachusetts with her mother and step-father, a Professor of English Literature at Harvard. Each morning he had driven her into Cambridge to drop her off at the Peabody School on Linnaean Street and each afternoon she had been picked up by her mother the moment school ended at two-thirty. Just two or three times in her whole early life she had slipped away to Brigham's, the ice cream parlour on Mass. Avenue, or mingled with the Harvard students in the co-op, but mostly her schooldays were carefully regulated by her Puritanical step-father's anxieties about the growth of permissiveness in the late '50s. She had first visited her own father in England when she was twelve and had immediately reacted to the casual freedoms accorded the daughter of an English county family. Her father was a soldier, a major then, in the Brigade of Guards, immensely tall, cheerful and not very intelligent. By the age of fourteen she was crossing the Atlantic twice a year whenever her father was on leave from Malaya, Cyprus, Germany or wherever his regiment was stationed.

He had married again, of course, a colourless Englishwoman of similar background, quite unlike her own determined, intelligent Yankee mother. But Virginia and her new-found step-mother got on well enough. She spoilt the child and pressed for her to stay longer in the hope that her husband would not insist on her having children of their own. For odd, impracticable periods of a term or two here and there she had even been at school in England, where she had absorbed the necessary nuances of her English rank and learnt to become proud, rather than simply amused, that her father was a baronet. At eighteen she had enrolled at Radcliffe but long before her four undergraduate years were up she was already travelling the Atlantic again every vacation. At twenty-one she left Massachusetts for good and came to live with her father.

I asked her if, in the last resort, she felt English or American.

'Both,' she said. 'But the curious thing is that although I was repressed in America and given all the freedom I wanted in England, still, I know, the most liberated part of me is American.'

We left the Blue Boar and drifted towards King's College. They were mowing the grass in front of the magnificent Gibbs building and we strolled slowly past towards the river bank.

Punts glided downriver, some expertly, others ineptly punted. Things had changed very little. More girls did their bit with the punt pole, there were many more jeans about than I could ever remember. But the voices sounded very much the same – more Rugby and Cheltenham than Manchester and Bradford Comprehensive.

I found her mood difficult to judge. Sometimes animated, sometimes grave but always somehow with this strong sense of herself, as a person, a woman. And yet as we sat there on the river bank I was aware of something else too, some struggle in progress. It was some time before I realised she wanted me to ask about her husband.

We lay facing each other, plucking grass shoots and chewing them.

'He had red tabs on his collar. He had authority. He had authority even over my father. I don't know why but I found that immensely exciting.'

I raised my eyebrows. She smiled.

'The significance wasn't lost on me. Even at that time.'

As she bent her head I could look down from the nape of her neck, down the undulations of her back to where bent back, crossing and uncrossing, her legs kicked idly in the air – like a schoolgirl in the body of a woman.

'What happened then – did he begin to ask you out?'

'No, not immediately. We met from time to time at various point-to-points. He would always come across and chat and be pleasant. But it was at a ladies' night at the brigade mess that I really first became aware that he was interested.'

'What did he do?'

'He told my step-mother.'

I burst out laughing.

'Look,' she defended him, 'he was obviously in a difficult position.'

'So he chose your step-mother as an intermediary?'

'Why not? He asked if I would accompany him on a weekend to Germany. His friend Hans von Arnitz has a hunting lodge near Mainz.'

'You agreed.'

'Of course. I was twenty-four. He was twice my age. He had solidity, respect from people of my father's generation . . .'

'There you go again.'

'I'm serious. He offered all those qualities I'd been brought up to admire.'

'And do you admire them still?'

'Yes,' she said slowly, 'yes, I think I do. But at the same time I've come to understand that that sort of society, the society of the English upper classes – responsibility and *bon ton*, dinner parties and hunting – can only express part of the personality. In all of us there's something less disciplined, more sensual . . .' She broke off.

Her light brown eyes wandered past my shoulderline to the river behind me. A splash, a squeal of girl's laughter which meant some aspiring punter had lost his pole.

I didn't turn my head. Slowly her eyes came back to meet mine.

'He's not a monster, you know,' she said. 'He's very kind. And he was an exceptionally efficient soldier.'

'That sounds like a requiem, if ever I heard one.'

She looked down at the grass without answering. Slowly her head came up level with mine.

'When you're next in London alone, will you phone me?' I said.

I could see by the rhythmic flare of her nostrils that she was breathing deeply. 'The General's holding a big conference in London next week.'

'Will you be going to it?'

'To the main meeting, yes. Afterwards he expects at least a day of smaller meetings.'

'You'll have time on your hands, then?' I said slowly.

She nodded. 'Some, at least, of which I'd like to spend with you,' she said and leaned forward and for three, four, five seconds placed her mouth on my lips.

Chapter 8

Driving back from Cambridge I was waved down at an army road block just outside Stevenage. In the last few months spot checks of this sort had become common practice in a good many European countries. For the British what they had believed was confined to Northern Ireland was now a part of everyday life.

The men in red berets and camouflage jackets came forward to surround the car. After my experiences of yesterday I was quite pleased to see them. The Parachute Regiment sergeant in charge of the squad was polite and hard-eyed. I was invited to get out of the car and open the boot. Two men ran gelignite detectors over the vehicle and two others examined the underneath of the Lancia by running angled mirrors mounted on small trolleys between the wheels. The remaining two troopers covered me with their machine pistols.

'Thank you, sir. Sorry to have troubled you,' the sergeant saluted as I climbed back into the car.

I pulled away from the road block and watched, in my driving mirror, the paratroopers flag down another car. Lighting a cigarette I switched on the car radio. The news was of more bomb incidents scattered across the British Isles. But there was no mention of what I was really listening for. I imagined by now that Mansfield and his European equivalents had moved against the names on Pushkin's list while I was in France. That would probably mean an announcement late today or tomorrow morning. I switched off the radio and drove fast towards the city.

Parts of London kill me. Not Whitehall, and the Horseguards Parade, Buckingham Palace, and the Tower . . . but smaller, more private corners. Like the craggy mulberry tree that sits on a handkerchief of sloping grass behind eighteenth-century railings overlooking the Thames at Chelsea. That tree was there before the Victorians banked the river, that patch of sloping grass is the last vestige of a water meadow where Thomas More walked arm in arm with his royal murderer. Traffic thunders past it now, TIR trucks for Amsterdam or Alicante; Vivas, Victors, Jaguars, Datsuns, Beetles, Renaults, Fiats and myself among the pulsating traffic, directing the Lancia as the lights changed green along the Embankment towards Jazz Oliver's flat.

I could have turned left at the mulberry tree, up Beaufort Street, across King's Road, towards my own flat in Elm Park Mansions. No prescience kept me away, no nagging presentiment of danger. Just the thought of a drink with Jazz, a recounting of the Honfleur story, a laugh at my intrepid leap from fishing boat to freighter and maybe dinner afterwards at the Aretusa on King's Road or my favourite Tandoori house on Sidney Street.

I could tell I'd made the right decision the moment I saw her face.

'What is it, Jazz?'

She led the way quickly into the sitting room.

53

'Stevens called,' she said over her shoulder, as she reached the sideboard and began pouring drinks. 'Mansfield's after you.'

I took the drink she handed me.

'He's got something for me?'

'No, Tom, he's *after* you. He's got men watching your place. Does he know about me?'

'You're my private life,' I said. 'Mansfield doesn't even know you exist. What did Stevens say?'

'He rang about three times. Didn't leave a name. But you can't miss that queer, plummy voice. He said it was because of a list – you'd know which list.'

'Yuh, I know. I picked up a list for Mansfield at the Tower of London a couple of mornings ago. What about the list?'

'Stevens said when they went round with the sack and bludgeon the birds had all flown. You know what that means?'

I nodded. 'It means Mansfield thinks I tipped them off.'

'Tipped who off?'

'The names on the list – in all probability the international leadership of Red Banner. And as if losing them weren't bad enough for Mansfield, he's also lost face before our informants.'

'Who were they?'

'An improbable Russian song-and-dance act named Pushkin and Tchaikovsky.'

She was nervous and strung up enough to laugh. But she got a quick hold on herself and told me to take it easy while she went out to buy steaks and a bottle or two of wine. This was clearly no evening to make ourselves conspicuous in one of the better-known restaurants. I peeled off a pair of tenners from the wad the General had given me and told her to pick up a couple of bottles of the Château Margaux '70 that we were both devoted to and got a sweet-tasting tongue in my mouth for the gesture. One of the really nice things about Jazz is that she believes a man's there to be turned on. She looks on men (I once had occasion to feign complaint) as nothing but sex objects. She and I both were feeling better by the time she left to buy the dinner.

I threw myself on to the sofa and lit a cigarette. What made Mansfield suspect me of tipping off Red Banner? That I could find out from Stevens. Maybe he was just guessing I'd seen the list. It was after all fairly standard Service practice to have a shufti at anything that came your way. Information – assessment – conclusion was the formula the training manuals hammered home. And it had all seemed fairly obvious and simplistic until

54

you began to see how many people in fact developed concepts backwards from a preferred conclusion to an assessment which fitted in the information available.

And what I lacked at the moment, I decided, was information. I'd also decided that only Stevens could provide it when the phone rang – I lifted the receiver and held it to my ear without answering.

'Thomas.'

It was Stevens's voice, without a doubt.

'It's me,' I said. 'Luckily I came straight here.'

'Very lucky, dear boy. A certain mutual friend is exceedingly upset with you.'

'Jazz tells me he's having my flat watched.'

'Microscopically.'

'But he can't believe I handed out a tip-off,' I protested.

'He can and does. Now listen, Thomas. Meet me at my club later this evening. I'll be able to tell you more then.'

I agreed and had just rung off when Jazz came back with the supper.

As she began work on the steaks and I opened the various bottles I told her Stevens was trying to find out exactly what had happened.

She turned away from the grill as I poured her the magic liquid. I held my glass to the light and delighted in the faint rust-coloured hue of the wine against the brim. And though strictly speaking it might have benefited from a couple of days standing and an hour or two breathing I still felt that singular black flavour was worth the eight pounds a bottle Jazz had paid. I can never drink wine of this quality without an overwhelming desire to rush out and proselytise the martini and scotch drinkers. But I am restrained by the thought of the impact of the big spenders of Manitoba, Melbourne and Manchester on the price structure of fine clarets. And my missionary zeal declines with the level of wine in the bottle.

'Stevens,' Jazz said, 'hadn't he seen the list too?'

I nodded. 'He typed a copy. But he couldn't possibly have memorised the whole list with addresses. And why should he tip off the Red Banner, and then give me the word? No, not Stevens, Jazz.'

No, the more I looked at it, through, round and over my second glass of claret, the more it looked to me like an internal conflict in the Soviet Embassy.

If Pushkin and Tchaikovsky were Military Intelligence, GRU

– as I believed – it was perfectly possible that they were being co-operative in order to smooth the path for the diplomats proper at Kensington Palace Gate. Readily conceivable was a situation in which the hard-line KGB didn't approve of this namby-pamby co-existentialist behaviour on the part of the diplomats, and had decided to blow it.

That still left the question, after the steaks and claret were consumed, of what the hell I could do to put myself back in right with Mansfield. The first step evidently was to see what Stevens had found out.

The Gay Night Owl is located in a basement under an antique shop in the King's Road not five minutes' walk from Jazz's flat. Women and straight men are excluded from membership, and when Jazz and I both presented ourselves at the studded leather door the reaction was a distinctly raised eyebrow on the other side of the Judas.

'Guests of Mr Stevens,' I said firmly.

The eyebrow relaxed. The door opened.

'For one dreadful moment,' said the tall, languid polo-necked doorman, 'I thought you were a pair of Luxemburger tourists who'd inadvertently stumbled on our little haunt.'

Jazz grinned. 'What would you say if we had been?'

'Oh, what I usually say, I suppose: tonight's orgy night – everybody's welcome if they've got clean knickers. They then *usually* leave without too much of a fuss.'

The club consists of two rooms divided by a doorless arch. The first room, the bar, contained about eight or nine men of all ages. They stood in pairs drinking and talking, soberly well-dressed for the most part. It might have been the saloon bar of any City pub. As we passed through, the kaleidoscope of conversations seemed to be about share prices, house buying, schools for the children . . . Yet every one of them flickered hostile eyes at Jazz as she passed.

We could see through the arch that six or seven of the red-clothed tables were occupied by diners. Stevens sat alone at a corner table watching the pretty young male guitarist.

He stood up immediately he saw Jazz. They had always got on well, each recognising, I feel fairly sure, the promiscuous sensuality of the other. He greeted us both, and asked us to join him in another bottle of wine.

'Only if you can follow a Château Margaux '70,' Jazz said.

56

Stevens's eyes widened: 'Who has to?'

'You do, I'm afraid. We've just drunk a bottle each. Anything less would be a fearful anticlimax.'

'Which is presumably one worse than no climax at all. Very well . . .' he signalled the waiter, 'Harold,' he said, 'you've got a bottle of Warre '63 on your list. Nurse it in this direction, will you?' He turned to Jazz. 'You *do* drink port?'

She said she did.

'Good,' Stevens expanded, 'and we might even save a teeny glass for the guitarist there. I think he's awfully good, don't you?'

Jazz said he was super. I said I thought he played as if he had two broken thumbs but, of course, Jazz and Stevens weren't talking about his playing.

They put their heads together. 'You've probably noticed,' Stevens murmured, 'those quite *remarkable* thighs.'

'He does go both ways, I suppose?' Jazz wasn't going to waste any precious lust on the boy if it were pointless. Stevens assured her that he had it on excellent authority that the boy, Andrew by name, was open to the widest possible range of suggestions for one so young and toothsome.

The waiter brought the port already decanted, and as I poured three glasses they were speculating on whether or not he used a sponge to pack his jeans – or could that really be all *him*. Reluctantly Stevens turned his attention away from the boy. Briskly he recounted what he had found out. Mansfield had been put in charge, about a month ago, of co-ordinating European efforts against Red Banner. When the Russians decided, for their own purposes, to provide a list of Red Banner commanders, Mansfield appeared on the point of making the biggest coup of his professional life. He planned eleven simultaneous police raids in eleven European cities for last night. But when the various heavy mobs had battered down the doors they'd found no one at home.

'All eleven had been tipped off?' I must admit I was beginning to get a strong hunted feeling.

Stevens nodded: 'They left pans boiled dry on the stoves, television sets still on, papers burnt and crushed in the grate. Not just a tip-off, but a fast, efficient one.'

'And Mansfield,' I asked. 'How did he react?'

'Can't you guess? The Department has been in an uproar all day. Rumours, counter-rumours, but the final picture is, unfortunately, clear enough . . .'

Mansfield had apparently recognised that someone at the

Russian Embassy in London might have been responsible for the tip-off. He knew from long experience that in Soviet Embassies the KGB, Military Intelligence, Diplomatic troika doesn't always pull in the same direction at once. But if the KGB were responsible for the tip-off there wasn't a damn thing that Mansfield could do about it.

In any situation, however, impotence is what Mansfield finds hardest to accept. So with no more intention than of filling investigatory gaps he had begun to examine the single possible section of the chain of events in which he wasn't impotent to act – the period between my receiving the list and handing it over to him.

Stevens of course had denied any knowledge of the contents of the envelope. Mansfield's next move was the devious one. He'd run a saliva test on the envelope gum and checked it against mine and Stevens's records.

'Yours, Thomas, I'm afraid,' Stevens lisped, 'was rapidly established as the guilty tongue.'

Chapter 9

Jazz woke me at sometime after ten with the morning papers. She was dressed in a crisp blue denim skirt and a white shirt. Her fair hair was brushed but her round face had not yet received its morning quota of Elizabeth Arden. She stood over me looking almost virginal.

I slipped my hand under her skirt and gave her thigh a good morning hug almost from force of habit. She didn't resist but then she didn't go mad about the idea either. I had told her about Virginia last night after we'd left Stevens's club, and she knew our relationship was about to run into one of its more platonic periods. It had happened before to both of us, and had certainly not worried Jazz. Which is just another of the things I really like about this girl.

I opened the papers and spread them across the bed. The General's publicity machine couldn't have used advice from Barnum and Bailey; every paper carried Deedes's revelation of the hi-jacked freighter on the front page. Most carried a photograph of the General himself, and they all featured prominently his denunciation of the government cover-up and his insistence on far tougher measures against the terrorists. Central to his demands was of course his call to reintroduce capital punishment for a wide range of terrorist crimes. This was really going to put the Government on the spot, because they knew full well that the majority of the British electorate wanted the return of hanging. The Government's problem was that a significant part of the party would not countenance hanging under any conditions and a vocal section of the young, callous and insensitive to the bombers' victims, would beat their breasts and rend their hair at the iniquity of a society which proposed to hang the murderer.

But the General's demands didn't stop at hanging. He proposed a massive recruiting drive (mostly I guess among members of Action England) for the creation of an armed anti-terrorist force with stop and search powers such as the police and army exercised. At this point I just couldn't go along with him. I had seen enough of the CIA, SDEC and even our own Intelligence services to know that a few rotten apples could soon corrupt the barrel. Ten years in the barrel with Mansfield had taught me that.

The tabloids, who go to press later on the whole than the rest of Fleet Street, carried the follow-up story: the jubilant claim of Red Banner to have engineered the freighter hi-jack. Together the two stories represented a body-blow to the Government.

I lay back on the pillow to think about my own situation. Stevens's advice last night had been to use the contact facility that Pushkin had given me and tip-off the Russians that somebody in their Embassy was not playing straight. Armed with more information from Pushkin, Stevens felt it might be possible to clear myself with Mansfield.

In the cold light of morning, as they say, I wasn't too sure. Yes, Mansfield knew I had looked at the list, but he also knew that in our business that was not too unusual. Perhaps in his anger at his loss of face before his European colleagues he had overreacted. Perhaps by now he had had second thoughts.

I got up quickly, got dressed and asked Jazz to take a walk with me. She readily dropped her paint brushes, took off her smock and was waiting for me at the door as I finished dressing.

We walked up Lawrence Street past the superb William and Mary houses which Jazz coveted and reached King's Road by way of Oakley Street. We crossed King's Road quickly and slipped, via Dovehouse Street, through the slightly anonymous area of the old workhouse and Chelsea Women's Hospital until we emerged on to Sidney Street. At the flower shop opposite the Gothic revival church of St Luke's we bought a large bunch of roses. Then, while I killed time in the churchyard, Jazz went on to check the situation at my flat.

I sat among the shouting, pushing children and the sleepy-eyed young brothers and cursed Mansfield. Why should he think *I* tipped off Red Banner? Or maybe he didn't. Maybe it was just another example of the vindictiveness I had seen him use time and time again against others. Then again, maybe by now he had called the whole thing off.

She was back in a few minutes. She had gone up to the flat and rung the bell, having so far seen no sign of the Special Branch. A man in his late twenties wearing a suit, shirt and tie but all very recognisably King's Road in style, had opened the door to her.

'Chelsea Flower Deliveries,' Jazz had told him, proferring the bunch of roses, 'for Mr Tom Hart.'

At that moment my Latvian *émigré* neighbour and his manic long-fanged Alsatian emerged from the next-door flat and headed for the lift. The red-eyed, psychopathic quality of the brute (I'm mostly talking about the dog – but I wouldn't mince words about his owner either) diverted the attention of the young detective and Jazz was able to see past him into my flat. It had been gone over by a ransacker with a tidy mind. The contents of every drawer were stacked in front of the writing bureau, pictures had been removed, the television set eviscerated.

The detective had taken the flowers and glanced at the note on which Jazz had scrawled a message loaded with sexual innuendo.

As the Latvian and his dog disappeared into the lift the detective produced his warrant card and asked Jazz for a description of the woman who had sent the flowers. Jazz gave him a description to start any man's mouth watering.

'Did she pay by cheque?' the detective asked.

'No. Cash. Three pounds-twenty including delivery,' Jazz told him, and added, 'One of the pounds was a Bank of Ireland note, if that's of any interest.'

The detective thanked her and watched her from the doorway as she walked back down the corridor and rang for the lift.

I had given her a careful route-plan back to St Luke's churchyard which would prevent a car following her, and as far as I could see she was clear of anyone following on foot.

So Mansfield was still out for my blood. I had to extricate myself from this situation as soon as possible. Jazz and I agreed to meet later that evening and I found a public call box and looked up the number of the Royal Hotel. I dialled, and when the receptionist answered I asked for Mr Pushkin. She replied with hardly a hesitation and without asking my name. If I were to come to the hotel, Room 18, third floor in two hours' time Mr Pushkin would be there.

Obviously he was expecting a call. I left the hot-house atmosphere of the phone box. Without really thinking I crossed the road to the Wellesley Arms and ordered myself a large scotch.

It slipped down easily, without ice or water, and I pushed the glass across the counter for another. The euphoria of the last few days had disappeared. I was no longer employed by the General and my present chances of getting back into the Department were non-existent.

This last year the sociologists have published work on the psychological impact of unemployment from every conceivable angle. Of course they've had plenty of material to work on – redundant executives, salesmen, car workers, printers, building labourers . . . the whole spectrum. Not surprisingly, however, studies of redundancy in my line of business have been thin on the ground. In the four months since that interview with Mansfield I suppose only Jazz and Stevens had kept me anything like sane. It wasn't just that I had too much drinking time on my hands; it was, as much as anything, the lost sense of purpose, the special loneliness, the envy of watching men drinking up, checking watches, announcing they 'must get back'. Back to noisy offices, to scowling secretaries, to back-biting colleagues, it didn't matter. It was something to get back *to*.

No, not just too much drinking time. Too much thinking time too. I didn't mind admitting I wasn't as hard as I used to be. My tour of duty in the United States had shown that, I suppose. Or much more, if confirmation were needed, the accident the other day on Ludgate Hill. It was strange, and disconcerting, the way the image of the dying driver crumpled on the wet kerbstone had returned to me, sharp but fleeting, in these last few days. Self-analysis is not my bag and I couldn't really get past the idea of the senselessness of the accident. Maybe I'd talk to Jazz about it after all. She'd listen and be sympathetic and comforting. But then why should I need comforting for a sense of loss for an anonymous death?

Two or maybe three large whiskies later I decided to phone Mansfield. I left the pub and returned to the greenhouse heat of the call box. Checking his personal line number in my notebook, I dialled.

The phone was picked up immediately.

'Sir, this is Tom Hart,' I said into the receiver. Then remembered I'd forgotten to insert a coin. I fumbled for a ten-pence piece, pressed it home just before the pips stopped and tried again.

'Sir, this is Tom Hart.'

There was a pause at the other end which I guessed meant Mansfield was signalling to his secretary to have the call traced. That meant I had two minutes to be quite safe.

'Yes, Tom . . .' his voice was fruity with friendliness.

'You've put the SB on me.'

'What makes you say that, Tom?'

'They're in my flat – they've run a security check on everything but the mice behind the wainscot.'

'Why should they do that?'

'Let's stop the games, sir. You blew out on the Red Banner list.'

'You know that's what the Russians gave you?'

'Of course I did. Look, there's not a man in the Department who wouldn't have taken a shufti at the list. I did only what everybody else would have done.'

'There's a difference, however,' Mansfield said, 'you're no longer in the Department.'

'What difference does that make?' I asked him. 'I still have nothing to gain by tipping off Red Banner. And you know very well there's a much more probable explanation.'

'Which explanation's that, Tom?' He was luring me on, playing for time. I cradled the phone between my chin and shoulder, slipped off my watch and propped it in front of me as I spoke. One hundred seconds to go. I began to explain fast.

'The contact I met at the Tower was a Military Intelligence man. They've always taken a more liberal attitude than the KGB.'

'True . . .' he drawled. I could imagine his watch on the desk in front of him, too.

'And we know,' I pressed on, 'that London has Koloniev as senior KGB officer – and there's no one more hard-line than Koloniev.'

'I don't need a lecture on the opposition, Hart. If you've got something to say, say it.' Clever – annoy me – divert my attention from the time – less than fifty seconds.

'There have been a dozen occasions when we've profited from a GRU/KGB struggle. We know they don't always agree.'

'So . . .?' I was getting nowhere. I knew it. Twenty-five seconds.

'So this time Koloniev decided to throw a spanner in the works.'

'Koloniev, you think?'

'Why not? It fits. He's old guard. Yeshov's appointee, a Beria man for years.'

'But we don't even know he saw the list. The whole GRU operation may have been conducted without his knowledge. Or can you prove differently?'

Five seconds.

'No,' I said. 'Not yet. But I'm going to try.' Time up.

I put down the phone, picked up my watch and left the call box, walking rapidly in the direction of Kensington.

From the corner of Ixworth Place I saw the police car arrive.

The Royal Hotel was built in the '80s or '90s of the last century to accommodate middle-class travellers arriving at Paddington station.

Talking to Mansfield had had its usual effect on me, and the pumping adrenalin of hate had set me walking at too fast a pace across the park so that I arrived at the Royal Hotel almost ten minutes before the appointment time.

These Anglo-Russian Intelligence contacts – and they are more frequent than either side would like to admit, especially on the subject of China – have to be treated with a certain amount of delicacy. I therefore decided not to wait in the hotel lobby but to take in about four blocks in a slow circle which would bring me back to the hotel on time. It was thus that I was walking slowly down an unknown side-street when I saw just ahead of me a squat, stocky figure getting out of a black Citroën.

Pushkin saw me almost as I saw him. Locking the car door he raised a hand in greeting and waited for me to approach.

'Mr Hart . . .' he leaned forward and shook hands.

'I arrived early – I decided to take a walk,' I explained.

'In fact,' he told me, 'my colleague is already waiting for you at the hotel.'

'Tchaikovsky?'

He smiled. 'Yes, Tchaikovsky.'

We walked together down the sunlit side of the street. His

rolling gait brought our shoulders into contact on every second step.

'How long have you been in London?' I asked him.

He cocked an eyebrow in my direction, 'Surely your files . . .'

I had no objection to telling him, 'I no longer have access to the files. I'm what might be called an "occasional employee" of the Department these days.'

He nodded: 'Yes, I have heard.' He paused: 'How long have I been in London? Three months, four. Not long. But long enough to know I like it here. It seems to me that you have managed for the most part to live with the contradictions of your system. Is that apathy or maturity? I haven't yet made up my mind. Take this Paddington quarter we are walking through. I understand it is one of the city's main red light areas.'

I said it had a fairly seedy reputation, certainly.

'And yet,' he went on, 'is it not true too that it is also a quarter owned principally by your Church of England?'

I laughed: 'To their profit and embarrassment, no doubt.'

'Yes, a city of great fascination,' he mused.

'But then I'm sure Kiev is too.'

'Ah, you remember.' He was clearly delighted. 'No, sadly Kiev suffered much in the Great Patriotic War. We lost our incomparable Kreshchatik, our main boulevard and hub of the city. And our Kiev-Pechersk monastery and its Cathedral of the Dormition.'

'The Germans?'

'Some say.' He shook his head mysteriously.

I didn't press the point. We walked a few more steps in silence. Then he continued: 'One night,' he said, 'just a week or two after the Germans had occupied the city, that would be in August or September 1941, I was out with my younger brother. I was about fourteen or fifteen at the time. We were watching Germans, these strange, smartly-dressed soldiers with their special vehicles for everything. A huge convoy was rolling along the Kreshchatik towards the front further east at Konotop – or perhaps even Kharkov, they were advancing so fast in those days. We were watching the convoy, Mr Hart, and if I remember the last trucks had just passed through and the crowds were milling around almost in a holiday mood.'

'A holiday mood?'

He nodded. 'We were Ukrainians, not Russians. A holiday mood. When suddenly there was a vast explosion in the children's store two or three hundred yards from where we were standing, my brother and I. And then another behind us. And in the shouts and screams and panic another explosion and another and another and another. And they continued, Mr Hart, until the whole of the centre of Kiev was a blazing, exploding fire storm. The Ukraine is not unfamiliar with disaster, Mr Hart. The richest farmland in the world has seen great famine, wars have been fought across it, its Jewish population has been attacked in pogroms and massacred in gas vans and shootings. But we saw the destruction of the Kreshchatik and the monastery and cathedral as something different. The entire written record of Ukrainian history was destroyed in this catastrophe. Overnight we had become a people without a past.'

I walked along beside him waiting for him to continue. But he had finished.

'And who benefited from all this?' I asked. 'The Germans, presumably?'

Again he smiled. 'Yes, some say.'

We turned into the courtyard of the hotel and mounted the steps. I followed his broad back to the lift, noting the nod of recognition he received from the receptionist.

The lift took us to the third floor. It was a somewhat old-fashioned elevator whose doors did not open automatically. As it came to a stop Pushkin turned to me, his square thumb pressed over the button which opened the lift doors: 'The man you know as Tchaikovsky also comes from Kiev. As children we sold chestnuts in the Yevbaz, the Jewish market-place, for enough roubles to buy a glass of flour.'

'Sounds pretty capitalistic to me,' I said.

He smiled: 'Ah, during the German occupation we were forced to revert to naked capitalism to keep alive. But then the competition was not as stiff as it might have been. The SS had rounded up all the Jews of Kiev and shot them in the ravine outside the town.'

He pressed the button and the doors slid open. 'Sergei Sergei-vitch, the man you know as Tchaikovsky, compiled the list we passed to you.'

We walked down the hall, again with Pushkin in the lead. In front of Room 18 he stopped and rapped.

No answer.

Pushkin frowned and delved into his trouser pocket to take out a bunch of keys. He chose one and opened the door with it. I was a step or two behind him as he walked forward into the room, but I could almost feel the shock-wave pass through him.

Taller than he was I could see over his shoulder. Tchaikovsky lay on the floor, his jacket off, his hands secured by white insulating tape behind his back. His head was covered with a plastic bag which had been taped tightly round his neck. His dead eyes stared through the misted plastic and the running drops of condensation which had once been his breath.

Pushkin was down on his knees beside his friend. I'm not sure how long it took him to rip off the plastic hood and untape his wrists. I'm not sure how long I stood looking down at Pushkin cradling his friend's head in his arms. I'm not sure now what I felt or thought.

After some seconds or perhaps minutes I turned and walked into the corridor. I checked the service stairs and found they came out at a small courtyard at the back of the hotel. One side of the courtyard was stacked with empty orange boxes and the wisps of royal blue tissue paper shifted and rustled in the slightest breeze. For another indefinite period I stood staring at the boxes. Then I went upstairs again, along the corridor and closed the door behind me as I entered Room 18.

Pushkin had got Tchaikovsky's body up on to the bed. He turned as I entered.

'You checked the back staircase?'

I nodded: 'Nothing.'

'Thank you.' He sat on the bed beside the body, stroking the head. I lit two cigarettes and handed him one.

He turned to me. 'Sit down then, Mr Hart. Let's talk.'

I sat down, then saw for the first time a bottle of whisky and two or three tumblers on a sideboard.

He followed my eyeline.

'Please do,' he said. 'For both of us.'

I poured two very large whiskies and put one down beside the bed. He was still stroking Tchaikovsky's forehead but he had closed the eyes.

'You know,' I said, taking a long draught of whisky, 'that when we went to arrest the names on your list they had all gone.'

'I knew some of them had. Not all.'

'Somebody had tipped them off. My guess is someone in your Embassy didn't approve of the co-operative course you had taken. Koloniev perhaps?'

He thought for a long time, stubbing out his cigarette and taking up the whisky glass.

'You asked me if it was the Germans who had destroyed our Kreshchatik and the monastery and the Cathedral of the Dormition. No, Mr Hart. They were dynamited by our own NKVD in order to provoke German retaliation on the Kiev population. To make co-operation between the invader and the people impossible. The NKVD has now of course become the KGB, but its senior officers today take the same view of co-operating with the enemy.'

'You mean Koloniev could have done this?' I looked down at Tchaikovsky.

He remained silent.

'Or, more likely,' I pressed on, 'that Koloniev informed Red Banner that your friend was responsible for compiling the list.'

Again he was silent. I poured more whisky for both of us.

'What will you do?'

He stood up. 'I will continue to carry out the orders I have received. Those are to co-operate with Western European Intelligence forces in the annihilation of Red Banner. That means tracing Sergei Sergeivitch's contact and assembling a new list with up-to-date addresses.'

He finished his whisky in a gulp. 'Now, Mr Hart, perhaps I can ask you to go out and buy one or two items for me.'

'Of course.' I guessed what he was about to do – construct a scenario that wouldn't fool Special Branch for a moment but would cover any embarrassing situation that might arise in the Coroner's Court.

'Lipstick,' he said. 'And perhaps a lady's cigarette lighter. That should be enough.'

I went out by the service staircase and bought the lipstick and lighter in a row of shops behind the hotel. I returned to the hotel again by the back staircase and knocked on Room 18. Pushkin opened the door and silently stretched out his hand for my purchases. From where I stood I could see that he had turned back the bed and rumpled the sheets. Unscrewing the lipstick he pressed his index finger and thumb together and smeared them red. Then pressing his hand down on the pillows he achieved the rough outline of a lipsticked mouth on the white linen. As he tossed the lighter casually on the floor the sun emerged from behind the clouds and threw the swaying shadow of Tchaikovsky, hanging by the neck from the central lamp bracket, across the empty bed.

Pushkin stepped out into the corridor and closed the door behind him.

'We'll announce that he was about to be posted back to Moscow tomorrow. Nobody in the Embassy will be looking for trouble over this.'

I left Pushkin in the rear courtyard where the tissue from the empty boxes rustled in the breeze. He had not himself mentioned the name Koloniev since we entered Room 18. But I knew that's who he was thinking of. And I found it hard to imagine a worse enemy to make in this life than the affable Mr Pushkin.

Chapter 10

The pubs were open by the time I'd crossed the park on my way back to Chelsea. I stopped off at the Grapes in Knightsbridge, made a second stop at the Markham in the King's Road, drank up there but got no further than the Chelsea Potter before I stopped again.

The Chelsea Potter is one of those King's Road pubs that has hardly changed in the fifteen or twenty years I have been using it. It was the first pub in which I had ever bought a drink (aged 16, two years under age for the premises) and it had been one of the proudest moments in my life. I had matriculated that summer and had managed to get a vacation job as reserve stoker in a block of flats in the King's Road. The manager, a vigorous, broad-shouldered man of medium height and a native intelligence beyond his education, had elected to show me the job himself.

My first impression of the boiler room, with its six enormous boilers, its vast black water storage tanks, its lines of heavy overhead piping and its vast mounds of coke was of a hell-hole out of the days of the Industrial Revolution. When crunching footsteps over the coke dust made me turn I couldn't at first believe my eyes. The manager, Bob Woodhouse, previously immaculate in a Savile Row suit (second hand from the Aga Khan himself, he told me later), was dressed in a pair of baggy slacks and an old cardigan which, as he crunched forward, he was already peeling off to reveal a tattered, once-white singlet underneath.

'Right, son,' he said. 'Get your shirt off.'

I took off my jacket and shirt while he opened the feed doors to the boilers and squinted through the blast of heat at the congealed mass of white coals inside.

With no words wasted he explained that the job in hand was to transfer the coals of boilers three and four into boiler five, rake and clean boilers three and four and build up five for the day.

'Let's get a move on, then,' he said and bent to pick up a poker two inches thick and almost ten feet long. Lancing it deep into the boiler he thrust and battered until the white-hot mass of coals began to split and shatter under the impact.

I took up a second massive poker and attacked the other boiler. Unable to contemplate stopping while he, a man approaching fifty, thrust and smashed the white hot cinder with frenetic energy, I worked in the 90° heat until my legs trembled, my hands lost their grip and the sweat carved runnels in the coal dust on my arms. Two hours later we stopped. 'That's the job, son,' he said. 'Seven o'clock tomorrow morning. Still want it?'

I suppose it was the first real challenge of my life. I'm still not sure if I was too cowardly or too brave to say no. In these situations we never know. I nodded: 'Seven o'clock. I'll be here.'

For five weeks I raked and shovelled, sweated and trembled with exhaustion. At the end of every day Bob would come down, look over the result, eye my heaving, retching figure half-doubled over the coke shovel, and estimate tomorrow's needs. 'You'll want about another half ton shifted up front, Tom,' he'd say, and pick his way carefully in his Aga Khan suit across the coke and up the concrete stairs.

I came to will a word of praise from the man. Because I knew that on my day off he was down there alone, sweating and grunting and shovelling – finishing in two hours what it still took me a full day to get through.

My vacation was almost over. I'd finished up at Whitelands House and been paid off by the second porter. Sadly I'd not had a chance to say goodbye to Bob Woodhouse. My father and I lived together at that time in Astell House, a smaller block of flats than Whitelands but under the same management. I had nineteen pounds in my pocket and had invited for the first time in my life, my father, a retired naval officer, to have a drink on my earnings. He was a tall, wispy, not very forceful man. He had smiled across his pipe smoke and decided to humour his son.

I chose the Chelsea Potter – perhaps partly because I'd heard Bob Woodhouse drank there occasionally. Now I can no longer really remember if that was the reason. But we entered and shouldered our way to the bar and there he was.

He winked – no more – and turned back to his drink. I touched his arm and he looked round quizzically. I introduced my father and offered them both drinks. Bob Woodhouse asked for a plain tonic water, my father for a small whisky. As I tried to signal the barman my father was politely enquiring how I'd got on as stoker.

'I'll say this for him,' Bob Woodhouse said, knowing full well I could hear every word, 'the boy certainly knows how to work.'

But then, what I'd never come to terms with was that the other side of the Bob Woodhouse coin carried the face of Mansfield.

It was almost eight o'clock before I finally stepped out unsteadily down King's Road in the direction of Old Church Street and the Cross Keys.

The main bar was fairly full when I arrived and I took my large scotch into the garden at the back. From there I could see a good selection of the customers, mostly young twenties, students maybe or something on the fringe of the rock world. The economic situation didn't seem to be affecting them very badly. They still stood with their pints of bitter telling each other what a simple job it was to solve the country's problems.

I finished up my scotch and ordered another at the bar thinking I really should ask Jazz over to join me. Her flat was no more than a minute or two's walk away, and she used the Cross Keys and the King's Head about equally as locals. But then if I asked Jazz to join me now I wouldn't get in much thinking about Virginia. Instead I'd talk about Mansfield and Red Banner and Tchaikovsky in his plastic hood. And I really needed to get away from all that for an hour or two.

I was about to take my scotch back to my seat when a young man in jeans and roll-neck sweater, pale long face and frizzy blond hair, leaned back on the counter and said in answer to some unheard comment from his friend:

'Red Banner? They've done what they set out to do, that's all. They've demonstrated the impossibility of a capitalist structure for this society.'

'How?' I said.

He looked round at the stranger who was injecting himself into their conversation. He shrugged.

'The same way the IRA demonstrated the impossibility of Unionist rule in Northern Ireland.'

'How?' I said again.

'I should have thought it was obvious. All the repressive measures of the Government failed to defeat them.'

'Repressive?'

'Torture, beatings, internment without trial. I call that repressive.'

'The torture and beatings are a figment of your imagination, laddie,' I said. 'And internment was the only way to deal with an organisation that openly murdered witnesses.'

'You've been reading the *Daily Telegraph*', he sneered.

'Listen,' I said, 'what sort of society would you get if Red Banner had its way? You'd be the first to get a power drill through your knee-cap.'

'Oh, belt up,' he said, laughing at his friend.

'Come on, Johnny.' The friend tried to move him away, looking warily at me.

'Wait a minute.' I turned him round by the shoulder. 'I'm asking a question. If Red Banner's willing to blow the legs off an eighteen-year-old girl to get what it wants . . .'

He laughed, shaking his head at my astounding ignorance of Red Banner's methods.

'Red Banner,' he said, spelling it out as if for a five-year-old, 'is only interested in destroying property. That's what all the fuss is about in the capitalist press.'

'And Red Banner have never killed anyone, then?'

'Listen,' he jabbed a finger, 'Red Banner gives a phone warning to Scotland Yard every time a bomb's planted. It's not their fault if Scotland Yard deliberately drag their feet.'

'And why the hell should Scotland Yard do that?'

'So that middle-class rednecks like you can get all worked up about it.'

I hit him. A single straight-fingered jab into the ribs and a cut across the collar bone as he jack-knifed towards me. As the friend swung at me I hit him too, but luckily only caught the upper arm muscle instead of the neck I was instinctively aiming at.

Among the layers of cigarette smoke in the circle of shocked faces the two boys lay groaning on the wet floor. And then I saw Jazz and Stevens. She grabbed my arm and pushed me through the hostile crowd. Stevens behind me was talking, placating. In the engraved mirror at the door I saw him bending over the two boys.

I couldn't go – and I couldn't stay. I sat hunched forward on Jazz's sofa drinking black coffee while she stood with her cup, leaning against the wall, looking down at me.

What had I come to? Against two defenceless twenty-year-old students I had used skills as deadly as a gun. Fortunately I had been too drunk to use them properly and a torn shoulder muscle and a cracked collar bone were probably the most they'd suffer. I was already suffering worse.

I looked up at Jazz, unable to form words.

'Wait till Stevens gets here,' she said. Then, God bless her, she came and sat down next to me and hugged me.

We sat like this, not speaking, for a few moments until Stevens's step was heard in the passage outside. Jazz carefully took her arm from around my shoulder and stood up to let him in.

He entered the room, his round face grave, and stood in front of me rubbing at a point on his forehead where his hairline had receded. I had noticed the habit in the past when he was concentrating hard on an A & E problem at the Department.

I said nothing. Jazz stayed in the background making a long job of pouring him a brandy.

'They're not too bad,' he said at length. 'The first one's probably got a damaged collar bone. The other one, thank God, you missed.'

I nodded my thanks to him and then to Jazz who had poured me a brandy too.

'You're going to have to get away for a bit, Thomas,' Stevens went on. 'The whole thing with Mansfield's getting you down.'

'I'm drinking too much, I know that. But I want my job back. And before that can begin to happen I have to clear up this Red Banner business with Mansfield.'

'Did you see Pushkin today?' he asked.

I nodded. Then haltingly I told them about Tchaikovsky. Stevens moved his head up and down slowly throughout the account and rubbed at his hairline. Jazz stood in the half-shadow against the wall looking shocked.

'So I can't leave,' I told them. 'Not even for a few days. If I can deliver a new list to Mansfield that'll clear me completely. Pushkin will deliver it to this address as soon as he gets it.'

'Does he think Koloniev tipped off Red Banner?'

'He didn't say so in so many words. But he thinks so, I'm sure of it. He grew up with Tchaikovsky, they were together in Kiev during the war. I wouldn't like to be in Koloniev's shoes if Pushkin decides he's responsible for Tchaikovsky's death.'

Jazz had gone into the kitchen to start scrambling eggs. Stevens and I sat opposite each other sipping brandy.

'There may be another lead opening up, Thomas,' he said after a few moments. 'Entirely confidentially of course, but just before I left the office tonight news was coming in from Germany about

72

an attempt to hi-jack a train in a siding at the Krefeld marshalling yards.'

'A Red Banner operation?'

'We don't know yet. But the train carried, among other things, twenty or thirty tons of gelignite. It was well guarded, of course. But then the operation was well planned. A diversionary attack on the headquarters of the Railway Police drew off most of the guard. The attackers then moved in to unhook the gelignite wagon and shunt it to a waiting locomotive hook-up. What happened next is not clear, but obviously the German security forces responded quickly. The attackers were panicked into trying to hook up a moving wagon to the locomotive. One of the hi-jackers slipped and was crushed between the two. He's still alive, just. But in the next week or so he may prove a useful source of information.'

'Who is he?'

'Horst Gehlen – his name appeared with a Hamburg address on your list.'

'Anything known?'

'Strangely enough, not too much. No outstanding left-wing background. Matter of fact, he was something of a Nationalist in his university days. The Heidelberg National Club. That sort of thing.'

'There are Fascists of the Left and Fascists of the Right. It's a hairline difference between them,' I said.

'Agreed. But the immediate point is this. Get out of London for a few days, Thomas. Breathe some country air. In the meantime Jazz can take any message that Pushkin has for you – and I'll keep an eye on the recovery prospects of Herr Gehlen. Information from either side could exonerate you with Mansfield.'

'Okay.' I didn't feel in any position to refuse. Then Jazz came in with steaming platefuls of scrambled eggs and we sat around talking and joking and trying to forget twenty-year-old students with broken collar bones and Russian eyes staring mistily through the condensing droplets on a plastic bag.

Chapter 11

The next morning I drove in a Fiat 128 hired in Jazz's name to the Spread Eagle in Rye. Late summer is my favourite time for the Romney Marshes when the mist rolls in like gunsmoke from the sea and covers the old pony trails the smugglers used to use. From my upper-floor bedroom at the Spread Eagle I could look out at night across the marsh, above the layer of mist, towards Dymchurch. Tall trees, church steeples, the roofs of tithe barns and farmhouses all floated at anchor on this silent sea, illumined from below by the occasional glow of a car's headlights on the Rye-Dymchurch road.

The Spread Eagle Inn served the Dymchurch traveller before Henry V led his host to Agincourt, before even the Black Prince stood at Crecy. It had been burnt and rebuilt in a century lost to record and is now an inn perhaps of the sixteenth century, perhaps a hundred or two years older. Time and the style of building had not changed enough to tell.

It stands as a whitewashed, rambling half-timbered building with steep tiled roofs and swallows' nests in the deep, moon-shadowed eaves. The rooms are either small or large with no uniformity or consistency apparent in their lay-out. They have fireplaces and fires from late summer on and thick black timbers line the ceilings. The beds are ornate, mostly four-poster, and mostly hideously uncomfortable. But there is no piped music.

That evening I had dinner alone, drank two bottles of burgundy, one white one red, and declaimed Dryden's 'Secular Masque' to myself in a room that was already old when Dryden was born.

> All, all of a piece throughout;
> Thy chase had a beast in view;
> Thy wars brought nothing about;
> Thy lovers were all untrue.
> 'Tis well an old age is out,
> And time to begin a new.

Time to begin a new? Was it? As a teacher of Slavonic languages in a small university somewhere? So that I could get ahead with the new translation of Turgenev I'd often thought about? Perhaps . . .

And Virginia? Forget about her. Mansfield? He'd find out sometime that I hadn't tipped off Red Banner. And Jazz – well, perhaps she'd like to become a don's wife and seduce all the undergraduates as Joan Burtle did in my day. Perhaps . . .

I ordered up another bottle of burgundy and drank it slowly while I thought it over. But the more I thought of a new direction, teaching, or translating, or in commerce with the Soviet Union, the more I realised that, for me, there was no fire in the prospect. It wasn't that I needed the physical excitement of the world I had lived in for the last fifteen years. But I had been a member of an exclusive club that embraced everybody from every country engaged in Intelligence work. And I couldn't imagine accepting a situation in which I was no longer a member.

Then it came to me. Half-way through my third bottle of burgundy, when by any reasonable calculation I was unfit to drive or play chess or make love, the idea came to me which would change my circumstances at a stroke.

Mansfield needed proof that I was not associated, for whatever crazy reason he imagined I might be, with Red Banner. That first point had to be cleared. In order to take me back into the Department he would also need some grand coup that I had engineered but for which he could take major credit. And both conditions I could fulfil if I could find out where the freighter-load of gelignite stolen by Red Banner was now being hidden. If I could pass *that* piece of information to Mansfield he could take all the credit he wanted for the gelignite's recovery.

I was excited. The fire was back where it had to be. I got out a large white sheet of paper and began to note down everything I knew about the hi-jacking of the *François Villon*. Information – assessment – conclusion. It took me the best part of the night, and about six sheets of paper, to detail the information alone. Then I went to bed.

I awoke the next morning at about 11.30. I took a long bath, got dressed and left the hotel for a brisk walk to clear my head.

The streets of Rye run steep and cobbled among the white-painted houses. It was a bright but cool late-summer morning and the leaves were already beginning to turn on the trees as I took the road down to the beach. I was anxious to get back to the hotel and go over my work of last night, but I knew that only hard physical exercise can have any effect on the numbing quality of my hangovers.

There were not more than eight or ten people on the beach, an elderly couple or two, three small boys playing ducks and drakes, a fisherman trudging along the shingle. I broke into a run.

My legs seemed weighted with stones, my chest ached, my breath wheezed through my teeth. I threw myself forward . . . another fifty yards, another fifty yards, another fifty yards . . .

The boys stopped hurling stones as I crunched past them. The fisherman glanced in a bored way, the elderly couples stared. I covered five or six hundred yards then promised myself relief if I made the breakwater, or that bobbing rowboat, or the rusting memorial of an invasion threat long past . . . At something short of the mile a pale haze filled my eyes and I hit the shingle, rolling and groping at the water's edge.

I lay still for a few minutes, flat on my back, eyes closed, sucking in air. Then I hauled myself to my feet and looked back down the beach. The old couples had gone. The fisherman continued to trudge. The three boys, small figures against a grey seascape, were pointing in my direction.

I felt wet and cold and ready for lunch. At a leisurely pace I jogged back to the hotel.

A shower, change, mixed grill and coffee later and I was ready to examine my night's work.

I concentrated first of all on what I could remember of Morel's description of the men who had conducted the raid. My notes read:

> Skilful seamanship. Six men. No obvious leader. Total silence throughout. Dress: black polo-neck sweaters, dark trousers, black tennis shoes. Weapons: Thompson sub-machine guns?? 759mm Mausers???

Not much to go on. The weapons meant little or nothing. The French crew's descriptions indicated the Thompsons – but the identity of the pistols carried by two of the men was more or less guesswork on my part. In any case, such weapons were free floaters in any gun market in the world. No, much more interesting was the organisation of the group. I remembered at the time being impressed by the French crew's reports, confirmed by Morel, that the whole action was conducted in total silence. The more I thought about it, that had to mean professional. But in that case what was a professional – Russian GRU, British Secret Intelligence Service, French SDEC or American CIA – doing leading a Red Banner operation? Or more intriguing, were all six of the men professionals? And if they were what did that say about the make-up and real aims of Red Banner?

Professional? Yes, the whole operation had a really profession-al look about it. It was quick, silent, efficient and no one was hurt. I put down 'professional' in the tentative assessment column.

I next turned my attention with the aid of another large brandy to the plywood superstructure that had been netted near the sea area where the *François Villon* was hi-jacked. I reread my notes:

> Motor sailer. Length – 18 metres approximately. Well-handled. Morel notes *Jamaica Storm* for his log. (Then details of the boarding approach.) Honfleur 6.30 a.m. Plywood con-struction, white and pale blue. Extension of wheelhouse and raised aft decking. *Jamaica Storm.*

This looked more promising.

I took the sketch of the motor ketch Morel had given me on the quayside at Le Havre and examined it closely for the first time. I was astonished at the careful detail he had recorded. He had of course only drawn what he saw that night. But on a second sheet he had drawn to scale the outline of the plywood super-structure we had seen fished up at Honfleur.

When I was last in Rye I had taken the girl I was with – Barbara? Bette? Bianca? – to a pub in the centre of town, and had re-coiled in alarm at the white polo-neck sweaters and Harrods yachting caps clustered round the bar. But today it seemed just the place for me.

I walked down the steep Cinque Ports street towards the centre of the town and found the pub in the market-place. It was a warm, old fisherman's pub deserving of a better class of customer. I chose the saloon bar, eased my way up to the counter and ordered a large malt.

I had planned to seek out a likely victim drinking alone. But I had hardly ordered my drink when the young-middle-aged, sandy-haired sea-dog next to me puffed on his pipe and observed, in a strong Scottish accent: 'I can see you know your whisky, friend.'

I turned and looked him over: did *he* know his yachts?

'It's a fine glass of whisky,' I agreed, lifting the smoky fluid to the light.

'My favourite's Glencarrock,' he told me. I took the hint and ordered him one from the barman. Glencarrock! I hoped he knew more about yachts.

Whisky is not like wine. After the first few observations, the ritual smacking of the lips and rolling on the tongue, there's little or nothing to be said. Malt whisky may be one of the supreme achievements of the drinking man, but we quickly moved on to other things.

My new-found friend, Sandy Macdonald, proved to be a Scottish Nationalist of some conviction, arguing for a totally independent Scotland with all ties severed from England. I told him I couldn't agree more.

He pulled back a little and looked at me closely.

'But you're not Scots,' he protested.

'No,' I said.' I'm a Home Rule for England man myself. Think of all the plum jobs there'll be going this side of the border when all the Scots go back to Edinburgh. Where do you work yourself, Sandy?'

He looked thoughtful and explained that Scottish independence didn't mean all Scots should give up their English jobs. After all, there was no really suitable employment in Scotland.

I nodded understanding. Before we came to blows I turned the conversation to boats. Next to a dependent independent Scotland boats were clearly the love of his life.

I had chosen well. Sandy Macdonald, unbelievably knowledgeable in this field, was the world's leading boat bore.

He talked while I bought. Of his own Macwester Pelagian designed by C.S.J. Roy, of a dozen other sloops and ketches with this or that capability or fault . . . he was a difficult man to stop.

I seized the opportunity as he ritually savoured his fourth malt.

'Sandy, you could be just the man to help me out with a little problem.'

'Say on, friend,' he said. But I could see he was already nervous that it might cost him something.

'It's a puzzle. But right up your alley.'

I drew the two sheets of paper from my hip pocket and spread the main drawing out on the bar.

'What is it?' I asked.

He looked closely, took out a pair of horn-rimmed spectacles, put them on and subjected the sketch to a minute examination. I was hopeful.

'No idea,' he said at length.

'No idea?' I couldn't take back all those malt whiskies now.

'It's a very well executed sketch,' he said, shaking his head. 'But the actual boat, I just don't recognise at all. Tell you the truth, Tom,' he said, 'it's a bastard.'

I agreed.

'What I mean is there are elements of at least two different motor sailers here.'

I began to smile and invested in another malt.

'Approximately eighteen metres,' he mused. 'It's a big one. I'm strongly reminded of *Ballyhoo*. You observe the buttock lines run out to a reverse raked transom stern?'

I said I did.

'It's this midship section that bothers me,' he puzzled. 'You see the distinctive flats and rounded corners, the slackish bilges with just a hint of tumblehome . . .'

I gave him a nod of encouragement.

'But *that*' – he stabbed at the plywood section – 'that's completely out of place on a boat like this.'

I pulled out the second drawing, and dropped it on the bar next to the main sketch.

'Subtract that,' I said, 'and what've you got?'

He laughed. 'Simple when you know how,' he said. 'It's the new aluminium-hulled sloop Simons designed, of course. Nice trick that.'

'How many of them exist?' I asked him.

'It's custom-built.'

'You mean there's only one of them?' I tried to keep the excitement out of my voice.

'Strictly speaking, yes. In fact Simons used the same basic design in dozens of them.'

'But you can recognise this one from the others?'

'That's asking a bit much, friend,' he said, taking up the challenge. 'I'll say this much: it's not the one they did for Billy Grantham at Cowes.'

'Simons,' I asked,' is that a company?'

He looked at me in complete bewilderment. It was like asking a similar question about Robbie Burns.

'S.J. Simons, down at Hythe. Simons the boat-builders.'

'Sure,' I said. 'Well, thanks for your help, Sandy.' I was already backing for the door.

'You're not going without the other half,' he said, reaching into his pocket. In his deep state of cultural shock he was apparently going to buy me a drink.

In a call box outside my hotel I looked up the number and called Simons the boatbuilders. After explaining myself to a receptionist and secretary I was put through to Mr John Simons. I could almost imagine him pulling judiciously on his briar.

'This is Rye police station,' I told him briskly. 'Inspector O'Sullivan. I want your help with a trace we've been asked to do by London.'

'A what's that, Inspector?' the Kent voice asked.

'A trace. We're looking for a man who just might have bought one of your boats. I'd like to send my sergeant down with a sketch I want you to look at.'

There was an uncommunicative grunt from the other end of the line. 'What would you be wanting this man for, Inspector?'

'I'm not at liberty to disclose that at this stage, I'm afraid,' I told him. 'But I'd very much appreciate your co-operation, sir.'

He considered: 'One of our customers, you say?'

'Just a possibility, Mr Simons.'

'I can't see it being one of our customers you're looking for,' he said slowly. 'They've most of 'em been buying from us for years.'

'Nevertheless, if you would see my sergeant . . .'

'We close at five-thirty, Inspector. The place is empty by then.'

I told him I'd make sure my sergeant arrived before that. But he was still far from being ready to help. He clearly assumed one of his boats had been recognised by the coastguard on a clandestine trip across the Channel. A piece of minor smuggling, in all probablity. Under pressure from his own local police or coastguard he would probably have given in easily enough, but he wasn't going out of his way to be helpful to a foreign authority.

I dropped my voice to a confidential low. 'Between ourselves, Mr Simons, and I'll ask you to respect a confidence . . .'

'Of course, Inspector.'

'. . . it's officially a missing persons trace we're on to. But I think I can tell you that we'd be not surprised to find it was very much more.'

He fell. 'I'll be waiting for your sergeant myself, Inspector. Whatever time he gets here.'

I replaced the phone and returned to the hotel, packed my case and decided to call Jazz before I left.

She was pleased to hear from me but cautious. No, she hadn't heard anything from Pushkin yet.

'What is it, Jazz? Something wrong?'

'No . . .' her voice sounded slightly strained, 'just that I thought you were down there for a rest. If Pushkin calls I promise to let you know.'

I rang off with a sense of unease. That was not Jazz as she should be. She was worried about something, something connected with me. I saw the answer when they delivered the afternoon papers. Major-General Sir Richard Deedes had called an emergency conference at Central Hall, Westminster for tomorrow. He had invited the leaders of similarly concerned groups from Europe. Von Arnitz would be there. And so presumably would Virginia. So Jazz's concern was that I'd cut my holiday short and return to London. Of course she was right.

Stevens phoned me about fifteen minutes later in evident response to a call from Jazz. He was speaking from a call box.

'Thomas, call me back at this number. I'll wait.'

I knew what he meant. Hotel receptionists are notorious eavesdroppers. I left the hotel and hurried down towards the market-place. At the first phone box I called the number Stevens and I had arranged the day I left.

'Thomas, dear boy,' Stevens's voice came through on the other end of the line, 'how are you enjoying your break?'

'Jazz asked you to call me, right?' I interrupted.

'True.'

'She's worried I might be coming back to London. Is that it?'

'It is.' Stevens's voice hardened. 'Listen, Thomas, Mansfield is not giving up. He's had Special Branch distribute your photograph to the metropolitan police. He believes you're in London, probably with a girl. So as long as you stay where you are you're safe until Pushkin comes up with something to exonerate you.'

'What about the German injured in the train hi-jack – what was his name . . . Horst Gehlen?'

'He died last night, Thomas. No, I'm afraid all your eggs are in your friend Pushkin's basket at the moment.'

Not quite, I thought. But I wasn't going to tell Stevens about my plans just yet.

'Have you spoken to Mansfield?' I asked him.

'This afternoon. He's in no mood to be told anything. The pressure's on him from the Director to produce something – either Red Banner suspects, the hi-jacked gelignite – or you. Admittedly you come a poor third in the pecking order, Thomas, but you're still very much on the great man's mind.'

'I'm coming back today,' I told him.

S. J. Simons's was a pretty little collection of ancient and somewhat tumble-down buildings on the sea-front just outside Hythe. Looking more like a farmyard than a boatbuilders, it was only finally redeemed by the two gleaming aluminium hulls mounted on a pair of ramps at the water's edge.

I parked the car at the most important-looking building and got out. Looking up I saw John Simons standing in the doorway.

He matched his telephone persona exactly. About fifty-three or -four, thick grey hair, a ruddy outdoor face, cautious, genial as he extended his hand.

'Sergeant Porter.' I shook hands. 'Mr Simons.'

'Come straight in, Sergeant,' he said and turned and led the way into the offices.

A big country girl with big thighs and big breasts was brewing tea in the untidy outer office.

'I asked Sandra to stay on late, just in case,' he explained.

I thought I knew what he meant. 'Is she discreet?' I asked with a wink.

His red face reddened further. He clearly wasn't used to any innuendo so close to the truth.

'Oh, aye. Aye, she's . . . that all right.'

Sandra came in with her pink sweater and very short pale blue skirt and filled a sizeable part of the small office as she handed round mugs of hot tea.

I looked round the room. It was as untidy as the outer office. Along one wall a draughtsman's desk was covered with sheets of blue paper carrying the outline of superstructures and sections of hulls. Anglepoise lamps peered down their noses at the clutter on the desk, at the fraying brocade top of the revolving workstool and the two patches in the linoleum under the desk worn down to the jute base by Simons's feet. Yet I was not forgetful of the new Rolls-Royce that peeked out of the garage as I had parked.

'Your health, Mr Simons.' I raised my mug.

He nodded, sipped at his tea and looked at me from under his shaggy grey eyebrows.

'Well now, Sergeant . . .'

I was already producing the sketches. I unfolded them and smoothed them on his desk in front of him.

'I believe Inspector O'Sullivan hinted at the serious nature of this business?' I allowed a flat Scottish whine to overlay my voice, faint as whisky on a Glaswegian's breath. As O'Sullivan I had indulged a delicate touch of Irishness. I'm not really that much of a performer, but I needn't have worried. As I should have realised from one look at Sandra, John Simons was unconcerned with nice distinctions.

He nodded conspiratorially. 'Yes. The Inspector as good as told me that it could be a matter of murder.'

I drew a quick breath at this fearful indiscretion on my superior's part and called his attention to the problem of the two sketches.

He recognised the hull immediately and confirmed that once the additional superstructure was subtracted it was undoubtedly their boat. So far so good. But the problem of closer identification arose because the superstructure had clearly been designed to disguise which it was of the many series using the one hull.

I asked him how many series had they made.

'We're on Mark VI at the moment, Sergeant,' he said proudly. 'And every mark has sold well above sixty boats.'

So much for Sandy Macdonald's dozens. Bloody hundreds, more like.

Dispiritedly I asked him to supply me with a photocopy of his sales list, and he took the opportunity to call in Sandra. As she busied herself on the copying machine with much coy squeezing past Simons in the restricted space of the small office, I asked him about overseas sales.

It was clearly hopeless. They had sold the first series mostly in this country. The second series had seen the growth of international favour and from there they had sold to every major country in the world. With a jaunty set to their yachtsman's caps owners of Simons's boats were listening to the slap of wave on aluminium hull in just about every sea and ocean around the world.

Sandra handed me the completed list and I read through the names automatically. It was interesting enough as a roll-call of the international affluent, but it had little to offer me.

I had hardly reached half-way down the list when I heard outside the crunch of gravel as a car drew to a stop. I glanced up through the window. I saw a white police Rover 2000 and a uniformed officer climbing out.

John Simons lifted himself to his feet. 'It's George Hopwood,' he said, 'he's seen your car, I expect. Wondering what it's doing here after hours.'

'Have a word with him, Mr Simons,' I said as calmly and authoritatively as I could. 'And don't mention my presence here if you don't mind.'

He looked slightly surprised.

'Uniform and plain-clothes branches sometimes tread on each other's toes. I wouldn't like the local people to hear we should have put this in their hands. As the Inspector hinted to you – at this stage an investigation can be a very delicate matter.'

I was ninety-nine per cent sure he believed me as he left the office and walked across the forecourt to meet the policeman. But I watched him through the window all the same. In order to cover my anxiety I talked to Sandra.

'This is a complete, up-to-date list, is it, Sandra?'

'As far as sales go, yes, sir,' she said. 'But I didn't want to say in front of Mr Simons – it's not going to help you much.'

Simons and the young copper were talking, indicating my parked car.

'Why not Sandra?'

'Well, because we sell a boat to someone and his name goes on that list. But inside a year or two he's probably sold it to someone else. We don't know. Or if we do, it's just by chance, reading the yachting press.'

Outside on the forecourt they were still talking. Here in the office I was already convinced my visit was a waste of time. But I didn't want to leave until the police car was clear of the premises.

'Whereabouts was this boat seen?' Sandra was trying to be helpful.

'The Seine estuary.' I looked away from the window. 'Near Le Havre. Or a little place called Honfleur.'

She shook her head. 'No, you don't find this sort of boat there. It's Deauville, I expect, a couple of miles along the coast. That's the place for yachts.'

I looked at her in surprise.

'Mr Simons delivered a boat there once,' she confessed ingenuously. 'I crewed for him.'

'You delivered one of these boats?'

'No, it was smaller. A Ramrod. But there were three or four of our boats there at the time. We visited all of them to do a maintenance check.'

I handed her the list. 'Mark them up for me, will you?'

She underlined four boats without hesitation. Against two of them she wrote the names of new owners – Captain Peter Fredericks and J. R. Dyson.

My head was singing. J. R. Dyson, Rob Dyson? Could they be the same person?

'Sandra, did you meet this man Dyson?'

'The owner of *The Cricketer*?'

I nodded.

'Oh, yes,' she said, her eyes opening at the memory. 'He was lovely.'

Not the way I would have described the Rob Dyson I knew: six feet two, two hundred pounds, a scar splitting his right cheek like an African tribal mark . . .

'Describe him.'

It was him all right. Big, blond, South African . . . Long before she'd reached the scar I had no doubts that J. R. Dyson and Rob Dyson were the same thug.

Simons came back apologising for the time he had taken. I told him to think nothing of it, offered up a silent toast to the slow-talking, quick-thinking Sandra and took my leave. John Simons and Sandra came to the outer office door to see me off.

They'd stay on, he explained, to finish off a little work. Later, no doubt, he'd cover with his wife by a long account of the visit of the Rye murder squad.

He could hardly keep his hands off her as I climbed into my car.

They both stood on the doorstep and waved goodbye, like proud new homeowners to the friendly building society man who had made it all possible.

Dyson. The more I thought about it, the better it looked.

Dyson was the sort of man that no Intelligence service likes to admit it has ever used – but must have at one time or another. In a word, he was a mercenary. A hard-bitten, short-tempered, vengeful South African who made his money (and plenty of it) working a 'dirty tricks' game for governments, companies, syndicates or even individuals if they were rich enough. He was one of the few professionals who had never trained with one of the national Intelligence services.

I had come across him once or twice and had seen evidence of his work on a few more occasions. What we had done in the '60s in defence (as we saw it) of liberal democracy, he had done for money, girls, fast cars – and now, apparently, yachts.

Totally without conscience, he would accept a commission from a group like Red Banner without compunction.

Chapter 12

I remember thinking that as a back-drop to the General's conference the next day the bombing of the Four Square Disco could not have been improved upon.

I began to get the first reports on the car radio shortly after I left Rye that evening. By the time I reached South London the story had been pieced together and the names of the dead and injured, and the hospitals they had been taken to, were being read over the radio, repeated and enlarged every ten minutes as later news came in. I drove into London feeling sickened as the BBC voice read the mournful roll-call. Later I was to see the whole thing on the screen preserved by the chance presence of television cameras on the spot.

Like the shooting of Oswald it was one of those examples of television *vérité*. The cameras had been set up for a world premiere on the other side of the square to film the arrival of the Queen and members of the Royal Family when the bomb or bombs exploded opposite in the packed disco. Red Banner claimed that this was their only way of bringing the realities of life to the attention of the enemies of the proletariat. Those members of the proletariat whose sons and daughters lost their eyes and limbs in the bombing may have felt the cost was a trifle on the high side.

The Royal Command Performance was due to begin at 8.30 that evening, with arrivals of the royal party and the stars of the film to be completed by 8.20.

As ever for these occasions a fairly large, mostly young crowd had gathered to watch and afterwards dispersed across the square, streaming past Shakespeare's statue in search of coffee and hamburgers and some good loud Rock. The Four Square therefore filled rapidly and by 8.30 the manager was turning people away at the door.

I suppose on its two upper floors the place holds something over 600, and the average age was probably not much more than seventeen or eighteen. They were mostly school kids on their night out in the West End or young shop assistants and working boys. And since it was Leicester Square there was also a fair proportion of foreign students from the West End schools of

English and a good number of Dutch and German and French and Italian au pair girls. There was, I imagine, the same sort of racial mix as I had seen on other nights as they queued to get in – a good many West Indian youngsters as well as Greek and Turkish Cypriots from the Soho restaurant families.

At 8.22 the news desk at the Press Association in Fleet Street had received a call. The journalist who answered it says that the voice sounded excited and definitely slurred. It had peremptorily ordered the journalist to take down a message, and had read off a statement about bringing the realities of life to the attention of the 'royal class enemies'. During the statement, which he insisted on having read back to him, two hundred pounds of gelignite were ticking away on an alarm-clock detonation device underneath 600 dancing teenagers.

The journalist had tried to break into the statement as soon as he realised a bomb was involved and extract enough details from the caller to give the security forces something to get started on. But with a crazy, punctilious concern for each sentence and the correct placing of full stops and commas the caller had insisted the statement be read back for errors. And still the bomb ticked on.

By the time he was satisfied and had ordered the Red Banner signature to be added to the statement it was 8.27 p.m. The bomb, he had then announced, was in the Four Square Disco at Leicester Square. It had been timed for 8.35 p.m.

Even so it was possible, because of the police contingent already in the square for the Royal Command Performance, to do something in the eight minutes accorded by Red Banner.

All PA journalists have the number of the direct line to the Bomb Squad at Scotland Yard. This night it was a matter of fifteen seconds to dial, give the code signal, place and time. This message was immediately radioed to police cars in the square.

Chief Inspector Jack Longfleet was the senior police officer in the square. He grabbed a crowd control bull-horn from one of his officers and raced across to the Four Square. Six officers followed him.

Youngsters were already beginning to stream out of the disco as they arrived. Hot, sweating, coatless, clasping hamburgers and Coke bottles they flowed out into the gardens in the middle of the square, chattering and laughing with nervous relief.

The tension was palpable. By now every television camera was pointing at the disco and, when the film was transmitted, a tasteless director had superimposed a clock with a sweep second hand on the screen.

At 8.32 the bomb exploded. No additional malice on the part of Red Banner need be adduced to account for the premature explosion. Any policeman knows now that alarm-clock devices are seldom completely accurate. Jack Longfleet knew it. So did the six officers who followed him into the disco and died there with him.

The explosion tore the façade off the building, revealing the two upper floors like the open front of a doll's house. The top floor from which the bulk of the remaining youngsters were being shepherded out partially collapsed and for a full ten minutes after the explosion chairs, tables, chunks of masonry and injured kids rolled down the sloping floor and fell into the street below.

I sat with Jazz watching the harrowing scenes, the numbed anguish of some, the high courage of others, until the whole building, speckled by minor fire outbreaks, burst into flames. Then I stood up and switched off the set. I couldn't help thinking that I might have the source of the gelignite that exploded tonight.

Chapter 13

The din was deafening. Between the 'Sieg Heil' roars from the hostile crowd and the rhythmic chant of 'Action England' in response, motorcycle police radios crackled and the vehicles backed up along Whitehall as far as Trafalgar Square sounded their horns in pointless protest against the delay. From where I stood in Victoria Street the entrance to the Central Hall, Westminster was a sea of waving Union Jacks relieved occasionally by the red cross of St George. Two parallel lines of policemen were struggling to hold back the left-wing protesters and keep open the way into the hall for the main body of the demonstration which was reported to be crossing Westminster Bridge at that moment.

From time to time a particularly determined attack by the crowd would burst through the lines of helmeted policemen who, with linked arms and heels digging into the tarmac road, were trying to keep the two sides apart. Then for a brief few minutes five or six young men would hurl themselves at the flag-bearers and struggle to wrest a Union Jack or St George's Cross and carry it back as a trophy. But the defence was as bitter and determined as the attack, and flag-poles would be jabbed into faces, splitting noses and damaging eyes, while Cola bottles shattered and burst round the flag-bearers like exploding hand-grenades. Then the police Special Patrol would move in, pulling and dragging the attackers clear, dispatching them back into the crowd or frog-marching them to the waiting lines of Black Marias parked in Tothill Street.

Then, from the direction of the river, the sound of kettle drums was heard, and the head of the marching column of Action England supporters turned into Parliament Square. I found it impossible to make any estimate of numbers, but by the time General Deedes, at the head of the marchers, had reached Central Hall the column stretched back down Victoria Street, past the House of Commons and was still flowing into Parliament Square from Bridge Street. It was very far, in terms of numbers at least, from the miserable fiasco that left-wing commentators had predicted.

It had been reported in this morning's papers that the police had applied to the Home Secretary to ban the demonstration, but public feeling about the recent Red Banner bombing was running far too high to have conceded yet another victory to the Left. Trapped between Right and Left the Government's principal energies were devoted to maintaining itself in office.

I had obtained a ticket for the Conference easily enough that morning by presenting myself as the Editor of the *British Industrial Review* and resting a copy on the desk as I spoke. The Action England security man beside the desk was not to know that the *British Industrial Review* was a cover magazine printed (one undated issue only) by the Department and used by its operatives at their discretion. For other purposes and with suitable impartiality the Department also prints *Socialism Tomorrow* and *East European Commentary* also in single, undated issues.

Getting the ticket had presented no problem. Getting into the hall was a different matter. I moved back past the police barrier, turned right at New Scotland Yard, and came down Tothill Street from the other direction until I was stopped by the police guarding the Black Marias. I showed them my ticket and explained my problem, and they directed me into a rear entrance to the Central Hall where thirty or forty people were having their tickets checked before being let through. One of them was Virginia.

I got past the barrier and pushed through the crowd until I had caught her up. She turned as I held her arm.

'What are you doing here?' Alarm flooded her face. 'Richard told me that he'd heard the police were looking for you.'

'How the hell did he know that?' I was astonished at the effectiveness of the General's information system. She brushed it aside. 'He finds out these things. What do the police want you for?'

We were standing in a long corridor with people pushing their way past us as we talked, and the sound of martial music crashing around us from the main hall. I couldn't explain here.

'I can't explain now. When can I meet you?'

'I don't know!' She shook her head doubtfully. 'Richard plans to motor back to Cambridge after the conference.'

'You could make a quick drink around mid-day, surely?'

Again she shook her head. More decisively this time. 'No, it can't be done. There just won't be time.'

'You mean you'd prefer not to,' I said slowly. There was a sudden silence as the music stopped.

'I mean what I said.' Her tone was curt, but her face was troubled. 'I'm sorry.'

I nodded. 'What number's your ticket?'

She fumbled in her bag. 'Fifteen,' she said. 'B row. The bands have stopped playing. I think I'd better find my seat.'

'I'll help you,' I said. 'I'm just a couple of rows behind you.'

Central Hall looked like nothing as much as an American party convention. What had been achieved by General Deedes's organisers at what must have been virtually nil notice was genuinely impressive. Each Action England district group had been supplied with a St George's Cross standard with the name of their area in black and gold across the top of the frame.

Stewards and ushers with Union Jack armbands were everywhere, and the podium was draped with alternate English and Union flags.

I showed Virginia to her seat and found mine a row or two behind her. We were barely in time. I had just sat down with a suitable mumble of apologies to my neighbours when the lights dimmed in the hall, spotlights lanced down through the cigarette haze to illuminate the podium, and the band broke into 'Land of Hope and Glory'. Like the last night of the proms the whole hall rose to its feet and sang as Major-General Sir Richard Deedes led Freiherr von Arnitz and perhaps a dozen others on to the podium.

As the last strains of 'Land of Hope and Glory' died away and the body of the hall sat back in their seats, the General began to introduce by name the men on the podium. Each one received a round of applause and then took his seat. I noticed a high proportion of foreign names among them, but von Arnitz was the only man I recognised.

As the last man was seated the General began his speech.

Although you see this hall at Westminster draped with the Union flag and with the flag of England's patron saint, Action England is not just a patriotic society. It is a movement which represents ideals of humanity and justice which are of course European ideals. They are the ideals which every European country received from the Greeks, they are the ideals which, though frequently trampled on (by us Europeans as much as by others), have still been kept alive over thousands of years by Europeans and by those whose societies were shaped by the European experience.

Ladies and Gentlemen, today in Europe and throughout the Western world these ideals are under savage attack. I do not have to remind you of the bloody and tyrannical nature of our opponents. Last night, in one of the most insensate and murderous actions in this capital's history, over sixty young people lost their lives and the toll of injured is still not finally known.

Today we welcome in our midst the leaders of Action movements throughout Europe. Freiherr von Arnitz from Germany, Marshal Fausto Amarotti from Italy, Meinheer Piet Gravius from Holland and General Jean-Jacques Linquier from France.

In some countries these movements have been established almost as long as our own. In others, notably Germany, the movement is new but already it is gaining rapidly in adherents.

Ladies and Gentlemen, we represent no class or section in our different countries, we are open simply to men and women who believe passionately that the ideal of freedom must be defended with all the vigour of which a State is capable. And that vigour is not apparent in the activities of any single European government today.

There was deafening roar of applause at this point, and I looked down at the back of the head of Virginia just below me. She was motionless in the semi-darkness.

I must admit that the General's speech was masterly. He did

not bay for blood, but he made effective play with the fact that somewhere in Britain or on the Continent Red Banner, whom he identified as the principal grouping of the enemy, had in their possession something approaching 200 tons of gelignite ready to be used again in bloody incidents like last night or, even more menacingly, in one single, massive explosion in the centre of a city.

I was reminded of Pushkin and his beloved Kreshchatik.

The General continued with a discussion of the death penalty. He was preaching to the converted, and he knew it. But he made the points in an orderly fashion: that to claim that the abolition of the death penalty did not affect the murder rate is a politician's evasion, because those statistics related to what can be termed family murders; that though hard-core fanatics may not be deterred by the certainty of capital punishment less fanatical adherents and apologists for terrorism would hesitate to become involved, thus striking at the infrastructure (one of the General's favourite terms) of the movements; and finally that you cannot ransom a dead man – and innocent hostages were daily put at risk by the Government's craven unwillingness to hang convicted murderers and their accomplices.

The converted applauded wildly.

Then the General got down to cases. The Action England committee had decided to continue with a series of practice Alerts, the first of which would take place in ten days' time. The purpose of the exercise would be to demonstrate the speed with which, in an emergency in support of the Civil Power, key points in the economy could be protected from wreckers and railways and power stations actually run on a voluntary basis. The General was careful to make it clear that there would be no occupations, that cross-roads and level-crossings would not in any way be impeded. But I had the feeling that at this point he was sailing close to the wind.

The audience were more rapturous than ever at the prospect of action.

Among the wild cheering and storms of hand-clapping I saw Virginia rise in front of me and make her way along to the end of the row. For a second she glanced up to see that I was moving too, then made quickly for the Tothill Street exit. By the time she reached it I had caught up with her.

We showed our passes and walked out into the sunshine. She looked tense and purposeful. I couldn't fathom it. She had left the hall making sure I was following – why exactly I wasn't sure.

I decided to let her make the running.

We had turned out of Tothill Street towards St James's Park when she began.

'Why should the police be looking for you? I don't understand. Is it anything to do with what my husband wanted you to find out for him?'

I told her as quickly as I could about the Red Banner list, the tip-off by, in all probability, another branch of the same Embassy which had supplied the list, and finally Mansfield's suspicion that it might have been me.

'Why should you have done it?'

'Vindictiveness or hard cash. Most tips of this sort involve a little of both.'

'But you didn't?'

'No.'

She looked at me as we walked. And nodded. The subject was closed.

We walked slowly without speaking along Birdcage Walk, then towards the lake and stopped on the bridge to lean on the stone parapet.

'I have an apology to make to you,' she said at length. 'I have behaved very badly. I am, I admit it, a very confused woman, Mr Hart.'

'Mr Hart? What happened to Tom?'

She looked at me a moment before continuing. 'I owe you an explanation. I tried to give it to you when we had lunch together, or rather afterwards when we sat by the river.'

'You began talking about your husband?'

'Yes. But I thought perhaps it wasn't the right time to go on. Now I have no choice.'

She had me completely baffled.

'I immensely admire my husband,' she continued. 'I think, listening to him today, whether or not you agree with all he was saying, you must respond to his sheer ability to enthuse people, to direct them . . .'

Was it *power* she idolised? Could that be it?

'I find him,' she went on, 'a significant man.'

'And me?' I asked.

'We're talking about my husband,' she said sharply. Then, more softly, 'I find I can, and want, to give him my loyalty. In every respect but one.'

I could hardly believe my ears.

'I'm still a comparatively young woman,' she looked across the water, 'much younger than he is. I find it impossible to accept the celibate life he quite obviously prefers. We have not slept together for over eight years.'

'And during that time there have been others?'

'Once or twice only. I've been very circumspect. I'd hate him to know. And frankly it just doesn't seem necessary.'

I was ready to explode. 'So when we met in the garden at Cambridge, you had a few glasses of wine and booked me down as a likely stallion. Is that it?'

She looked at me without answering.

'Well, is that it?'

'I thought perhaps we might sleep together two or three times, yes.'

'You thought you could do it safely – without any danger of involvement with this second-rate private investigator your husband was hiring?' I couldn't separate the mix of anger and dismay I felt.

'I thought I could do it without a sense of disloyalty to him.'

'What went wrong?' I asked savagely.

'Our second meeting. Or rather, when I lay in bed that night and thought about it. I began to have doubts. I began to see dangers.'

I didn't really know what to think. What she was saying I wanted to hear. But I couldn't take the cold-blooded way she had marked my card.

'Look, don't you see what it is? You've a father-daughter relationship with him. What you admire about him are the qualities to ascribe to a father. It's no good,' I said desperately. 'It's rotten.'

She was very quiet. For a moment or two I thought she was going to leave. Then she turned her face towards me. 'I'm aware that it might be a certain immaturity in my make-up that makes me feel so intensely for a husband who has no physical interest in me. But after ten years of marriage to him I can only tell you that is how I *do* feel. I'm unlikely to change now.'

'Then what's the danger you were talking about?'

'The danger of my not wanting to break off a relationship I'd started with you.'

'You'd have to make a choice; you'd do what you wanted in the end.'

'But it's a choice I could never make. Because my sense of loyalty to him would be undiminished. Don't you see – it's different for most women, for most wives who have affairs?'

94

I didn't see. Not at all. And I didn't like this way of talking about it. I thought the direct way out of this impasse was probably the best. 'Will you stay with me in London tonight?' I asked her.

She shook her head.

'Or now, this afternoon? The meeting'll go on for hours yet.'

Again she shook her head, shuddering slightly with distaste.

'I'm sorry,' I said, 'I didn't mean to suggest I bundled you into a hotel room for an hour or two. I can imagine how you'd feel about that.'

She opened her bag and took out a bunch of keys.

'What are those?'

'The keys to my aunt's flat in Chester Square.'

'Your aunt's away?'

'Yes. Until tomorrow.'

'You mean we can go there?'

'We *could* go there, but no.' She put away the keys. 'I just wanted to show you that it is not simply lack of opportunity.'

Small flotillas of ducks headed purposefully in arrow formations towards the old lady on the bank below us. They must have recognised her lined face, or the dun-coloured coat or perhaps the broken heels of her shoes. Certainly they knew she was about to delve into that brown paper bag and throw handfuls of crusts into the water.

For them there were no disappointments, no dangled keys. She tossed out crusts in all directions and the ducks, abandoning the neat flotillas to the instincts of greedy anarchy, squawked and dived and fought for each crust. The old lady obviously enjoyed every moment of it. But to me it was a sad sight.

I turned angrily to Virginia, but a woman with two small children had stopped on the bridge next to us. I watched Virginia snap her bag closed, then I took her arm and moved her a yard or two away from where the woman was lifting one of the children better to see the ducks fight on the lake. The second child squealed protests at the unfairness of the world.

'What in God's name are you doing?' I turned Virginia to face me.

'That hurts,' she said, looking down at where I was holding her arm.

I let it go. 'You didn't owe me any apology, you know that. You could have stayed in the meeting and in all probability never seen me again. You know that too. You left because you wanted to leave. Because you wanted to see me.'

'Yes,' she said.

I was thrown. I'd expected an argument. I took out a cigarette and lit it. I could feel her mood had changed again, to the point at which she was looking for a lead. But I had no idea which direction we might go. In particular I was afraid to say something that might break that fragile submissiveness which I had seen once or twice before.

'Talk to me,' I said. 'Doesn't matter what about. Just talk.'

I looked at her beautiful but troubled face as she looked out across the lake. She nodded.

'You know, Tom,' she said slowly, 'when things change so very fast some people get left behind in the headlong rush.'

'Like little old ladies of the Distressed Gentlefolks Association who live in squalor with two or three pieces of superb furniture from the old country home?'

She shook her head.

'I was brought up to believe in the wealth and power of the United States of America and the values of the Commonwealth of Massachusetts. My step-father drove a Volkswagen because to him an American car was a grossly ostentatious piece of machinery.'

'Exuberant,' I conceded.

'When I came to live with my father in England I was shocked. I believed Europe was a continent of starving millions. I didn't realise that there was wealth here too. My mother kept the fact from me. It was like a secret from a tainted past.'

'You were shocked. But you took to the new style of life.'

'Timorously, I suppose, at first. It seemed so carefree – almost careless. It took me a long time to realise that the English upper classes were as remote from everything happening around them as my New England step-father. Both had set their faces against change.'

'Privilege always does. It's the way of the world. Your step-father had tenure at an old and rich university. Your father was a landowner long after most great estates had been broken up. Why should either of them welcome change?'

'I suppose you're right. They had a lot in common – though it didn't seem that way to me at the time. I only saw the differences.'

'Is your father still alive?'

'No, he died last year. The estate passed to his younger brother. I always knew it would.' She looked at her watch. 'I really must go,' she said.

I felt empty, impotent to move her. Angry at all this wasted talk, angry at myself.

'You asked me to talk,' she said. 'And now I've talked too much.'

I shook my head.

'You see,' she persisted, 'I feel I've lived a very special sort of life. In some land of time stood still.' Her pale brown eyes looked up at me. 'I don't think I can leave that land, Tom.'

'Is that why you so admire your husband? Because he's got his shoulder against the hand of the clock and is pushing as hard as he can go?'

She shrugged slowly, almost shivered in the chill wind that was coming off the lake. She was hurting herself, I could see that.

I reached down and held her hand. She entwined her fingers in mine as she said: 'I want this to be the last time, Tom. I don't want to see you again.'

We stood holding hands while people moved past us, back and forth across the bridge – two men in black overcoats and bowler hats, the old lady still throwing crusts to the ducks on the lake below, a soldier looking for an unaccompanied girl . . .

I slipped my arm round her waist and she came forward, responding.

'It's impossible, Tom,' she said.

'I don't see it like that.'

'But it is. Believe me it is.' She pressed herself hard against me. 'I desperately want just to fuck with you, Tom,' she said. 'But I'm sure, before we knew it, we'd find ourselves making love.'

The Aeroflot cargo jet taxied towards the small group of dark-overcoated men on the concrete apron. From where I stood in the main building, buying my air ticket to France, I could see out across the Gatwick Airport assembly area, past the huge Laker Airlines DC 10, to where the group of men were arranging them-selves into two ranks facing inward.

As the Aeroflot TU 144 came to a halt the faces of the men turned away towards the cargo loading sheds and those who wore hats removed them as a long black hearse crept across the tarmac and came to rest between the two lines of men.

It remained there between the ranks of now hatless mourners for less than ten seconds, then pulled forward to where a bright yellow aircraft loader stood ready to hoist Tchaikovsky's coffin into the plane.

I pocketed my air ticket and took up a position near the wide glass window to watch the group of men returning across the windswept apron. They straggled now, pairing off to talk together as they clamped their wide Russian trilbies on their heads and struggled to keep their coats from being wrapped around their legs by the gusting wind. Only Pushkin walked alone, a little to the side of the group, alone and staring at the white concrete of the apron. From where I stood I could see Koloniev clearly. He was unusually tall for a Russian, something over six feet two, with thin, broad shoulders and a very slight stoop. He carried a grey Homburg hat as befitted his senior position in KGB, and the wind harassed his thick grey hair. Over ten years I had studied so much film of this man that I felt all his movements and gestures were intensely familiar to me. I had seen him run his fingers through windswept hair in airports in India, South America and the Middle East. I had seen him drop an arm round the shoulder of his companion in Prague, Cairo and Havana. And I had spent hours Russian lip-reading the banalities of his comradely greetings in the hope of a word of significance slipped in among them.

Men like Koloniev are a menace to our world and to their own. Long years ago he had forgotten why he did what he did. He had become a blind functionary of a system.

They piled into their big black chauffeur-driven cars and drew away from the airport in close convoy. Pushkin, I noticed, took care not to share the same back seat with Koloniev.

Chapter 14

End of season Deauville is the saddest place I've ever seen. The tall ornate houses back from the sea-front are boarded and shuttered against wind and vandals. The planked boardwalk is empty of middle-class French families and the spiritless channel waves heave against the jetty, heavy as oil. A few cafés and tea-houses remain open in some brave but futile gesture against the onset of winter. The shops that sell seamen's striped jerseys and green glass globes in rope nets are deserted and mostly closed.

In the early evening the green cross of a pharmacy shines like a welcoming inn-sign among the shuttered cafés and brasseries; a cinema or two remain open but apparently without custom to be lured by the poster drawings of the 1940s, red-lipped starlet with split skirts and flowing hair. The sea wind, ever present, shakes the suspended overhead lights and thumps noisily on the parked 2CVs. In October Deauville sits on the Normandy coast like a city abandoned to the approaching invader.

It's hard to imagine now that for the international jet-set of the '20s there was no place like Deauville. It was here that the girls wore shorter skirts and more pointed shoes, wriggled more, talked more, danced more and *gave* more than anywhere else in Europe. It was here that the bloods in blazers and cream trousers gambled more at the casino or the race-track, sipped more champagne out of more ludicrous receptacles, proposed more marriages and more propositions, and drank more toasts to absent friends decomposing in the Flanders mud than anywhere else in Europe.

One remnant of this life of long ago remains in the yachting fraternity of Deauville. They hang on long after the summer visitors have returned to Paris, loath to miss an opportunity to re-scrub a deck or paint a bowsprit. They are to be seen, even in early October, along the quayside or in the tea-houses in canvas shoes and reefer jackets exchanging words of timeless banter. I had already confirmed *The Cricketer*'s mooring from one of them and was sitting at the zinc bar of a small locals' café waiting for dark. I knew enough about Dyson to have a healthy respect for his animosity. And that I certainly planned to arouse. But I was going to have to be certain that no casual visitor disturbed our interview – and for that the hours after midnight seemed indicated.

I drank the first bottle of burgundy with what the patronne considered unseemly haste. But she gave me a new glass with the new bottle and folded her arms across her narrow bosom to watch my progress on the second. It was an indifferent Brouilly. When I ordered a large brandy to chase away the taste she rolled her eyes and set the whole bottle on the bar.

We chatted a little as I made my way down the neck to the label on the bottle. She told me how the Resistance had used her bar as a meeting place until the Gestapo had discovered she served the best sea-food in Deauville and began to patronise her cooking. I asked her if the Gestapo were good tippers. The very best, she assured me, the very best tippers she had ever come across – bar none. If you ask, I thought, you learn a little more about the human condition every day.

The side-street sloped steeply to the quayside. By letting the hired Peugeot run down silently, without engine or lights, and braking just before the corner, I had positioned myself just fifty yards from the quayside and Dyson's boat.

I reached in the dark for the hold-all on the seat beside me, pulled it on to my lap and unzipped it. From it I took my passport (Roger Synian, journalist) and a pair of binoculars, decent quality but not expensive. Last of all I unclipped one of the leather handles of the hold-all. It was tight-packed with lead shot and wielded as a blackjack it could reduce a man to a reeling, dizzy wreck in one. As I said, I'd a healthy respect for Dyson. I slipped the leather blackjack inside my coat-sleeve under my left armpit and let it hang from a button I have on all my jackets for just this purpose. On Mansfield's team all the field-men had developed their own little self-protective idiosyncracies. This was mine. I had found that a normal frisk-search usually failed to reveal it.

I sat from about nine-thirty to midnight studying *The Cricketer* through the binoculars. In practice it meant I kept them trained on the one circular porthole through which I could see movement. I counted and recounted, identified and re-identified the heads that bobbed back and forth. Three girls – three men, I made it. Drinking, dancing, having fun.

I wasn't. The hire car was small, cramped and cold. And I was not anxious to switch on the engine to get the heater going. But I did have the rest of the bottle of brandy I had bought from the bar round the corner, and I swigged at that from time to time and carefully smoked a cigarette, shielded in my cupped hand.

At this time of the year there weren't many boats moored at Deauville. The nearest to *The Cricketer* was some 75 yards further down the quay. Beyond that I could see the lazy movement of deck lights as the waves lifted the big boats and the faster bobbing mast lights of the smaller fry.

At just after midnight a man and a girl emerged on to the deck of *The Cricketer*, followed by a tall figure in a dark rollneck sweater that I could easily identify as Dyson. With laughter and back-slapping he saw them on their way before returning below himself.

I had almost another half-hour to wait before the saloon door opened again and the heads and shoulders of another couple could be seen turning and talking to someone below them in the saloon. I rolled down the car window and listened to the voices. They came across the intervening space clearly enough but in a language I couldn't identify. Dutch perhaps, or Afrikaans. After a few moments' banter this second couple mounted the companionway on to the deck and, clasping the hand-rail, unsteadily edged down the gangplank and on to the quayside.

I allowed their footsteps to fade down the cobbled quay and took another swig of brandy. I was within distance of finishing the bottle, I noticed without too much alarm. With four guests gone, I calculated Dyson was now alone with his girl.

Taking the car key from my pocket I fitted it into the ignition and set the gear in first. Then I climbed carefully out of the driver's seat and jammed a wad of Kleenex into position to stop the car door closing completely. I wanted to be sure I was set for a quick departure if it proved necessary.

The quayside was deserted as I crossed to *The Cricketer*'s gangplank. I made no attempt to conceal my footsteps across the deck and as I reached the entrance to the saloon I heard Dyson's voice inside.

'Jan, is that you?' Then something in Afrikaans mixed with a splutter of laughter.

He pulled open the door. Stripped to the waist he looked even bigger than I remembered. I was standing three rungs up the companion ladder so that when I kicked out I caught him hard in the solar plexus, toppling him backwards into the brightly lighted saloon. Then I saw that I had miscounted. There were *two* girls, one dark-haired, one blonde, both open-mouthed, staring at me from the curved benches at the end of the saloon. I also saw that both of them were in various stages of undress.

As I jumped into the saloon and kicked the door closed behind me I was already reaching into my sleeve for the loaded leather strap. Dyson's head came up with a dazed look in his eyes and I aimed a wristy squash stroke that wrapped the leather round the back of his skull with a dull thwack. Then I turned my attention to the girls. They were scrambling across the leather bench grabbing up sweaters and skirts. As I looked across at them they stopped – slowly, like clockwork toys running down. They were convinced that they were the real object of the attack on Dyson.

I needed them both to know that they were safe as long as they didn't try to intervene.

'I've an old score to settle with Dyson' I said. 'Understand?'

They looked at me, eyes bright with tears, the blonde overwhelmed every two or three seconds with a violent, shivering spasm.

'Stay over there. For your own sakes,' I said. 'Stay over there.'

They looked down at the heaving, retching figure of Dyson on the floor. The end of the strap had whip-lashed round to catch his upper lip. They looked at the blood and the visible rate of swelling and understood what I meant.

Somewhere, of course, he had a gun. And that I had to get to first. While the two shivering girls dragged sweaters over their heads I pulled out the bureau drawers. The gun was in the top one. I pushed open a port, dropped the gun out and turned in time to see Dyson pushing himself to his feet.

Rocking back on trembling legs, he crashed like a drunk into a sitting position on the floor. 'What in God's name? . . .' he spluttered.

'Tom Hart,' I said. 'Remember me?'

He nodded and retched at the same time. The girls, I noticed, were fascinated.

'For Chrissake . . .' he tried again. But his blond head fell forward on to his chest. I could imagine the wave of nausea that overcame him every time he tried to focus.

'I'm going to ask some questions, Dyson. You're going to give me the answers. And if you don't – you and I are going to put on a show for the girls.'

'Are you off your head?' He spumed blood through his distorted lips.

'I want to know about Red Banner,' I told him. 'I want to know about the job you did for them.'

He lifted his head and fought to focus on me. His eyes were red, and tears were running down his cheeks.

'Can I have a drink?' he mumbled.

I told him to forget it. But I badly needed one myself. I eyed the whisky bottle and the glasses on the table next to the girls. Dyson wasn't in a sufficiently submissive state yet for me to relax.

'Red Banner . . .' I reminded him with a twirl of the strap.

'Who sent you?' He was beginning to feel very sorry for himself. 'Did Mansfield send you?'

'Dyson, your time's running out. Red Banner – tell me all about it.'

'I don't *know* Red Banner,' he started, but the strap cut him short, jerking his jaw like a punch from a steam hammer and leaving a sharply marked welt across his face that immediately began to seep blood.

I was feeling bad. I knew if Dyson held out any longer I had to have a drink. It wasn't that I felt any pity for him – I had only to think of the Four Square Disco to quell that. But I couldn't explain that to the girls who were, in all probability, just there for a well-paid threesome. And the disgust and terror on their faces I was finding hard to take.

I looked down at Dyson. He wouldn't be saying anything for a while. I pointed to the blonde nearest the whisky bottle. 'Pour me a drink ' I ordered.

She stood up trembling. 'Whisky?'

She was French I nodded and watched her take the bottle and overfill the glass. As she handed it to me she burst into tears.

I motioned her back on to the bench. 'How long have you known him?' I asked the other girl.

She swallowed hard. 'Me, a week. Anne-Marie longer.'

'How much longer?'

'A few days.' The blonde was still crying.

'Does he pay you? For this . . .' I indicated the bench. The dark one understood. She nodded.

'Pays well?'

She shrugged.

I took a long draught of the whisky and shuddered under its impact. Dyson was groaning and would have to be attended to again. The blonde was crying in uncontrollable bursts of hysteria. The other girl watched me with button-black eyes.

'Get out,' I said. 'Get out and go home.'

Neither of them moved.

'You've got somewhere to go?'

The dark-haired girl nodded slowly.

'Then go there.'

Very deliberately she got up, never taking her eyes off me for a second. Then she raised her friend to her feet and edged her past me. I opened the door for them and they scrambled up the companion ladder. The blonde girl, I noticed, wore only one shoe.

I closed the door after them and crossed to watch them through the porthole. They reached the quayside and began to run, the dark-haired girl looking back over her shoulder every few steps.

I knew of course that I didn't have much time. Both girls had removed their tights and had draped them over the bench before I arrived. I took both pairs and bound Dyson's hands behind his back.

He was conscious now, in a semi-bemused way. His face had swollen grotesquely and was already colouring around the mouth and under one eye.

I decided on one more go at him before I took him across to the car. I took the ice bucket next to the whisky bottle and emptied the water and melting ice-cubes over his head.

He gasped and began to mumble. 'Mansfield. What does

Mansfield want?'

'Forget Mansfield,' I told him. 'Just concentrate on your answers. Where did Red Banner contact you?'

His blond hair stuck flat against his skull. He half sat, half sprawled against the bulkhead watching the dangling leather strap.

'They came here,' he said. 'They sent someone . . .'

This was better. I took another gulp of whisky and looked out at the quay. There were no signs of life. Under the street lamps I could see the thin sparkling drift of rain. I turned back to Dyson.

'Let me have a drink,' he begged. 'You mad son of a bitch, let me have a drink.'

He'd known what he was doing when he heisted the gelignite for Red Banner. However pathetic he looked at the moment he wasn't going to get a drink.

'All right. They wanted you and your boat to hi-jack the *François Villon*. Did they tell you it was carrying gelignite?'

He looked up at me and nodded.

'Did they tell you what it was for?'

He was watching the leather again. He knew what the gelignite was for.

I brought the strap down hard on his shoulder. As he gasped with pain I asked him again. 'What did they want it for?'

He was mumbling pretty incoherently, his head dropping forward under the thudding pain he would have in his shoulder. I slipped the leather back in my sleeve and jerked his head up by a handful of wet hair.

'I want to know where they've got that gelignite hidden, Dyson. I want to know if I have to kill you to find out.'

I had just decided I would have to get him to the car when I heard the footfall on the deck above me.

I checked through the port and saw across the street the dark-haired girl. She was watching the man Dyson had called Jan move up the companionway towards the deck. That probably meant that the man already on the deck above my head was the first of Dyson's friends to leave that night.

I kept talking and hauled Dyson on to his feet. I was in trouble. Of course I should never have released the girls, but I really had no choice – I couldn't have stood them there much longer. I was definitely getting soft. Thank God. In this business, as Jazz has often reminded me, soft means human.

But right now soft meant dead. I don't think Dyson had twigged that the 7th Cavalry were surrounding the fort as he rocked and swayed and mumbled behind the door. At least I didn't until he dropped the act, and snapped his forehead down across my eyebrow in a perfectly executed pub-brawler's head butt. The room went misty green.

The next seconds were an explosion of shouting voices and dull thuds about my head and body that I could feel as impact but not as pain. In a sea-green reverie I was transported back to pillow fights in a prep school dorm.

Slowly the anaesthetising green mist receded and I became aware of throbbing pain and pairs of feet. Three men and then a girl with white high-heels and bare, brown, stockingless ankles.

'Who is he?' a voice above me asked. Jan, I guessed by the accent.

'His name's Hart,' Dyson's voice said. 'He's a legman for British Intelligence.'

'He's mad,' the girl's voice trembled. 'He's like a mad dog.' The French accent was heavy with hate.

'Get him to his feet,' Dyson said. 'He's got a blackjack, so watch it.'

Two faces bent into my eyeline and hands gripped me and pulled me to my feet. I let my knees buckle but in truth I didn't feel too bad. There's a certain hysterical euphoria that can take over immediately after being beaten up. Maybe it's the adrenalin pumping, I don't know.

'Find that blackjack,' Dyson said. 'I could use it.'

One held me up while the other searched. He did a pretty thorough job, but he found nothing.

'I tell you he's got some sort of blackjack.' Dyson pushed Jan aside. 'You don't think he did this with his bare hands, do you?' He was gesturing to his swollen face.

'He's got nothing on him now,' Jan said irritably.

'For Chrissake, you saw it.' He turned to the girl.

'He was hitting you with a leather strap,' she enunciated clearly. 'About so long.' She held her hands a foot apart.

'A lead-weighted leather strap,' Dyson lisped through swollen lips. 'Get his jacket off, Piet. He's got it on him somewhere.'

Piet, the other man, stepped behind me and began to peel off my jacket. For a second my hands were free and the strap handle was exposed as Piet dragged back the jacket.

I snatched at it, ripping the button from the cloth and kicking backwards with my heel in the same movement.

Piet yelled, the girl screamed, Dyson's hand came up too late to stop the strap catching him a partial blow across the face. He

105

reeled back, blocking Jan.

By the time they recovered themselves I was through the door. Somebody was a second or two behind me and grabbed at my ankle as I scrambled up the companion ladder. I kicked back again and my heel sank into a soft breast. The girl screamed with pain and tumbled back, blocking the way to the three men behind her.

She had given me maybe four seconds. As I crossed the gangplank they were still trampling over her to get to the deck. As I raced across the road they had reached the gangplank. As I threw open the door of the car they were streaming across the road.

I slammed down the clutch and turned the ignition key. It fired, and as I lifted my foot and gave it gas the car jumped forward at Jan and Piet who were in the lead.

The door, swinging open, caught one of them and sent him sprawling in the road. The others scattered as I wrenched the wheel and turned on screaming tyres along the quayside.

I was high on adrenalin. I leaned out and caught the door, slammed it closed and sped through the town towards the Trouville exit.

It was some time between one and two in the morning, and the streets were totally empty. The rain which had started while I was in *The Cricketer* had left the cobbles treacherous and the tarmac brimming with reflected light.

As I joined the N 813 to Villerville and Honfleur I saw the headlights behind me.

Of course they could have been anybody's headlights, but I wasn't going to take the chance. I put my foot down. Behind me the driver did the same.

The N 813 to Honfleur is hardly more than a country lane, deep-set between high hedges and overhanging trees with slopes and gradients which follow the natural undulations of the cliff top, unevened by highway engineers. I was already driving far too fast, fighting at even the gentlest of bends to keep the car on the road and unaided by the effect of the powerful double-banked headlights behind me distorting and reshaping the shadows of the trees and high hedges.

I was very scared. But somehow the flow of adrenalin had stopped and I was in danger of succumbing to a nervous weariness which began to make even the idea of surrender attractive. Death, they say, comes when you let it. Defeat most certainly does.

As we approached the sparse street lights of Villerville I knew that I had to find out about the other car. The white-on-blue Villerville-sur-Mer sign, the first dozen houses, the Credit Agricole bank had all flashed past when I saw the slip-road open in front of me. I don't think I really thought about it – certainly it was in no sense a decision. I hit the brake, half-turned the wheel and was skidding fast down the slip-road as the headlights of the other car brushed past me.

Ahead was the beach. Between the shuttered houses there was nowhere else to go. The slip-road ended in a concrete ramp. I drove down it and accelerated across the shingle, the wheels hurling pebbles that rattled and thumped upon the underside of the Peugeot. I reached the wet sand, ribbed but firmed up by the action of the waves, braked the car to a sliding halt and switched off the lights.

To my left the limitless menace of the heaving sea. To my right a shadowed jumble of beach houses, cliff face and trees. The other car appeared to have continued on down the coast road to Honfleur.

I wheeled down the window because I was suddenly hot and sticky around my shirt collar and reached for the brandy bottle in the glove compartment. There were still two or three good mouthfuls left. I lifted the bottle to my lips and held the hot liquid in my mouth before swallowing. Do sea-birds never sleep? Swooping and cawing across the sand at me, climbing and banking only seconds away from the windscreen they dropped behind the car to dig at the sand surface torn up by the tyres.

I lit a cigarette and took another gulp of brandy. It was a long time since I had felt quite so alone.

The really heavy rain had stopped and the droplets that scattered across the windscreen now were little more than sea mist, driven inland by the wind. I took out my binoculars and focused them on the cliff face. Hardening from the shadow a clapboard beach house, three storeys high . . . a set of steep steps . . . a tangle of black bushes and stunted trees . . . the ramp at the end of the slip-road . . . I raised the glasses to the cliff top. The street lamps silhouetted a line of shuttered holiday homes but revealed that there was no alternative way down to the beach for a car.

I swung the binoculars back at shingle level past an upturned rowboat and what looked like an abandoned mussel stand and stopped again at the ramp. But this time the shadow formation was different. My heart was racing as I adjusted the centre screw for a finer focus. Two enormous pale eyes seemed to stare blinking at me from the depth of shadow.

By now I was shaking with cold and fear. It is basic training on a night binocular search to rest the eyes from time to time. But I was too scared to stop looking at the strange rhythmic blinking of the eyes. Finally I rested the binoculars and stared across the three hundred yards of shingle. The moon was out at sea behind my head so that my car cast a shadow on the wet sand. I followed my own car tracks back to the ramp then raised the binoculars again. This time I understood. Their car itself was lost in shadow but the action of the wiper blades cleared the windscreen to reflect the moonlight on alternate slow sweeps.

Then, as I watched, the double headlights flooded me with light, the engine burst into life and the car nosed fast down the ramp and was bucketing across the shingle towards me.

The engine fired on the first turn of the key. In a series of fast gear changes I got the Peugeot moving across the hard ribs of sand. Through the open window I could hear the spurt of sea water under the wheels as I raced the Peugeot along the water's edge, my foot flat down on the accelerator, the engine emitting a strange flat whine and the sea spray slashing at the side of my face.

The car behind me which I could now see was a big black Citroën seemed, if anything, to find the sand at least as heavy going as my own car, and for three or four hundred yards at a time I would have the impression that I was pulling away from my pursuers. Then the sand would somehow change in quality or I would be forced to swerve into the shadows by a sharp protruding rock and the Citroën would be up on me again, fifteen, ten yards away, striving to draw level so that it could force me into the sea.

Then, in an unexpected change of tactic, the driver suddenly pulled away and pointed the Citroën up the beach ploughing through the heavy shingle, losing ground to me as I raced ahead. Merely driving had absorbed all my energies and it was not until the Citroën turned and began to run parallel but behind me and higher up the beach that I understood the point of the tactic.

Ahead, I now saw, the beach made a sharp turn right round a modest headland. If I followed the waterline round the headland the Citroën could cut across the shingle and ram me into the sea.

I lifted the pressure from the accelerator to hold a little power in hand and the Peugeot bounced bravely along at 50, maybe 55 plus, staying with the water's edge while the Citroën churned shingle high on my right.

Then it turned. With its headlights blazing yellow it came charging down the beach like some monstrous sea animal, bucking and rearing over flat rocks and heaped shingle. At God-knows how many yards I stabbed down on the accelerator, and with a fast-rising engine whine the Peugeot jumped forward another ten or fifteen miles an hour. It was just enough.

With a scraping blow across my rear bumper that spun the Peugeot in a new direction up-beach, the Citroën plunged on nose deep into the sea, blowing and hissing and spluttering like the Loch Ness Monster.

I adjusted the wheel to continue on the waterline and had glanced in the mirror to see the doors of the Citroën fly open and men begin to tumble out when I caught sight of the groyne in the periphery of my vision.

Stretching as a solid four-feet-high timber wall from the cliff face deep into the incoming tide, the groyne was designed to prevent the erosion of the beach round the headland. It was equally clearly going to prevent my escape.

I had turned the Peugeot up towards the cliff, thinking at least to put the width of the beach between me and Dyson and his friends, when I saw in the headlights a section of the timber wall where the sweep of the tide over decades had massed the shingle almost to the height of the groyne.

Aiming the car at this makeshift ramp, praying that the drop on the other side would be no more than a foot or two, I gave the Peugeot all the throttle I could stamp out of it.

With a desperate lurch across the heavy shingle and a frightening whine from the engine the car hit the shingle ramp, almost stopped on wildly spinning wheels, then jumped forward across the top of the groyne into the darkness beyond.

As the Peugeot flew through the air I could guess the trim of its flight by the crazy angle of the headlights. There was no possible way in which I could land on all four wheels. I braced myself as the rear off-side wheel struck rock, and sea, cliff and sky described a quick circle round my head. But the shingle absorbed the major part of the clattering impact.

I crawled out of the Peugeot to shouts from the other side of the groyne. Scrambling forward on the shingle I wasn't aware of being badly hurt. I got to my feet and began to run for the cliff.

The big round pebbles turned my ankles at every step and the dark rocks forced constant changes of direction. But I ploughed on towards the headland, looking back only to see a flashing light as Dyson, Jan and Piet climbed the groyne and headed after me.

I couldn't believe Honfleur was so close. As I struggled forward on legs leaden, as in nightmares, the mass of the headland suddenly seemed to fade and first one or two then many more of the quayside lights of Honfleur twinkled in the rain and mist.

I knew now that I could win – that if I could drive my aching legs another half-mile I would be in the middle of the town. And that somehow there I could get help.

It was no carefully formulated plan because such plans aren't best made when your knees are trembling and you're wheezing like a sex maniac, but it offered hope. And hope I needed more than a fresh pair of legs.

I reached the stone steps that led up the cliff-side, still well ahead of the other three and had made it 50 or 60 feet above their heads before they arrived below. They caught me in the flashlight beam and Dyson called on me hoarsely to stop.

I looked down and saw that they were as exhausted as I was. Jan carried a shotgun but as he pointed up towards me Dyson pushed it aside. The rock overhang would have made it useless at that angle. I started on again up the steps.

'Hart . . .' Dyson's voice floated up to me. I continued on round the next rock outcrop and looked down. They hadn't moved.

'It's time to talk, Hart,' Dyson yelled up at me. If I believed that I'd believe anything. I stole another couple of steps higher and shouted down: 'You had your chance earlier in the boat. You could have talked then.' I took a couple more steps up.

'Listen to me, Hart. You choose. Make it down here and talk, or you're done for.'

With my foot I rolled a rock over the edge that bounced and sprang towards them in a shower of earth and stones. As they scattered I turned and ran for my life.

From the cliff top into Honfleur itself was no more than a few hundred yards downhill. I was under the street lights and sliding on the wet cobbles by the time Dyson and the others reached the top of the cliff.

My problem now was to avoid being trapped between Jan

with the shotgun at one end and Dyson and Piet at the other end of one of the narrow backstreets of the little town.

I ran straight on down the N 813 until it became the Rue des Capucins and turned into the narrow Rue des Lingots, an ancient paved and guttered alley lined by half-timbered houses which were already crumbling when Bonaparte had stayed in one of them as a young man. My footsteps clattered on the paving stones making concealment of my direction impossible. Behind me I could hear the running footsteps of Dyson and the two men. I turned quickly into the Rue de l'Homme de Bois and at the Lycée took the stone steps down past the house that had once belonged to the painter Boudin. I knew immediately I had made a mistake.

Below me in one of the ruelles leading off the Rue de la Prison I could hear a single running man. Above me, more footsteps. I threw myself into a deeply shadowed opening that seemed to lead back to a courtyard. For the moment, gasping mouthfuls of the cold, mist-laden air, I waited.

I was about half-way down the 36 stone steps and could clearly hear the exchange between Jan, at the bottom, and Dyson above. They must have stopped, facing each other while Dyson probed the shadowed doorways with the beam of his flashlight. I saw it first dig into the doorway opposite, reveal for a second the intricately carved woodwork of the door jamb, then leap on to banish the shadow in the doorway of the next house.

Then suddenly, startlingly it jumped the stone staircase and was lighting the entrance to the courtyard where I stood.

At the same time, cautiously, Jan began to mount the steps.

'Any sign of him?' Dyson's voice floated down from above. I could see Jan now, taking a step at a time, shotgun at the ready across his chest, peering into the doorways on either side.

'He's here somewhere,' he said. Then swung round quickly at the squeak and rattle of an auberge sign swinging in the wind somewhere further down the steps.

I had two or three seconds only. I came out of cover like an express train to hit the half-turned Jan with a shoulder charge that hurled him and the shotgun down the steps. He crashed in a cry of pain near the bottom, the shotgun clattering into the darkness. As I ran on down past him all around dogs were barking, windows were opening, French voices were raised in alarmed enquiry across the narrow streets.

But I was clear. Jan, I guessed, was probably out of the hunt for the rest of the night, and Dyson still had the wet slippery length of the staircase to descend before he could take up the chase again.

Pushing myself to the limit now I doubled back to cross the Rue de l'Homme de Bois, hurled myself into a narrow alleyway and emerged on the Rue Haute not more than a few yards from Morel's house.

It was where I was aiming for. But I needed at least a minute clear of them. I stood and listened. There was no sound behind me. I rapped hard on the darkened window pane.

The seconds passed. I rapped again. This time I heard Madame Morel inside call irritably, 'Attendez.' I rapped again harder. I could hear Dyson and the others now turning off the Rue de l'Homme de Bois.

They were getting close. I could hear their tired, flat-footed running steps stop as they inspected an alleyway, then start up again at a jog-trot to the next one. Dyson wasn't the sort of man to give up.

In the Morels' front window the light went on and the curtain was lifted. Madame Morel bent towards the window pane and squinted out at me. The alarm on her face reminded me of what I must look like. She dropped the corner of the curtain and I heard her move towards the door. But light was still spilling through a curtain crack out on to the wet cobbles. If Dyson turned into the Rue Haute now with that shotgun I would be finished.

Their voices were not 30 yards away when the bolt shot back and the door opened. I stepped straight inside and snapped off the light. Madame Morel looked at me, no longer in alarm but with a calm, silent enquiry. I gestured towards the street outside where footsteps and voices could be plainly heard.

'I will make coffee,' she said, and disappeared into the back room. I checked that the door was firmly closed behind her and crossed to stand before the crack in the curtains. Dyson stood not five yards away, cradling the shotgun, his head turned to watch Jan limping towards him. A few yards further down the road Piet was bent forward, his hands on his braced knees, trying to recover his breath. Dyson looked at the two men in disgust. His own face was almost unrecognisable. Swellings around the mouth and under the almost closed right eye gave him a grotesque, piratical look. His blond hair was plastered down on his head and like the other two his clothes dripped water. But he still wasn't giving up.

'He maybe knows someone here,' said Piet, straightening up.

'Maybe,' Dyson peered restlessly up and down the Rue Haute,

'or else he's holed up in some corner of a dark alley. We'll keep looking.'

'Listen,' said Jan, limping forward, 'I say we call it a night. We run around like this any longer and we'll have the police called.'

'The French don't call the police,' Dyson snapped. 'They bawl you out and go back to bed. We're okay for a bit longer. Let's start looking.'

He flicked on the powerful flashlight he was carrying and threw it to Piet. 'He turned into this street. We try every doorway . . . every single courtyard. And we find him.'

They moved off as Madame Morel opened the door behind me. She had remembered to turn off the light first.

'Coffee, monsieur,' she said softly.

I sat with her in the kitchen at the back of the house and drank coffee by the light of an oil lamp. She asked no questions, and apart from telling me that her husband was away on a voyage she simply waited quietly for me to decide how much I told her.

I explained to her briefly that one of the men outside, and probably all three of them, were responsible for the hi-jacking of her husband's freighter. I told her that with any luck they could be in jail within a matter of hours.

I borrowed the phone and direct-dialled Stevens in England.

He had lived, ever since I knew him in a picture-postcard cottage on the river just outside Maidenhead. I could imagine him now as the phone began to ring, climbing in his white silk pyjamas from between the black, fine cotton sheets and padding across the bedroom to the telephone in the exquisitely furnished sitting room. It was a house where every last detail of furniture and furnishing had been lovingly considered, bought and placed by Stevens. The total effect was such that it was hard to imagine even the smallest Berlin-glazed figure being positioned anywhere else but where Stevens's taste decreed.

He lifted the phone. 'Maidenhead zero-seven-nine-five-one.' He waited, then carefully repeated the number. From the last digit I counted eleven seconds and put down the receiver.

It was a signal he recognised. I could imagine him now cursing me as he pulled trousers and sweater over his pyjamas, checked his keys, collected his top-coat and let himself out into the early-morning Thames valley mist.

The telephone box we had arranged to use was about a hundred yards from the cottage. I gave him five minutes and dialled the number. After half a dozen hollow clicks it began to ring. Stevens lifted the receiver.

'My dear Thomas,' he said. 'I do most sincerely hope that this is important.'

'It's important,' I assured him. 'I know who hi-jacked the freighter.'

'You do?' He'd already forgotten the walk through the mist.

'You remember Dyson, Rob Dyson? South African contract man?'

'Oh yes. I know Dyson.' Stevens was thoughtful. 'A very likely candidate indeed.'

'More than a canditate,' I told him. 'I put Dyson under pressure tonight. He admitted it.'

'Where *are* you, Thomas? Jazz is worried out of her mind.'

'I'm fine,' I said. 'Tell her no need to worry now. When Mansfield hears this everything's going to be okay.'

'Thomas, have you read last evening's papers?' His voice showed his concern.

'How could I? I'm in France. Dyson has a boat at Deauville.'

'I see.' His voice dropped. 'Look, it may not be that simple to clear things with Mansfield straight away. He's issued your photograph. The story is you're wanted for an eternal-triangle murder of a Russian diplomat.'

'Tchaikovsky! Why the hell should I have killed Tchaikovsky?'

'Of course Mansfield knows no girl's involved,' Stevens said. 'This is just the press cover story. But listen carefully, Thomas – because in Mansfield's mind, at least, it all makes sense. It goes like this: You had access to the Red Banner list when you picked it up from Pushkin at the Tower. Saliva tests indicated it was you who opened and examined it. That same day every name on that list ran for cover. Now here's the connection with Tchaikovsky. Whoever tipped off Red Banner knew that the only way to prevent Mansfield getting a fresh, up-to-date list was to cut the link between the Red Banner traitor (whoever he was) and the Russians. And that link was Tchaikovsky.'

'All right,' I said. 'I accept the reasoning. I think that's why Tchaikovsky was killed. But why look in my direction? Pushkin thinks it could be n his own Embassy. And with Koloniev in charge of KGB there, it's almost a certainty.'

'Mansfield prefers his own version, Thomas,' Stevens said quietly. 'If you come back to England you'll be picked up immediately.'

'You don't imagine I used my own passport?'

'No. But Mansfield has issued details of all your old cover passports to the police. If you're using one of those . . .'

I was.

'. . . they'll have you as soon as you land. Stay in France, Thomas, find a small pension somewhere that won't ask for your passport. And God forbid *I* should suggest it but find yourself a girl. They make the best possible cover, I'm reliably informed.'

I told him to forget the advice – I was coming back to England. The longer I skulked around in France, the more certain Mansfield would become I was his man.

'All I have to do,' I insisted, 'is to put Mansfield on to Dyson. From the moment they pick him up I'm in the clear.'

'Where's Dyson now?' Stevens asked.

'God knows. But one thing's sure – he won't go back to his boat. He'll lie low in France – or maybe try to make it back to South Africa.'

There was a long silence on the other end of the line.

'Thomas,' Stevens's voice sounded troubled, 'let me put Mansfield on to Dyson. I'll tell him you phoned me.'

'All right,' I agreed. 'But I'm coming back all the same. Remember I'm still expecting something from Pushkin.'

Again there was a long pause at the other end of the phone. 'I'll get a new passport to you,' he said at length. 'Where will you be tomorrow, sometime after mid-day?'

I thought quickly. I couldn't stay in Honfleur, that was certain, in case Dyson had Red Banner friends in the area. 'Rouen,' I told Stevens. 'Pension du Gros-Horloge.' It was a discreet little hotel I'd used in the past.

'Good.' I could envisage Stevens nodding over the receiver. 'I'll send a passport out to you tomorrow.' He paused. 'I can't persuade you to stay out there a few days longer?'

'No. I appreciate the concern. But I've got to come back.'

'Very well, Thomas. But take care.'

The phone clicked and I was left with a dialling tone.

Chapter 15

It was raining heavily as I left the Morels' house. My raincoat was torn in several places after last night's activity, and the dark patches across the shoulders and down the chest showed that even Madame Morel's stove hadn't made much impression on the soaking fibres. But with rain falling like this, in long straight columns of water, I looked less conspicuous in a torn raincoat than in none at all.

I kept my collar up and my eyes open as I hurried along the quayside. Even the heavy rain couldn't keep the French house-wives indoors, and I splashed along behind short, fat ladies with brown leatherette shopping bags.

The falling rain spurted crowns of water from the Vieux Bassin as I hurried along the Quai Ste Catherine and turned into the Place Thiers. Honfleur is a small town and the principal streets and squares with banks and shops and cafés number not much more than a dozen or two. If Dyson and the others were still here they had a good chance of intercepting me as I tried to leave town. But unless they deployed more than the three of them they would have to rely on luck. Small as it is, there are still numerous ways of leaving Honfleur.

Before saying goodbye to Madame Morel I had borrowed her phone book, rail and bus guide and the previous day's copy of the *Indépendant Honfleurais*, the local paper, and had spent half an hour studying the possible exits from the town.

Three taxi stands or two self-drive car firms at the Cours des Fosses and the Rue de la République could take me by road to Caen, Le Havre, Rouen or Paris; the railway station used an autobus service to Lisieux or Evreux after which no part of France would present a problem by rail; and at St Gatien internal air flights could get me to Tours, Lyons or Paris. But flights to England had ceased a week or so earlier with the end of the season.

If Dyson were mulling over the same information he would be stumped. *I* knew I was heading for Rouen. All he knew was that the chances were I was getting out of Honfleur. With the man-

116

power he had, picking up my trail again could be no more than luck.

But luck he almost had. I was about to cross the Place de la Porte de Rouen towards the waiting autobus which would take me as far as Lisieux when I caught sight of a shop-window clock which showed 9.30. I reacted with a start, checking my own watch quickly because 9.30 was the departure time for the autobus. My watch showed several minutes before half-past, but the activity of the driver across the square made me think that crashing the Peugeot and rolling around in the shingle had perhaps affected its timekeeping. I stopped an ancient pensioner on his way to collect his Tuesday morning benefits and sheltered under his umbrella as he consulted a silver timepiece which he drew from under folds of thick black overcoat.

It was he told me, in beautifully ponderous, deep-throated French, five-and-twenty minutes past nine. I thanked him. He added the intelligence that his watch had not strayed one minute in 65 years. I agreed it was remarkable. He offered for my consideration a deep dent on the obverse where flying shrapnel had hit the silver casing as his regiment of infantry had scrambled through the mud and wire at Verdun. I congratulated him on his escape.

While these courtesies were being exchanged I was watching, from under the lip of the old soldier's dripping umbrella, Dyson's dark-haired girl-friend get on to the autobus and check the passengers in the high-backed seats.

The old man listened to my accent and concluded I was German. 'No one can match you Germans for stamina,' he said, proud as if he had worn the spiked Uhlan's helmet himself, 'except possibly the British. The Guards or those Highland Infantry in their skirts.' He chuckled at some obscene memory from the distant past. 'I fought in Russia too, you know.'

My surprise encouraged him. I watched the light raincoat of the girl move back down the bus towards the exit.

'My goodness yes,' he said. 'They were funny fighters, the Bolsheviks. 1919 it was, and Clemenceau sent us over with the British to take Petrograd. You know what they told us? Show a revolutionary an Allied bayonet and he'd turn tail and run.'

'And did they?' The girl stepped down from the bus and made towards an English Mini-Cooper parked a few yards along the road.

'Did they?' The old man guffawed with laughter. 'We never gave them a chance. The first sign of *their* bayonets and *we* turned tail. We d heard that story from the generals too many times already.

The driver was getting into his bus and the dark-haired girl was pulling away from the kerb in her Mini. I thanked the old man for his company and ran across the square, keep ng the bulk of the bus between me and the departing Mini-Cooper.

As I climbed aboard and settled into a seat I looked back to see the old man trudging on his way. I wondered now hat Europe had abandoned war, how else would Europeans get to know and like each other. There didn't really seem to be an effective substitute.

Rouen rustled up a few shafts of cool October sunlight to welcome me and I hurried from the station down he Avenue Jeanne d'Arc conscious that the bus journey to Lisieux and the train on to Rouen had taken the best part of the morning.

There isn't much of the old city of Rouen remaining since the British shelling – the price of liberation in 1944 – but there are still a few old streets left around the cathedral. The Rue du Gros-Horloge is one of them, a paved walkway dominated by an ancient stone archway into which is set a massive and colourful clock from which the street takes its name. I checked into the pension just behind the arch and left a message with the concierge that I was taking a brandy in the Café Six and would be back within the hour.

I strolled back under the great clock and settled at a table on the walkway. When the waiter came out I ordered a black coffee and a very large Calvados, the fine strong cider-brandy of Normandy.

It was time for a grim financial reckoning. Mansfield's unhealthy interest in my movements meant that it was nearly five days since I had been to a bank, and the General's original fee was running out fast. I counted out my money and found that, in francs and sterling, I had barely eighty pounds left. The coffee was, as ever, good. The Calvados, a farm-distilled product from the Pays d'Ange, was even better. I immediately ordered another.

I was still sipping my second Calvados when I heard her voice behind me. Of all the emissaries I had expected Stevens to send for some reason I had not imagined it would be Jazz.

Even the French waiter grinned at our exaggerated greeting – and he hadn't even been tipped yet. I sat Jazz down, feeling a warmth and affection for her that I wanted her to know about.

But she cut me short.

'Tom,' she was looking me up and down for the first time, 'what in God's name have you been doing to yourself?'

'You mean the coat,' I laughed, lifting the tattered corner of my raincoat.

'No, Tom. Not just the coat. I mean the black marks under your eyes. The unshaven chin. The bruised face. I mean the torn coat, the battered shoes and the scratched hands. What are you on there? . . .' she indicated my glass. 'Meths?'

I could see from her expression that what she was saying she meant. I offered her a Calvados, but however much I extolled its virtues she refused. Her plan was straightforward. Buy a shirt and razor. Back to the hotel to shave. After that lunch. I capitulated.

I told her the Dyson story as I showered and shaved and she listened in silence. We left the hotel and walked slowly towards the Place du Vieux Palais where I planned we'd have lunch, and I still couldn't get much out of her.

The Auberge de l'Ecu de France is a 500-year-old tavern on the old main square of Rouen, a square they call the 'Place du Vieux Palais', as if the building of the Old Palace was incomparably the most important event that took place here. No mention of that day over half a millennium ago when the English soldiery, the 'Goddams' as the French called them after their most cherished swearword, yelled and cheered as the piled faggots were lit under the remarkable woman who had led the armies of France against them. No mention that in this square, opposite the low leaded windows of the Ecu de France, Joan of Arc was burnt to death on the morning of 30 May 1431 by order of the English Lord Talbot. He was killing, of course, in a cause he knew to be just. As so many had done since. As I had done when there had seemed no other way. He had seen perhaps, that fierce Lord Talbot, that some one person has to carry the guilt, then try to wash the blood free from their hands alone.

I poured Jazz some good Chablis and waited for her to speak.

'You know why I've come, Tom,' she said finally.

'Because Stevens got in touch with you. He gave you a passport for me.'

'Yes,' she nodded slowly. 'He gave me a passport for you, but that wasn't the only reason he wanted me to meet you here.'

'What else was there?'

She sipped at the Chablis. I could see the misery clouding her face. 'Tom,' she stretched out and touched the back of my hand, briefly like the peck of a small bird, 'Tom, you've got to face the facts. You're not going to get back into the Department.'

'Listen, Jazz.' She had no right to talk about facing facts. 'Listen to me. If Mansfield acts fast he can have Dyson under lock and key. And any offer of a deal will make him tell us where that gelignite is hidden. Then what happens? Mansfield recovers the gelignite and the Director and Home Secretary call him in to give him a special pat on the back. Mansfield takes the credit – and I get a back-hander in the form of reinstatement in the office. You see, what you don't understand, Jazz, is that this whole Red Banner deal looks like my best break since Mansfield put me out to grass.'

'Tom,' she said, desperately, 'how can you say that with the whole British, and, for all I know, French police forces looking for you as a Red Banner agent – and a murderer?'

'It's a Mansfield smokescreen. Stevens knows how he works. He needs to be seen to be on the track of something. At the moment the most important thing for Mansfield is to recover that gelignite. But until he can do it the hue and cry for me keeps his bosses happy. I know this man, Jazz, you don't.'

'Stevens does.'

'I know him better than Stevens. I've lived with him, worked with him . . .'

'Killed with him?' Her head jerked up.

'We did a lot of things back in the fifties and sixties, Jazz. I still think most of them were right.'

She nodded and I could see she was crying. She sniffed a couple of times and took a tissue to her eyes. 'I brought some money, Tom. Over five hundred pounds. How'd you like to show me Florence?'

'Five hundred pounds?'

'Yep . . .'

'In yen?'

She managed a grin. 'Let Stevens sort this whole damn thing out for you, Tom. He's a good friend. Most of the money comes from him.'

The waiter arrived beside our table and I ordered oysters, Bouchée de Reine and civet of wild boar for both of us. Even the claret didn't make Jazz's eyes sparkle.

'I'm sorry about Florence, Jazz,' I said as the waiter left, 'but I think you know how it is.'

'Tom, I asked you to show me Florence – not to screw me on the Ponte Vecchio by moonlight.'

We finished the oysters and Bouchée de Reine in silence, and I poured and ordered wine as we both drank rapidly through the first bottle of claret.

'What about Virginia?' Jazz asked as the waiter poured from the second bottle. 'Are you going back because of her?'

'I'm going back because of my job, Jazz. Because I can't imagine being without it. Because in a way I don't understand, part love, part hate, it's become dear as life to me. You must know that by now. I've talked to you, Jazz. I've tried to explain. Good God, you know what I've been like. You know I've been drinking too much, whoring around . . . You know I've been going to pieces without it.'

'Stevens says having the job is the only way you can keep believing it's all been worth doing in the past.'

'Stevens has a sharp mind in that fat, ugly body. But I want the job back because I'm lost without it. It's as simple as that. And what I really want to know at the moment is why Stevens is so damn keen to keep me over here out of the way . . .'

'Oh, for God's sake, Tom,' she exploded. 'He's trying to help. *I'm* trying to help. But you don't make it easy.' By now, I saw, she was really crying.

We left the restaurant with the rain still holding off, and I put my arm round her shoulders as we walked back to the pension. She didn't say anything but I could feel from the way she leaned in towards me that we were still friends. That somehow we'd always be friends.

We drove out of Rouen by Avis hire car at just after five and took the Paris autoroute. By about seven we were pulling into the vast parking area of Charles De Gaulle Airport at Roissy-en-France.

Jazz bought the tickets and we mingled with British football fans returning from an Arsenal-Nancy Fairs Cup match and slipped through passport control with no problems at all.

Aboard the Air France European airbus Jazz snuggled up close under a blanket that covered us both. 'You bastard,' she said with a friendly grimace, 'to think we could have been on our way to Florence.'

121

Chapter 16

I paid the taxi off at Corby Hall, the medieval merchant's house moved brick by brick from the City of London to Chelsea, and hurried a protesting Jazz off along the Embankment. She was tired and a bit drunk and not too sure why we couldn't have taken the taxi all the way to her flat. But I explained that the relationship between Scotland Yard and London taxi drivers has caught more murderers than mug-shots, fingerprints and Identi-kits put together. And I, I reminded her, was the current subject of a massive murder hunt.

In fact she didn't need reminding. London Airport had been a harrowing experience for Jazz, believing every unlicensed mini-cab driver who sidled up to us was a plain-clothes detective. Fortunately, though, I knew how difficult it was to identify a man from one single-dimensional photograph and I felt reasonably secure despite tabloids on the newsstands with my face occupying an average five double-column inches.

We mounted the steps to Jazz's flat and she fumbled with keys for a moment before opening the door. Last night I had slept no more than a couple of cramped hours in the wicker chair in front of Madame Morel's stove, and as I walked through the hall I could only think of hot coffee, a shower and bed. Jazz flipped on the sitting-room light. The room was neat, chintzy and very welcoming.

'I'll make coffee,' she said, and disappeared through the swing door to the kitchen. I was standing in the middle of the room savouring the buzzing tiredness in my head and listening to the rattle of cups through the thin partition when the door to Jazz's studio opened behind me. At all events it must have opened behind me, but the hissing voice was the first thing I can recall hearing.

'Step forward – face to the wall,' the voice said. As I reached the wall in front of me I risked a quick over-the-shoulder glance to see Pushkin standing in the studio doorway. His face was set hard. In his hand he carried a silenced pistol big as a power drill. I didn't recognise the make but it must have carried a .45 bullet big enough to knock a man's head off.

'Raise your hands above your head. Press the palms flat against the wall.'

I did so. He moved up closer behind me and kicked my feet backwards until I was angled with my weight heavily on my hands. A powerful hand caught my right ankle and forced me to bend my knee. I was standing, stork-like, on one leg as he shoved a chair under my raised ankle so that the high back bit into my instep. It was a position much favoured by the instructors at the GRU training school at Voronezh.

He frisked me rapidly and efficiently. *He* would have found my blackjack. He had stepped back when the kitchen door swung open and Jazz, still wearing her coat, came in carrying two cups of coffee. She stopped in utter amazement, staring at me propped ridiculously against the wall.

'What, in God's name? . . .' her voice tailed off as she saw Pushkin.

'Come in and sit down. Over there.' I guessed Pushkin had indicated the sofa. Jazz crossed out of my eyeline towards it.

'You too, Mr Hart.'

I hopped inelegantly free of the chairback and, under Pushkin's hard, watchful eyes, joined Jazz on the sofa. Pushkin sat on the arm of a chair opposite.

'Who is he, Tom?' I could hear from Jazz's voice that she was very scared.

'He's that friendly Russian I was telling you about.'

'Pushkin?' She couldn't believe it.

I nodded, watching him as closely as he watched me. 'Let's have it,' I said to him. 'Have you and Koloniev been burying the hatchet?'

I don't think he understood me properly. He rested the heavy barrel of the gun on his left wrist. 'Your own department has concluded that you killed Sergei Sergeivitch,' he said. 'Why?'

I slowly took out my cigarettes, handed one to Jazz and lit them both. 'Is that why you're here?'

He inclined his head once only. The menace he exuded got to Jazz. I felt her shiver on the sofa next to me.

'Have you already made up your mind,' I asked him, 'or are you ready to listen?'

Again the single inclination of the head, his eyes unblinkingly fixed on me.

I started slowly. 'My Department believes I warned Red Banner that you were supplying us with a list. They believe I then killed your friend Tchaikovsky, Sergei Sergeivitch, to cut the

123

link between him and his contact in Red Banner.'

'Are they wrong, Mr Hart?'

'Yes. They believe this because they are not prepared to accept that Koloniev or someone in your Embassy would go this far to torpedo co-operation between the two Intelligence services.'

'Why should I believe that you did not kill Tchaikovsky? You arrived early, I remember. You had the opportunity.'

'I arrived at the hotel a few moments before you. I decided to take a walk to use up the time.'

'Immediately after we entered the room and found his body, you left to check the rear staircase. You already knew there was a rear staircase? – the one you had used when you first entered the hotel, perhaps?'

'No. I guessed there *might* be a service staircase. There was.'

Jazz looked from me to Pushkin anxiously. She was aware that I had so far failed to score a really telling point. 'Let's take this very slowly,' I said. 'Obviously I could be working for Red Banner. I *could* have tipped the names on the list you gave me. But if I had then been ordered to destroy the link between your Embassy and some unknown traitor in the Red Banner organisation – why did I stop at killing Tchaikovsky?'

'Go on, Mr Hart.' He wasn't offering any help.

'I think you know what I mean. Why didn't I kill you as well? After all, you both gave me the list. I assume you *both* knew where it came from.'

'In fact only Sergei Sergeivitch knew the source of that list,' he said.

'But I wasn't aware of that.' I was fighting for my life now. 'You came here looking for proof that I didn't kill your friend. The proof lies in the fact that you're still alive yourself.'

His face remained set.

'Whoever killed Tchaikovsky was aware that he alone knew the Red Banner traitor. And to me that points to someone in your own Embassy. Did Koloniev know that Tchaikovsky kept his contact to himself?'

'Yes. It is standard practice. But then Koloniev did not have access to the Red Banner list – so he could not have warned the people named on it.' He paused. 'You see the problem, Mr Hart?'

'So we're looking for someone who had access to the list *and* knew that Tchaikovsky kept the source of his information to himself. *I* qualify on the first count only.'

Very deliberately he flicked on the pistol safety catch with his thumbnail and slid the massive weapon into a holster inside his jacket. Then he sat there with his hands linked over the bump like a peasant who has just stolen a chicken. 'May I join you in some coffee?' he said to Jazz with a smile of outrageous charm.

I've never seen Jazz so eager in her life – and that's something of an admission in itself. She scrambled off the sofa, beaming relief, and propelled herself through the swing door of the kitchen. Through the thin partition I could hear the cups rattling a lot more than usual.

'I won't apologise to you, Mr Hart. We are professionals. But I regret Mrs Oliver was here. I am afraid I made her nervous.'

'She'll be all right,' I assured him, listening to the rattle of cups from the kitchen.

'Then let us talk seriously.'

'About Koloniev?'

He shook his head. 'I have nothing definite there. I saw the report he wrote on Sergei Sergeivitch's death before it was sent to Moscow. It was harsh, but perfectly consistent with his stated opposition to the course we have been instructed to take by the Foreign Ministry.'

'So that leads nowhere?'

'Not at the moment. But there are others. I was able to ensure that I was the first to examine Sergei Sergeivitch's desk at the Embassy.'

'You found something?'

'That is why I'm here, Mr Hart. And why I had to be absolutely sure about you first. You see, I have the name of Sergei Sergeivitch's man.'

'His Red Banner contact?'

'I believe so. A Mr R. O. Sugden teaches art at the North Western polytechnic. For the last three or four years we have commissioned background reports from him on student attitudes. When Sergei Sergeivitch came to London Sugden was assigned to him as his responsibility. We work of course, as no doubt your Department does, on the basis of minimum necessary information . . .'

I nodded. Essentially it meant Department members were only told what was absolutely necessary for them to know.

'. . . But on two occasions,' Pushkin went on, 'when Sergei was absent from the country I took his place. That is how Sugden became known to me.'

'And what makes you connect Sugden with the Red Banner contact?'

'I counter-signed a payment from Special Funds two weeks ago.

125

It was for four thousand pounds for the Red Banner list.'

'Sugden's name was mentioned?'

'No, Mr Hart. You perhaps do not understand. It would have been a serious breach of security for Sergei Sergeivitch to have revealed the name to anyone except the residential officer in charge of Embassy security.'

'If he knew the name of Tchaikovsky's contact,' I said, 'why couldn't you get it from him?'

'I'm not sure how much you understand about the workings of our Embassy, Mr Hart. But if we are to work together some things will have to be explained. Each month Military Intelligence, myself and Sergei Sergeivitch, meet with KGB under Koloniev for an exchange of information. This exchange is presided over by the senior residential security officer. When specific information is discussed it is always covered by the use of code names and numbers to maintain the minimum necessary information concept. Senior members of GRU, like myself or Sergei Sergeivitch, or of KGB, like Koloniev, can apply for the coded information to be released to them by the residential security officer; but of course a convincing case must be made and the instance recorded. Perhaps you already know all this?'

'I had no idea you were that distrustful of each other. Most of this must be new practice.'

He smiled grimly. 'We are mortally afraid of defection, Mr Hart. The whole object of our system is to ensure the defector carries with him no more information than is strictly necessary.'

'When Tchaikovsky was killed surely you or Koloniev applied for the release of the name of the Red Banner contact?'

'Yes,' he smiled, 'we both immediately applied. But the residential officer refused our applications and assigned one of his own men to investigate.'

'Do you know what happened?'

'Only that the investigation indicated that the contact had left his address a matter of days before.'

'No doubt as soon as he pocketed Tchaikovsky's four thousand pounds.'

'No doubt.'

Jazz came in with the coffee. She had taken off her coat, brushed her hair and renewed her lipstick. She handed round the coffee and I came back to the point as Pushkin exercised his considerable charm on an already mesmerised Jazz. 'What makes you think this art teacher, Sugden, is the contact?' I asked.

He sipped his coffee. 'I signed Sergei Sergeivitch's application for the Special Fund on the morning of the twenty-first day of last month,' he said. 'He drew the money from the Embassy accountant that same morning. By the afternoon he had returned with the Red Banner list. I only realised the significance of the date when I examined Sergei's desk diary. Each twenty-first of the month had a mark against it to indicate a regular meeting with a contact. Now, Mr Hart, the two occasions I had substituted as Sugden's contact had both been on the twenty-first of the month. So why did not Sergei Sergeivitch strike out his regular meeting with Sugden in favour of the far more important meeting to buy the Red Banner list? Or why did he not request for me to meet Sugden instead?'

'Because it wasn't necessary if Sugden was the Red Banner contact?'

'Exactly my way of thinking, Mr Hart. What is your opinion?'

'It won't take long to check whether Sugden's just left his address.'

'No,' he agreed. 'But it may take much longer to discover the new whereabouts of Mr Sugden.'

We agreed that I should start the investigation and call him in when I had traced Sugden. As earnest of my intention to co-operate fully I described in detail my trip to Deauville to see Dyson. Throughout he nodded gravely. I suspected he knew Dyson, or at least knew that Soviet organisations had used him almost as often as we had for their dirty work.

'You are not suggesting that Dyson is a member of Red Banner?' he said as I finished.

'No. He wouldn't have any interest in an organisation of maniacs past the fact that they were paying him to do a job.'

He stood up. 'Good. Then I think we see eye to eye?' He smiled across at Jazz. She was taller than he was, but the physical presence of the man was clearly coming over to her strongly. As they shook hands something was tickling at the back of my mind. The four-thousand-pound payment for the Red Banner list was a good deal more than the Soviet Embassy usually paid for information. Especially information which they then passed on to the West.

'Something is troubling you, Mr Hart?' Pushkin asked as he turned towards the door.

'Perhaps,' I said. 'To put it bluntly, I'm still not quite sure why your Foreign Ministry should want to be so helpful over Red Banner.'

He shrugged gently. 'Do you think we benefit from association with these killers? No, we too are part of the European establishment, Mr Hart. Their object is to destroy us all. But of course they will fail.'

'They've no trace of popular support in Western Europe,' I said. 'On the contrary – the hatred they arouse has coalesced into right-wing opposition groups like Action England, Aktion Deutschland and the rest.'

He smiled. 'That, I am sure, is precisely why our Foreign Ministry wishes to destroy these so-called social anarchist groups like Red Banner. We fear them less than we fear the possibility of a Rightist backlash in every country in Europe.'

'If you're worrying about a right-wing take-over by the Action groups your Foreign Ministry's wasting its time. I know the leader here in England. He's a General, all right, but he's not been bred in the army of a banana republic. His tradition is support for the Civil Power.'

'Let's hope you're right about Sir Richard Deedes and all the other Action leaders in Europe. Perhaps we are simply being alarmist. Time will tell.' He didn't seem too confident.

I headed Jazz's car north for Cricklewood and reached the Broadway in less than twenty minutes. I'm a Chelsea man by birth and inclination, and this part of London always strikes me as having all the frenetic gaiety of a big night out in Dnieperpetrovsk. Three mid-teenage youths moodily kicked at strewn newspapers outside the tube station. Two black girls dressed to the height of Cricklewood chic chatted with an elderly white who, as I got out of the car, half-turned to reveal a vicar's dog-collar. The girls giggled a lot and threaded arms and rocked on platformed heels but I was still prepared to believe he was recruiting for the local choir. They were not.

The phone book had listed an R. O. Sugden at 261A Cricklewood Broadway, and with the North Western polytechnic no great distance away I imagined I was probably on the right track.

I parked Jazz's Mini in a side-street and strolled past the two black girls who had now ditched the vicar in favour of two shambling Irish drunks whom they were good-naturedly insulting across a safe twenty-yard interval.

I followed the numbers around the Broadway and discovered that 261 was a Chicken and Fish and Chip shop, and clearly one of the centres of the district's social life. Groups of very young girls and long-haired teenage lads stood around outside delving into bags of chips, laughing and pushing each other or jigging happily to the music of the juke-box inside the shop. I moved through the group to the dusty green side-door which led to the flat above the shop. It was marked '261A' in very amateurish sign-writing.

I pressed the bell. There was no sign of a light in the window above. I pressed the bell again.

After a minute or two I decided to try the shop itself.

It was presided over by a young Cypriot/Italian/Maltese with a black hairy chest festooned with more gold chain than the Lord Mayor of London. I bought a couple of drumsticks of chicken and a Coke and tried not to remember my lunch at L'Ecu de France.

As the music from the juke-box died I waved my drumsticks at the man behind the counter.

'That flat upstairs still empty?' I asked him.

The Mediterranean scratched his hairy chest between his gold chains and showed me a mouthful of black teeth. 'You looking for a flat?' he grinned.

'I could be,' I told him. 'Who owns it?'

'My boss own it,' he said craftily. 'You want I have a special word with her for you? I got influence.' In a briefly obscene gesture he indicated how that influence had been obtained.

I shrugged. 'I haven't made up my mind yet. Sugden never liked it much.'

'You know Sugden?'

'I used to teach with him at the North Western poly. They tell me he's done all right for himself. Got a much better place.'

He looked at me thoughtfully. 'What's your real interested, Mister?' he said with a syntax that threw me for a moment.

Hairy-chested gigolo he might have been, but he wasn't a fool.

'I'm looking for Sugden,' I said shortly.

'What for?'

'Business.'

'Police business?'

'Business business. He owes me money.'

'He owes my boss money,' he said. 'If I catch him I teach him to run off without pay the rent.'

'That's what he did – a moonlight flit, uh?'

He laughed. 'Moonlight flipt? Yes, that's very good,' he complimented me on my command of the language. 'I tell my boss that one.'

'So you don't know where he's moved to?'

'No. They just up and go. My boss she phone his school. They say he moonlight flipt there too.' He nearly fell into the vat of frying chickens with laughter. I couldn't help liking him.

'You said *they* just upped and went. Did he have a girl?'

'She live with him. What for I never guess.' He broke into the jingle from a well-known television chocolate commercial. 'Very good-looking chick. You want know – I getting on very well until my boss nearly catch me one day.'

'Bad luck,' I commiserated. 'You don't know where this girl worked? Maybe she was a teacher too.'

'No,' he said. 'I told you. Very good-looking chick.' And again he broke into the chocolate commercial jingle.

'What's that mean?' I pressed him.

'She the girl on the Alpert's chocolate box,' he explained patiently.' "Give yourself a sweet goodnight . . ." ' he crooned, '". . . the Alpert chocolate way."' An accompanying gesture elucidated his preferred version of a sweet goodnight. For a moment we both were in danger of drowning in a vat of corn oil. I dropped my chicken and Coke into the waste bin and turned for the door. 'You want to know something?' I said. 'I think you're going to make one hell of a success of life in this country as soon as you've been here long enough to get an Equity card.'

'What you mean – been here long enough?' He gave me a black-toothed grin. 'I born here, Mister. My boss just buy me the papers to prove it.'

Chapter 17

I pulled the Mini into the kerb outside Jazz's flat and let my head drop back on the raised neck-rest. It had been a heavy 24 hours, and Deauville and Dyson already seemed long ago. I guessed Jazz would be in bed by now, so I lit a cigarette and tried a little emotion recollected in tranquillity. The result was far from poetic. As I closed my eyes I saw the shining, wet cobbles of Honfleur disappearing under my running feet. I felt the sodden weight of the rain in my jacket as I sat before Madame Morel's stove, and saw my steaming shoes with the ragged, white, salt-water tidemark appearing as the leather dried. I experienced again my exasperation at Jazz, disappointment with Stevens and fear of Pushkin and again and again over the 24 hours the relief I found in booze.

Worst of all, I could only dimly see where I was going. Mansfield, Pushkin, Red Banner, Action England, the General and Virginia all appeared and disappeared before my closed eyes like a procession of the ghosts of Christmas past. And on top of all this I knew that time was running out for me, that on any reckoning of the odds I had to be spotted by some alert, intelligent young bobby in a matter of hours, or days at most, if I continued to ignore the risks.

I stubbed out my cigarette and rubbed my eyes. To my astonishment I found my cheeks were wet. I had been sitting there, smoking in the darkness, watching the images of my dilemma float past – and silently crying.

I put it down to exhaustion, but it frightened me. I knew I couldn't go on pummelling myself like this. But then I could see no other resolution. I dragged myself from the car, climbed the steps to Jazz's flat and let myself in with the key she had given me. The hall light was out, but as I opened the sitting-room door I was already aware of voices.

Stevens was sitting in the armchair Pushkin had used. He held a glass in his hand and turned a grim face towards me in a form of greeting. Jazz, equally sombre, sat opposite him on the sofa.

I pushed the door closed behind me. I cast about for an appropriate line but nothing came.

'Come and sit down, Tom,' Jazz said in the sort of kindly voice that had to mean bad news.

'You mind if I pour myself a drink first?' I asked. She looked at Stevens briefly and shrugged. 'Of course.'

I dragged my feet across to the table and began to pour a gin and tonic. 'I agree all that "hallo, how're you feeling?" routine's a bit of a bore, so let's give it a miss this time, shall we?' I said over my shoulder to Stevens.

I felt him start behind me. 'I'm sorry, Thomas,' he apologised. 'I'm a bit preoccupied. I didn't mean to be unfriendly.'

'Of course not.' I turned and faced them. I took a big pull on the gin and tonic. Again the coursing relief of tension through my body. I walked between them across the room. 'All right. Let's have the good news.'

Jazz got up. 'I'll leave you two.'

'What for?' I looked down at her as she stood beside me.

'I think it's best that you talk alone.'

131

Stevens nodded. They'd already arranged it between them. I dispelled a great wave of weariness with another gulp from my glass. 'Okay,' I said. 'Okay, okay.'

She pursed her lips as if she weren't far from tears herself, and walked quickly into the bedroom.

Stevens got up and began to pour himself another drink.

'Look,' I said. 'I've slept about two hours since the day before yesterday. Can we get it over with before I burst into tears?'

'Sorry, Thomas,' he said quietly, dropping clinking ice-cubes into his drink. He faced me. 'I did what you asked. I telephoned Mansfield this morning. I told him you'd phoned me from France . . . that you'd seen Dyson and believed that he was responsible for the hi-jacking of the gelignite on behalf of Red Banner.'

'What did he say?' I asked cautiously.

'He told me to come over to Northumberland Avenue immediately.'

'And when you did?'

He sat down heavily in the armchair. 'When I got there, Thomas, I was ushered into his office. There was another man with him.' He stopped. Then swallowed hard.

'Who was it?'

'But for what you had told me, there was no way of knowing. His face was an unbelievable sight. Unbelievable.'

'Dyson!' For a moment or two I simply didn't believe him. 'What in the name of God was Dyson doing there?'

Stevens hunched his shoulders miserably and looked at me from under his heavy eyelids. 'Mansfield told me to sit down. He wanted me to listen to what Dyson had to say.'

I laughed with relief. 'His version of last night, I suppose?'

Stevens nodded. 'The same as yours, Tom. In every detail.'

'You mean Dyson just sat there and confessed to the hi-jack?'

'No. He said that he'd had some friends round from a neighbouring boat. They'd just left and he was alone with a couple of girls who were staying the night when you burst in. He said you took him completely by surprise . . .'

'There's no other way to take Dyson. He's a big, hard bastard. I'd almost as soon face Mansfield himself.'

Stevens nodded impatiently. 'All right, Tom, the details aren't in dispute. You took a blackjack to him.' A shiver passed through his overweight frame. 'It was vicious, Thomas . . . I saw his face. It was appallingly lacerated . . .'

'You won't get me to sympathise with Dyson,' I said. 'Think of the young kids at the Four Square Disco. Think of all the people that don't have a hand or a leg any more because Dyson sold two hundred tons of gelignite to Red Banner.'

'But did he, Thomas?'

'He admitted it.'

'For God's sake, Thomas – what else could he do? "Berserk" was the word he used. He said you went berserk.'

'Look, I cut him about a bit. He won't win any beauty contests for a month or two. But there's no permanent damage.'

'You couldn't guarantee that. You could have blinded him with one of those blows.' Stevens was angry.

'All right, I could have blinded him. But he would have deserved that, too.'

I suppose I'd gone too far. He sat staring at me with his knees pressed together, and his drink held in both hands. 'I don't think Dyson had anything to do with the hi-jacking,' he said at length.

'So why did he chase me over half of Normandy that night? Did he mention that?'

'Oh, yes. And the next morning. He said frankly that if he'd got hold of you he would have killed you. As it was, as soon as he realised you'd probably got out of Honfleur he went straight to the French police and lodged a complaint for assault.'

That set me back a little, I have to admit. It was a pretty calculated risk on Dyson's part. I said so.

'Only if you still think he had anything to do with the hi-jacking.'

I got myself another drink, but it didn't seem to be having the same effect as earlier. I knew I had to keep myself on a tight rein: I couldn't afford to lose Stevens as a friend. 'Let's leave the French police for a moment,' I said with effort. 'Let's talk about him coming here. Why did he come to Mansfield?'

'Because he thought you still worked for the Department, of course. He thought you were acting under Mansfield's orders. He took the first plane over here this morning to tell Mansfield that unless you were called off he'd blow the Department through the open courts and to hell with any future work that he might lose.'

'Did Mansfield believe him?'

'Oh, he believed him, Thomas. *I* believed him. His threat to Mansfield was "call off your mad dog, or you won't have a Secret Intelligence Service left".'

It came in upon me like an enveloping wet cloak just how deep was the trouble I was in. I sat down and stared silently at the carpet between my feet. He had said Red Banner had contacted him, I was sure of that. But then what Stevens said made sense too. He was fighting for time as I held the blackjack over him. So what did it prove in the end: that you can beat a man into saying anything. My confidence was slipping rapidly from me.

'You remember New York . . .' Stevens began slowly. I wanted to shout, to storm about the room and yell that that was the lowest, the dirtiest trick to play. Instead I looked at him, trying hard to control the working of my face. 'New York was different,' I said harshly.

'Are you sure, Thomas?' he said insistently.

'I'm bloody sure,' I yelled at him. The bedroom door jerked open, and Jazz stood there white-faced. She looked from me to Stevens, then slowly closed the door again.

'In New York, Thomas, it was the wrong man. You had no real evidence, just some paranoid inner certainty.'

'Paranoid.'

'I'm sorry Thomas, I didn't mean to say that. But you were on the edge, you know that yourself. You were pulled back and given sick leave, after all.'

'That was the cover story to placate the Americans. We all knew there was no truth in it.'

Stevens remained silent. It was a simple mistake, surely he could see that. I'd jumped the gun on a suspect and persuaded the CIA to arrest the wrong man. Everything fitted except the last notch. All right, people like Stevens who'd not spent more than two years in the field in his whole life maybe couldn't understand that that's the way we often worked. Apply the judge's rules of evidence and more often than not your man would be sunning himself outside his dacha on the Crimea before we were ready to pounce.

I tried to take it slowly: 'In nearly fifteen years out, I made one single mistake. A big one, certainly. He was an influential politician and I put the CIA on him. But in fifteen years I'm surely allowed one slip-up.'

'Thomas, you put the CIA on him. But when they got to his house, the report said, he was beaten half to death.'

'Nonsense. I worked on him, I admit. But I knew how far to take it.'

'You worked on him and he confessed. To everything you asked him for. Is that right?'

I felt sick. I couldn't bear the thought of another drink. And then almost immediately I wanted one more than anything I've ever wanted in my life. It was true, of course, I'd pushed that aside. He'd confessed the sackful. He was a fat, scared little man with what he must have thought was a maniac hanging over him with a lead-loaded leather strap. I couldn't bear the memory of his fear-torn face.

I stumbled up and filled my glass. Sometime later, maybe five or ten minutes, Jazz came in from the other room. She was carrying an obviously full suitcase. She put it down near the door and sat down. I was clearly meant to ask about it.

I found it hard to get the words past the lump in my throat. My eyes were misting as I nodded towards the suitcase. Stevens sat silently nursing his drink, staring ahead.

'I'm going away, Tom,' Jazz said from the sofa next to me.

I nodded and swallowed hard. I just couldn't bring myself to ask her where she was going.

'I'm leaving in the morning, Tom,' she said. 'One of my Japanese friends rang and asked me if I'd like to go with him to the Munich Trade Fair for a week or so.'

I nodded into my drink. For a while we all three sat silent. I struggled to bring myself under control. 'You've both made it pretty clear what you think,' I said. 'But it still leaves me with a murder charge hanging over my head. I don't hear any practical suggestions for getting rid of that. Or have you both decided I *did* kill Tchaikovsky, after all?'

'Don't be ridiculous, Tom,' Jazz said sharply. But I was looking at Stevens. He, frighteningly, had said nothing.

'Well,' I said mock-reasonably, 'mine's a great job for attracting psychotics, we all know that.'

Stevens shrugged impatiently into life. 'We tried to get you to go away before, Thomas. This time frankly I think you've got to. You've got the passport Jazz gave you, you can easily get abroad.'

'And then what, for God's sake?'

'Then wait it out. Now that Mansfield knows we've been in touch, I'm free to talk . . .'

'He'll cashier you,' I said. 'For helping me.'

'I don't intend to tell him I've known your movements all along. I simply mean I can put your point of view.'

'You mean you'll tell Mansfield I'm a paranoid has-been, that my past record deserves the Dyson incident to be overlooked and that I had nothing to do with Tchaikovsky's death?'

'Something along those lines, Thomas. It's your only way out.'

'Then forget it.'

'Very well.' With great deliberation he placed his empty glass on the coffee table in front of him and stood up. 'In his office today Mansfield made it very clear what would happen if I encouraged any further contact with you. To stay in the Department means a lot to me too, Thomas.' He paused. 'Even so, I'd willingly give you all the help I could if I were able to believe . . . that you were right about Dyson.'

I stood up. I felt I just didn't know myself. I reached out and gripped his forearm. He blushed with embarrassment.

'I understand,' I said. 'I won't call on you again.'

'But you're going ahead?'

'I've got to unravel this whole business – for my own sanity as much as anything else.'

He ambled slowly towards the door, then turned back to look down at Jazz. 'Do what you can to persuade him, Jazz,' he said. Then, looking quickly at me, he said: 'Goodbye, Thomas.' And walked quickly into the hall.

We listened to Stevens let himself out, then to his footsteps clipping rapidly in his neat, short, womanish stride down Lawrence Street towards his car. Of course he had taken the precaution of parking it far away. His footsteps faded slowly in the silent room as Jazz and I looked at each other.

'Do you think I'm crazy, Jazz?' I asked her.

'I think you've had a crazy life, Tom. I think it's pretty amazing the way you've retained what you have of your old self. I've never met Mansfield, but he sounds to me like a vampire, sucking all the decency and humanity out of the men who work for him – then throwing them aside. I think he didn't succeed with you.'

'You mean, I took leave of my senses instead?'

She shrugged and sat looking miserably at nothing at all. 'This Japanese, Tom,' she said at length. 'I could phone him first thing in the morning.'

'Why would you want to do that?'

'Because much as I like Munich, Florence is a prettier city by far.'

I stood in the middle of the room and shook my head slowly. 'No, Jazz. Sorry.'

She stood up and walked towards the door. 'You don't have to apologise to me, Tom,' she was saying as she passed through into the bedroom.

The door closed after her.

I picked up my cigarettes and lighter and shoved them into my pocket. I looked round the room and let my eyes rest on the packed suitcase standing next to the door. It was like some desolate symbol of a marriage breaking.

I went through to the hall and let myself out into Lawrence Street. From the river not 50 or 60 yards away ectoplasmic snatches of mist floated towards me. I walked slowly down towards the King's Head and Eight Bells, then across the gardens and the road beyond and reached the river.

Leaning on the wet stone embankment I looked across the shimmering black water to where the red neon company signs of the Battersea paper mills threw bloody shadows on the smooth, sloping mud. A single car crossed the Albert Bridge and turned towards me and the West End. I dropped my head in my hands and squeezed my temples until the blood-red neon misted my sight. A small, small part of me said I could have been wrong about Dyson too. Why had it never occurred to me that it was just like New York? And think about that afternoon you went to the Royal Hotel. The double whiskies in the Wellesley Arms, the pointless phone call to Mansfield . . . and how much can you remember about the walk across the park to Paddington?

'Are you feeling all right, sir?' The voice behind me was friendly and solicitous. I turned, one elbow still on the stone embankment, and found myself looking at chest height at the silver buttons of a police uniform. Behind him a patrol car was drawn up at the kerb, the lone car, I realised, that I had watched across the bridge.

'Yes, yes, I'm fine, thanks. Just getting a little fresh air before I turn in.'

The young policeman eyed the river. 'Why don't you let us give you a lift home, sir?' he said.

'No, I've had a few drinks. If I don't walk it off I'll suffer tomorrow morning.'

I could see his face changing. The smile faded and was replaced by a moment of indecision, then he turned and called towards the car. 'Over here, John.'

I was too feeble and battered to make a move. He reached out and gripped me hard above the elbow. 'I'm going to have to ask you to come along with me, sir,' he said, his voice firm but a certain tense excitement already on his face. I had met that alert, intelligent young bobby that I knew I would. But I'd met him when the will to resist had already been drained out of me. As I walked with him towards the car I suppose I only thought of sleeping.

Chapter 18

The police car took me first to Gerard Road police station where I was searched and left in a statement room for an hour with a cup of tea. I had long finished the tea and was slumped fast asleep across the table when I was awakened and without explanation taken out to another police car and driven through the night to Putney police station. There I was shown into a cell, offered a sandwich and a cup of tea from the canteen, and when I declined was left alone to sleep. The low bunk's hard, rubber-covered mattress and the single, rough blanket did nothing to prevent me sleeping. When I was awakened again at 7.30 I had at least got in about three hours.

Sometime later I was again bundled into a car by two plain-clothes men and driven along the Upper Richmond Road in the direction of Barnes. It was only when we turned south across Barnes Common at the Red Rover that I realised for the first time where I was being taken.

For as many years as I had been in the Department we had maintained the euphemistically-termed 'Reception Centre' in a group of isolated houses in the middle of Barnes Common. As a site for an interrogation centre it was near-perfect, close to the West End and the Northumberland Avenue headquarters and remotely positioned on that massive swathe of ancient common land that cuts through London south of the river and joins up in Surrey with the vast Royal Park at Richmond.

I'm not suggesting isolation was necessary to drown the shrieks of tortured men in the thick mist that frequently hangs across the heath. Most of the techniques of persuasion were far too sophisticated. Deprivation was the principal weapon: sensory or sleep deprivation. And, somewhat nastier, the exploitation of phobias.

We turned up Mill Road towards the charming clutch of houses sitting alone among the white, early-morning ground mist and bumped across the unmade-up road and into the forecourt of one of the biggest. I was helped out of the back of the car and was surprised even in my exhausted state to discover how weak my legs were. The two Special Branch men positioned themselves on either side of me each with an arm under mine and half-walked, half-carried me towards the familiar door.

Old Uncle Jim, the doorman, was pretty upset to see me, that wasn't difficult to see. He hurried forward telling the SB to watch what they were doing and promised me a pot of coffee as soon as I was settled in.

I was put in a pleasant white room with a hospital-type cot and a view out through the leaded windows across the Common. At least they seemed like leaded windows. I knew that the lead was flattened bars of steel, each one of which would take an hour with a hacksaw to get through.

I dropped on to the bed and tried to fight off sleep. I tried to think ahead to my interrogations and my first meeting with Mansfield. But however hard I tried my mind clawed its way back to thoughts of Stevens and Jazz.

They say I was two days like it, and I wouldn't have believed them if it weren't for Uncle Jim. But I seemed to see him through the swirling Common mists bringing pots of coffee and collecting it undrunk, mopping my face with something cold and soothing and lifting my head to force pills and powders into my mouth. Sometimes I saw Virginia dancing naked across the grass at King's, or Jazz below a mound of classical cherubs, all, on closer inspection, with slit, Oriental eyes. And sometimes Stevens joined the orgy as the strangest cherub of them all.

According to Dr Gregson, a period of intense delirium was not an unusual element in a breakdown. He could have been telling the truth, I suppose. But then again this was the first time in over six months that I had not drunk nearly a pint of alcohol a day. When I was somewhat recovered I suggested to the urbane doctor that withdrawal symptoms was also a possible explanation of my condition. He said no.

On the morning of the third day I awoke feeling incredibly enfeebled but at least recognisably myself. Uncle Jim came in with a pot of coffee, and stood over me anxiously while I drank two cups in a row.

'I don't mind saying that I don't believe for a moment you killed that Russian,' he said, and glancing over his shoulder to where we both knew the standard microphones were installed he added, 'and I don't care who knows it.'

I thanked him for that and the coffee, and he asked me if I felt up to having a shower while he changed the sheets. I pulled back the blankets and eased myself into a sitting position on the side of the bed. Uncle Jim had gone off to get me a change of pyjamas and a clean dressing gown and I was pleased he missed the sight of me rocking around the room, trying to find my feet like some hopeless drunk. But such minor triumphs as reaching the door, turning on the shower and drying and dressing myself in clean pyjamas afterwards could barely keep at bay the empty sense of loss I felt. Or perhaps it was a feeling of betrayal and desertion that swept over me like the pain of love whenever I thought of Stevens and Jazz.

I'm not sure but I think maybe I was crying again when Dr Gregson came in for his morning examination. He asked me how I felt as he took my pulse.

'Olympic fit,' I told him. 'And if you were a doctor worth his salt you'd have me discharged today.'

He had very little in the way of a sense of humour, and continued to look bleakly down his nose at me as he tested my blood pressure and dragged my eyelids about while he examined my pupils with a pencil torch.

'I'm going to pass you fit for questioning,' he said finally. 'Do you have any objection?'

I recognised the formal nature of the statement with a sinking feeling in the stomach. The serious business was about to begin. I shook my head in answer. I knew well from experience there was little else I could do.

He left me with a vitamin injection and some pills to take every four hours, and I lay on top of the bed waiting for the knock on the door. When it came it was Uncle Jim.

'They want to ask you some questions in Room B1,' he said. 'Why don't you tell 'em you don't feel up to it?'

I told him no, and struggling into my dressing gown I followed him down to B1 interrogation room. As we paused outside the door he slipped me some matches and a packet of French cigarettes.

'Good luck,' he whispered. 'Don't let 'em get you rattled. Take it very, very slowly.'

I suppose it was like a surgeon going into hospital for an operation. I knew all the moves. First, as I entered B1, which was a heavily sound-proofed room without any furniture whatever, I would be left for two to four hours. Experience had suggested that this was an essential part of any interrogation. And although the psychologists were never short of a theory for its effectiveness I personally felt it was simply that all creatures can be divided into two broad types – those who hunt alone and those who prefer to hunt in packs. Man is one of the latter, and loneliness strikes him sooner and deeper than, say, domestic cats. We pay people like the good Dr Gregson fifteen thousand a year to wrap it up in antiseptic language.

But if you know the purpose of the exercise and aren't worried by the sinister bareness of the room, or the one central light, or the spongy rubber floor, and above all if you have a packet of Gauloises you can slowly smoke through, it all has a very different effect. When the two young opening batsmen for Special Branch entered the smoke-filled room three hours later I was stretched out on the rubber floor fast asleep.

I awoke to hear them wondering to each other where I'd got the cigarettes from. They fell silent as I climbed blearily to my feet and leaned against the wall while they carried in a metal table and three chairs. Things weren't starting well for them as we all sat down to the first round of questions.

'When did you first become associated with Red Banner?'
'I have never become associated with Red Banner.'
'Who did you pass the leadership list to?'
'I never passed the list to anyone.'
'What was the name of your contact in the organisation?'
'I have no contact.'
'Who ordered you to kill the Russian Sergei Dolsyncheff?'
'No one.'
'Why did you kill him?'
'I didn't.'
'What are your political attitudes to Red Banner?'
'Contempt for their policies – disgust with their methods.'
'When did you first begin an association with Red Banner?'
'I didn't.'
'What method did you use to pass on the list?'
'No method.'

And so we continued for a fruitless hour and a half. First with one, then with the other. My replies got shorter and shorter and at one point I lit another Gauloise. The two young men looked at each other but decided to allow it, so that by the end of the session I was feeling bored but distinctly relaxed and unworried. I knew that at some point Mansfield would turn up to conduct the investigation, and I knew that things then might become very different. *He* didn't much believe in exploitation of insecurities, sensory deprivation and the like. His system was the quick, unexpected kick in the balls which suddenly shattered your belief you were dealing with a civilised man.

Uncle Jim bustled in minutes after I was returned to my room.

He brought coffee and a copy of that day's *Guardian*.

In deference to the microphone on the wall I mouthed my thanks for the newspaper and he winked and left me.

I was careful to avoid excessive rustling of the pages but in the next couple of hours I read the paper from cover to cover. Government security forces were still trying to trace the whereabouts of the 200 tons of gelignite and, despite confident claims, appeared to be getting nowhere. The fear was that Red Banner planned one massive blast in the middle of a city which would go up with the force of a small atomic explosion.

On an inside page there was yet another profile of Major-General Sir Richard Deedes and reports of a long troubled debate in the Commons on the Action England Alert.

I had refolded the newspaper and placed it under the mattress for Jim to collect later. There was a rattle of the key in the lock and the door opened.

Jim put his head round the door. He looked worried.

'Mr Mansfield's downstairs, Mr Hart. He wants to see you right away.'

'Which room?' I asked him.

'The office.'

I nodded my relief. The office was on the ground floor. There were secretaries down there. Mansfield clearly wasn't planning any rough stuff just yet.

'The cigarettes, Mr Hart . . .' Jim said apologetically.

'Of course, Jim.' I gave him back the remaining cigarettes and the box of matches. Even Jim was afraid of Mansfield.

It was still a little before lunch, and I felt weak and hungry as I followed Jim down the staircase. In the main hall we stopped, and under the eyes of the armed front-door guard Jim knocked at what had once been the drawing room of a spacious Victorian family house. I heard Mansfield's voice inside and Jim opened the door.

'Mr Hart, sir,' he announced like an old family retainer, then turned back to me and nodded. I shuffled forward in my bedroom slippers, hands deep in my dressing-gown pockets.

Mansfield sat behind the broad desk that occupied one end of the room. The long, steel-latticed windows lit him from behind, and the pale shafting sun placed a sparkling halo round his fairish hair.

Silently he indicated an armchair, then got up and poured me a large whisky and water. He brought it across to me, and stopped before my chair.

'I'm sorry things have turned out this way, Tom,' he said heavily.

He handed me the whisky. So for openers it was going to be the saddened, avuncular Mansfield. I didn't mind. I'd get a drink or two out of it at least.

He walked back and sat on the edge of the desk looking at me.

'You're looking bad, Tom.'

I felt the three days' growth on my chin, and thought he was probably right. But I was feeling better. And it was not just the whisky. It was seeing him again, watching the old, well-worn posturing that I knew so well. It was only now that I realised how much I had dreaded this first interview.

'How did it all happen, Tom?' He poured himself a whisky and settled behind the desk to listen.

I knew my answer to that solicitude would determine the course of the interview.

'From the beginning?' I said.

He nodded and finished his whisky in a gulp.

'When you kicked me out of the Department . . .' I began. But he shrugged quickly.

'You were sick, Tom. You had been ever since New York. I couldn't keep you on. Don't you see that now? It wouldn't have been fair to you. . .'

Rubbish.

'. . . but more than that – I just wasn't sure who else you might settle on, believe them responsible for some action – and then take steps yourself.'

'Wait a minute,' I said, 'are you telling me that you let me go because I had become too much of a risk?'

'That was the doctor's opinion. I must admit it reinforced my own.'

I was shaking.

'I don't believe you,' I said. He was saying what Stevens and Jazz had said. I tried to control the movement of my hand but the whisky was slopping back and forth in the glass. 'Look, I *know* why you fired me. Because it was the best way you had of showing the Director you'd cut free of your own past. You fired me as a demonstration that the old days were over.'

He sat silent for a moment as the sun passed behind a cloud, and the halo faded from around his head.

'I didn't need a demonstration, Tom,' he said. 'When I was offered the deputy directorship I was also told by the nominations board that I would get the top job the moment George

Clarke retired. That's to say, next year – if there's any job to have by next year.'

He got up and poured scotch for both of us.

'I took the precaution of bringing this along. I know you've never seen it.' He pushed a bound document across his desk. 'I want you to take it away and read it, Tom. Then tomorrow we'll have another talk.'

He stood up abruptly and pressed the bell on the desk. Old Jim opened the door immediately.

'Show Mr Hart back to his room, will you? And incidentally I've signed an order that he's to have anything he wants.'

I left clutching the bound document and shuffled up the stairs after Jim. It was of course my medical report: that much didn't surprise me. But as Mansfield had pushed it across to me I had seen the name of the doctor who had compiled it – an old Department regular named Charles Hopwood-Elwes. I had known him for years, and knew that he wouldn't have compiled a false document for Mansfield even if they'd paid him in sixteenth-century miniatures, of which he was an obsessive collector.

I walked into my room and Jim locked me in after promising to bring up lunch. I asked him to make it a bottle of whisky and some cigarettes instead.

I dropped the document on the bed and stared down at it. Had Jazz and Stevens and even Mansfield been right? Was I going to have to face the truth about myself at last?

I sat on the bed with the whisky and cigarettes Jim had brought in, and opened the first page of the report. It dated from shortly after my return from the United States and had been compiled by four doctors under the co-ordinating hand of Hopwood-Elwes. During the examination I had been under the impression that the sole purpose was to produce a convincing document to placate the Americans. I realised now that this had never been the intention.

The first six pages were taken up with a detailed statement of my physical condition. Most of the terms were incomprehensible and to me entirely neutral in their portent.

The second section went on to a cold description of my two principal vices – drink and sex.

I am still not quite sure where the information came from but, while concluding I was not yet 'seriously disabled' by my daily intake of alcohol, the report listed twelve, dated days' drinking in New York just before everything blew up in my face. The combined quantities were astonishing. Eight American-sized whiskies before lunch on 19 February. A bottle of wine at lunch. Four vodkas in somebody's office during the afternoon. The best part of a bottle of whisky during the late evening. Had I really drunk that much? And how had they got the information? I had had a young assistant named Cooper at that time, and I suppose most of it must have come from him. Or perhaps they'd had someone checking at my favourite bars? Since most of my drinks were chalked up for payment at the end of the week it would have been relatively easy to compile fairly accurate totals. My problem was to decide whether to accept the evidence. I decided, with an effort, to do so. I *was* obviously drinking far too much during that period. Was I disabled? Strangely enough the report didn't seem to think so. Or at least not *seriously* disabled in terms of rationality and response. I moved on to the next section.

Sex has always been my salve for disappointment, my restorative of self-esteem. If I lack objectivity about my drinking I am totally aware, I believe, of the mainsprings of my sexual drive. I had to admit the report was too.

Several instances were detailed. Especially the booze and sex rampage I went on the moment I realised I'd fingered the wrong man. I knew what I was doing. I'd called every girl in my black book and never spent an afternoon or evening or night out of bed for ten days. Young Cooper had been assigned to track me from one set of crumpled bedsheets to another in the apartments of bleary-eyed ladies all the way across New York. I had ended up at Kay Walenska's place at the top of the Stanford building on West 86th Street. There I had stayed for two days in a haze of whisky-drinking and love-making until I could do no more of either, and I lay on the bed listening to the whooping police sirens far below in the night streets of New York. There Cooper found me.

I took a very large drink and lit a cigarette before turning to the next section of the report. It began gently with a résumé of my family circumstances – father a serving naval officer, mother died of influenza in the bleak winter of 1947 when Hart was eight. No brothers or sisters. Had lived with an aunt in Devon until his father retired early from the Navy in 1949.

Then followed details of my career at public school, comments by staff and excerpts from reports. Seen *in toto* like this they made me out to be something of a loner.

The description of my father – 'Hart's primary relationship', the document called it – underlined the loneliness theme. My father was drawn as a reserved, unemotional man not given to the enthusiasms of fatherhood. A lover of music, that most private of all the arts. A chess player. A gardener. Had I told them all this?

For a description of my mother they had obviously drawn a blank – for the simple reason I could remember absolutely nothing about her at all. I remember now that they had grilled me heavily on this point, even jokingly intimating that no American psychiatrist was going to find it convincing unless I'd had something to say about my mother. But I'd held out, and they'd finally accepted it.

Now here was a curious thing. A long passage describing Bob Woodhouse, the manager at the block of flats where I had worked as stoker for a few weeks when I was sixteen. The whole story was there, down to the meeting with him with my father in the Chelsea Potter and that comment: 'I'll say this for him – the boy certainly knows how to work.' I suppose they'd got that in one of the hypnosis sessions I'd agreed to undergo.

I began to have a weird feeling of fingers clawing back into my life. And it was unsettling because, at least so far, the report was doing no more than set down the facts – and I had to recognise them as real facts. I *was* pretty much of a loner at school. I certainly *did* always hope for something more from my father, some word of praise or even rebuke to replace that gentle, remote smile.

The report now began to discuss my aspirations, and for the first time an element of comment and conclusion accompanied the statements of fact.

It was decided that my ambitions had for a long time, well into my '30s, in fact, been sublimated in the day-to-day demands of the work. This, the report said, was of a nature to preclude introspection and normally provided a form of specious glamour which seems to have appealed deeply to Hart. But much more important, the all-seeing doctors concluded, Hart's dependent relationship with George Mansfield had resulted in a voluntary subordination of his own individuality and ambition drives. This period, just before my posting to New York, was seen as the watershed in my emotional development.

I would like to have been able to send the report spinning across the room, or even to have tossed it aside contemptuously as the usual wordy claptrap with which psychiatrists disguise their own lack of understanding of the world. But simply and without jargon it was beginning to build up a picture of me that, at least, *I* understood. I read on.

146

Under hypnosis I must have talked my head off because this watershed section was concerned almost exclusively with Mansfield. There were long verbatim question-and-answer sessions:

Q: When did you first begin to question what you were doing?
A: I don't really know . . .
Q: Try and tell me.
A: It's difficult because the two things seemed to go hand in hand – my increasing dislike of Mansfield and my doubts about the way he was handling some – not all – operations.
Q: You thought you could do it better?
A: By the time of my posting to New York I was sure I could.

I'd said all that and more. The thought raced across my mind that that was why Mansfield had sacked me: because I was affronted. But I pulled the idea in again with difficulty. That was another of those easy ways out. Like the whole New York business, like Dyson . . .? I turned painfully back to the report.

My arrival in New York marked a period that the doctors termed the 'revelation'. As far as I could understand the terminology (it had now become very much more technical), it seemed my own confidence and aggression grew as I became progressively liberated from Mansfield's influence. I think maybe they just meant I was growing up. But the stresses of independence resulted (they claimed) in my heavy reliance at this period on drink and sex.

Were they right? My head was beginning to reel. I thought I drank and slept around in New York because the booze was plentiful and the girls were very willing. It seemed a much simpler explanation.

Crisis, it seemed, followed revelation. By the end of my New York stay I was desperate for a victory – because only a victory would justify my belief in a Tom Hart independent from Mansfield. The evidence for paranoia now piled house-high. My reports were analysed by Mansfield for the doctors and torn to pieces. Of course this was hindsight on his part. I'd already been proved wrong. But several of my reports were quoted in the doctors' document – and they were terrible. Shot-full of suppositions which were unsupported by the evidence – a mish-mash of hearsay and desperate guesswork. Yes, I needed that victory badly – badly enough to enter the apartment that night and stand a 55-year-old man against the wall and take my leather

147

strap to his ribs until he squealed for mercy and was ready to confess to anything. Except that he had nothing to confess. The report concluded baldly:

We recommend that Thomas Hart be relieved from all Secret Intelligence work forthwith. Although it is not within our province to say so, we jointly conclude that it is unlikely that circumstances will ever favour his reinstatement.

It was signed by all examining doctors and counter-signed by my old friend Hopwood-Elwes.

Not too many men ever get to see a documentary comment on their lives. It was like being dead and reading the obituary – it was all in there somewhere, the story of a wasted life. Except I wasn't dead. I was still enjoying the Gauloise, feeling the sharp burn of scotch straight from the bottle. I want to go to bed with Virginia Deedes, therefore I am.

Mansfield was ready to see me shortly after breakfast. I followed Jim down the stairs and waited while he knocked on the door. Like yesterday he announced me formally, and I shuffled past him into the room.

I didn't know how I felt. I accepted the report's conclusions in almost every detail. I knew, obviously, that Mansfield had read the document but somehow I didn't care. I was much more concerned about myself.

He poured me a whisky and sat back behind the desk. He didn't want to talk about the report, he said, except to put it behind us.

'I took the advice of the doctors, and Hopwood-Elwes in particular. His view was that there was only one way to tackle the problem – and that was for me personally to attract as much of your anger as possible. His view was that, if I was willing to become the focus for your resentments, the pain of dismissal – retirement, if you like – would be more bearable. I don't mind saying, Tom, that I didn't enjoy my new rôle. However much your attitudes to me have changed in the last year I've always felt a considerable liking for you. I behaved as I did when I dismissed you on the doctors' recommendations. Those miserable little courier jobs were also part of the policy, to humiliate you into a total break with the Department, to make you see you'd get nowhere with a bastard like me running the show.'

He stopped speaking, and a heavy silence fell in the room. Distantly I could hear the heavy traffic riding down Rocks Lane on its way across Hammersmith Bridge.

'Of course,' he broke the silence, 'I never imagined for a moment that you'd get mixed up with Red Banner.'

Anger cut through my apathy.

'Look, I may have been chasing a shadowy father-figure all my life, but what I did was because I believed in a liberal society. And I believed that society sometimes had to be defended by illiberal methods. I don't believe in government by the bomb. Red Banner sickens me.'

'You still claim you had nothing to do with Red Banner?'

'Nothing. At the Tower I was given a contact point at the Royal Hotel in Paddington . . .'

'Which you didn't, in fact, pass on to me.'

'No. I was hoping to make myself indispensable if you wanted to recontact the Russians.'

'So you tipped off the Red Banner list to make certain I *would* need the Russians again?'

'No. I was in France when that happened. I was doing a private investigation on the hi-jacked freighter for Major-General Sir Richard Deedes. That's how I got on to Dyson.'

He nodded.

'Stevens delivered your message. When I received it Dyson was sitting in my office. Naturally he believed you were still in the Department, acting under my orders. He was in a murderous frame of mind, I can tell you. He wanted to know what I was going to do about "muzzling" you. That was his term.'

Mansfield got up and walked towards the window. Yesterday's sun was nowhere to be seen behind the heavy, grey November cloud.

'I bought him off, Tom, by issuing your photograph to the police and linking you to the killing of the Russian in Paddington.'

'You mean you don't believe I killed Tchaikovsky?'

He looked blank for a moment.

'Tchaikovsky?'

'His code name. Pushkin and Tchaikovsky.'

He nodded.

'I don't know if you killed him. I don't know if you tipped Red Banner. I *do* know that you beat up Dyson and I had to do something about it. He threatened to sue the Department. From someone who has worked for us from time to time I think you can appreciate the problems that would have caused. He meant it, Tom.'

'What do you plan to do now?' I asked him.

He sat down in his chair. Suddenly I saw him as a man on the far boundary of middle age, oppressed by problems.

'I'm going to drop charges against you,' he said. 'But as a condition I'll need to know where you are. I'll need to know that you are not pursuing Dyson across to France. I'll need to know that you are no longer in contact with the Russian Embassy.'

I waited for him to go on.

'I'll lay it on the line, Tom. In a certain state of mind you are a menace. To me personally; to my chance of becoming Director; and to the existence in its present form of the whole Department. You know very well I dare not take you through the courts on the Red Banner issue, although I could probably get a special investigative detention order on you from the Home Secretary. That would give me twenty-eight days to find that gelignite and to retrace, perhaps with Russian help, the Red Banner leadership.'

'Is that what you intend to do then, a special order?'

He let the breath flow from his body.

'I don't have to tell you the problems. The Home Secretary would give me an order this afternoon. But nobody in government can trust anybody else these days. Secretaries rifle file cabinets for the press and Opposition. This is the age of the calculated leak. The Home Secretary'd have to know the whole thing wouldn't blow up in his face.'

'You mean you'd have to tell him the Russians gave you a list – and you allowed the Red Banner leadership to slip through your fingers.'

I don't think I'd ever spoken to him so directly before. But he didn't react. He just nodded.

'So what I plan to do, Tom, is this. If you're prepared to sign a voluntary twenty-eight-day commitment order on yourself I'll drop everything against you.'

I looked at him in amazement.

'You mean voluntary committal to a mental hospital?'

'For treatment, yes.'

The new desk-bound Mansfield wasn't any softer than the old Mansfield I had known on operations.

'It's the only way I can placate Dyson, Tom. Other than that it has to be the Home Secretary's order.'

We sat in silence listening to the buzz of traffic. I stood up and helped myself to a scotch and lifted an eyebrow towards Mansfield. He handed me his glass and I poured him a large one. I could feel my relationship with him changing with each gesture, each response.

I had no doubts about what he was demanding. Voluntary

commitment meant more than a long, soft, tranquillised trip to Christmas. It also meant abandoning any thought of ever getting back into the Department. But then with the doctors' report on file there was no chance of that anyway. And somehow now the idea didn't hurt so much. Now that my festering resentment of Mansfield had been lanced and I saw him as a man, no longer young, somehow I didn't need the Department so much.

'All right,' I said. 'twenty-eight days. I'll sign the treatment order.'

Chapter 19

There was about my flat a feeling that it had been violated by the tidiest of burglars. The Special Branch going-over had been thorough and considerate. Everything had been carefully replaced in drawers and cupboards and on shelves. But not always in the right drawer or cupboard, and not always in the right place on a shelf.

I sat my two Special Branch escorts down in the sitting room and made some coffee for all three of us. The television set had been reassembled and my escorts seemed happy enough to watch the afternoon racing from Newmarket while I changed and packed a bag and muttered under my breath against the barking of my Latvian neighbour's appalling dog.

It was still early. We had an appointment with a Dr Hell-bronner at the Royal Maudsley Hospital at 4.15. If you're going to commit yourself voluntarily you might as well do it at the top people's hospital.

I kicked the bedroom door closed on the tedious details of runners and riders for the next race. I'm not a racing man – personally I agree with the Duke of Edinburgh that it has never been a matter for either wonder or dispute that one horse can run faster than another.

I walked to the window and looked out across the jumble of Chelsea back-gardens and mews below me. An iron fire-escape led past my bedroom. Two enormous pigeons perched there taking in the Chelsea scene with me. I loved this borough, populated by the rich and successful of London, the eccentric and colourful. And populated by lots of more ordinary people too, who had survived the changes since the war and had seen their own houses rise 40 or 50 times in value and still decided to stay rather than sell.

I looked at my watch. It was nearly three o'clock. Time I had finished packing. A month in the Maudsley – and then what? Time to begin anew. Yes, I really felt quite good about that now. I could close the door on a whole section of my life quite happily. One thing perhaps grated very slightly, but I had fairly easily been able to dismiss it from my mind. I could without difficulty accept the events in New York – that catharsis was over. But I still wondered if Mansfield had been right about Dyson. And I worried a little about how long I would continue to wonder about Dyson. I had been so sure. But then I'd been so sure in New York.

I sat on the bed. If I *did* decide to pursue Dyson would it simply be yet another stage in my pursuit of Mansfield's esteem? For a few moments I thought about that. But no, I disliked Mansfield, but I no longer felt that corrosive bitterness. And certainly the last vestiges of my old admiration for the man were long gone.

No, if I decided against the Maudsley and in favour of picking up the one lead I had – Sugden, the North Western polytechnic teacher, the man who had supplied Tchaikovsky with the Red Banner list – then I would be doing it for myself. For my own peace of mind in the life I would be leading when this last chapter was closed on my past.

Yet still I found it difficult to decide. I walked through to the sitting room where the Special Branch men were watching television and asked them if they wanted more coffee. They checked their watches and said yes, if we had time. I assured them all was well as long as we didn't leave it much more than a quarter of an hour.

I poured three cups of coffee, placed one each on the low table in front of the SB men and carried my own coffee through to the bedroom. There I put down my cup on the bedside table, picked up my packed suitcase and stepped out of the already opened window on to the iron fire-escape outside.

The taxi dropped me off at the bottom of Oakley Street, and I walked quickly round to Jazz's flat in Lawrence Street. I rang first, but I didn't expect Jazz to be there, and after waiting a decent interval I let myself in with the key she had given me.

I dropped my case in the sitting room and wandered around the flat. The studio was desolate, with white coverings draped across easels. There were some canvases stacked against the walls which I leafed through. About technique I knew nothing but I recognised in the subject and treatment of Jazz's painting a quality that defied precise definition but lingered somewhere in the area of compassion – or humanity, maybe. It wasn't that every picture told a story, but every picture certainly communicated a feeling. A surprising number of them were half-finished portraits of me.

I left the studio and looked into Jazz's bedroom – I would have given a lot to have seen her there fast asleep.

I made myself some coffee and settled down with the phone. Two calls to film production companies specialising in commercials was all it took before someone could tell me who made the Alpert's chocolate advertisements. A third call to that company, Finborough Productions, gave me the name of the girl they used – Sue Broadley – and the number of her agent, Jeff Ransom.

The whole operation had taken less than half an hour. I took up the phone again and rang Jeff Ransom. Slight suspicion in his voice was dispelled when I told him I represented Sovexport Trading, the Russian Government company in charge of the new range of Soviet-manufactured watches we planned to launch on the Western European market. I explained my principals had seen Sue Broadley on the Alpert's commercial, and asked me to make some enquiries about availability. I played it slightly green and said of course we couldn't guarantee anything at the moment (which he knew well anyway) but we had in mind a series of commercials using Sue and a boy in sports situations, ski-ing, scuba diving, etc – all aimed at underlining the toughness and reliability of the watches. Did he get the point?

He got the point all right – that ski-ing and scuba diving meant extended location shooting at a good fee to the girl and fifteen per cent to himself. Yes, he said, he'd be at the office until 5.30, later if I was delayed for any reason. For no good reason I gave my name as Adam Kirkup.

I put down the receiver, finished my second cup of coffee and was about to leave for Jeff Ransom's office when I was stopped at the door by the ringing of the phone. I hesitated a moment, then walked down the hall into the sitting room and lifted the receiver.

'Mr Hart?' Pushkin's deep voice purred down the phone.

'You're in luck, I've only just got here.'

'The press said the police were able to eliminate you from their enquiries.'

'It's a quaint way of putting things. In my case not to be taken too seriously. That's why I'm here rather than at home. Can you get here this evening – about seven?'

'I shall be there, Mr Hart.'

He put down the telephone.

Jeff Ransom's offices were in that section of Soho south of Shaftesbury Avenue which has rapidly become London's new Chinatown. I turned down Macclesfield Street, past De Hem's and was immediately aware of Chinese lettering on restaurants, strip-joints and abandoned cardboard boxes in the gutter. Every inch of this tattered section of the city spoke Chinese.

The inhabitants themselves, mostly from Hong Kong, stood on street corners and watched me without curiosity. But if they turned to speak together the dreamlike apathy of their manner would immediately dissolve to be replaced by a Latin vivacity of expression.

I turned past a chattering group of young Chinese boys and girls into Dancey Court, a cobbled relic of Jack the Ripper's London. Jeff Ransom shared an office with a company called Startime Enterprises.

I pushed open the door as far as it would go and squeezed my way into the minute reception hall. There was no one about so I thumped the brass bell and heard a chair scrape above and footsteps cross a linoleum floor.

Jeff Ransom introduced himself from half-way down the stairs and invited me up. He was a tall, pleasant-looking man who fitted none of my ideas of a theatrical agent. I didn't really feel that good about getting him excited about a project that would never come off.

Sitting in his bare office I began to explain that dealing with Sovexport was not quite like dealing with other companies.

'Red tape,' he nodded and I was fleetingly reminded of Swiss exercises going like clockwork. But he didn't smile so I pressed on.

'I've got two people from Sovexport over at the Embassy now. If we could get this girl across to see them before they leave for Moscow tonight we could save ourselves several weeks. And her chances of getting the job would improve if they saw her in person, I'd guess.'

'Oh yes, she photographs well but she's got it all there to photograph.'

'How far away does she live?'

He looked up his card index.

'She used to live in Cricklewood, but she's just moved. Yes, here it is. Parsons Green. Near Fulham Broadway. You know it?'

'Is she at home now?'

'Yes, I took the liberty of giving her a call. Said someone was asking for her – just to check availability. I'm not her sole agent, you see. More's the pity.'

'Could she be ready for me to take her along to the Embassy at about seven-thirty tonight?'

'I'm sure she could. Would you like me to ring her and see?'

I said I would. And he went back to the card index for the number.

'You might like to look through that top file,' he said. 'You may find someone suitable for the boy as well.'

I got up and pulled out the drawer of the filing cabinet while he dialled. Flicking through the composites I was surprised at the variety of his models. Somehow I imagined they would be all young and lissom. Not at all. There were ancient colonel-like gentlemen and maiden aunts, schoolboys and pretty little six-year-old girls. Sue Broadley's composite showed a sophisticated, attractive face in a yachting cap, smoking a long, thin cigar as she leaned out of a Mercedes SL. A second picture showed her emerging from the water on some Bermudan beach, a diaphanous dress clinging around the breasts and thighs. Behind me the phone call seemed to be going well. I shot the steel drawer closed.

'Nothing there?' he asked anxiously.

'I'll drop in tomorrow when I've more time,' I said. 'What did Miss Broadley say?'

'She'd be pleased to do it. She'll be ready any time from about seven onwards. Thirty-one A Chipstead Road. Will you be able to find it?' He was so anxious that nothing would go wrong.

I thanked him and he escorted me downstairs. Cramped in the small entrance hall, we shook hands.

'I do hope it works out,' he said again.

I said I hoped so too.

Pushkin arrived at Jazz's flat just after seven o'clock. We drank black coffee while I told him about Sugden's girl-friend.

I was unwilling to go into too much detail about my new access of self-awareness, but I felt I had to tell him something about Mansfield's ultimatum. I explained the 28-day voluntary commitment proposal and he nodded without asking further questions. At just before seven-thirty we set off in a taxi for Parsons Green.

Leaning back in the black leather seat Pushkin watched the King's Road slide past the window. Outside the Six Bells a group of youngsters milled around waiting for the disco to begin. At Beaufort Street half a dozen imitation Bhuddist monks with shaven pates and flowing robes imperiously stopped the traffic as they filed across the road. At the bend small knots of men and girls were entering the Water Rat for their nightly game of backgammon. By the time we reached the World's End it was an assemblage of black leather working boys from the massive council flats, gathered around a new motorbike with all the enthusiasm of a gang-bang.

I wondered what he made of it all. His thoughts were clearly travelling in the same direction. He turned to me and smiled.

'I shall miss being in London, Mr Hart,' he said.

'Where will you be this time next year?' I asked him.

'Who knows, Mr Hart? Who knows? And you?'

I shrugged.

Chapter 20

I paid off the taxi in Chipstead Road and we walked along checking the numbers until we reached the one we were looking for. There were three flats in the house with separate bells. I pressed the one marked '31A'. The click of her heels on the tiled hallway and the shape of her figure distorted by the glass panels preceded her to the front door. She opened it, smiling. She was made up with touching and meticulous care, but she wasn't really the girl of the photographs. The late-twenties sophisticate with the long thin cigar and the yachting cap was replaced in the girl before me – a pretty, pert-faced teenager, not more than a couple of years out of school. And what had happened to that goddess rising from the waves?

I introduced myself as Adam Kirkup, and after a momentary

hesitation I turned to Pushkin and introduced him as a trade counsellor at the Embassy.

'Do you want to leave straight away or do you have time for a drink first?' she asked.

I went through a watch-checking charade and concluded that we did indeed have time for a quick one. She led the way into the hall then through to the ground-floor flat.

It was a trendily decorated double room with probably a bedroom and kitchen and bathroom leading off it. Five or six new Spanish wickerwork chairs surrounded a circular, slate coffee table. Lights with red and blue and lime-green acrylic shades dangled from the ceiling to about two feet above the table, and Anatolian peasant weaves hung from the walls. Items of bric à brac from the last century supported the principal furniture: a polished, black-leather travelling trunk which served as a side-table; an old eel-and-pie shop menu board for the drinks tray; and a blue police station lamp, which sprouted plastic flowers. Most importantly there was no sign of Sugden.

She poured us whisky and herself a gin and tonic, and sat down opposite us. She was obviously a little ill at ease but Pushkin took over the conversation with a rambling and compli-mentary comment on her flat, on the housing situation in Mos-cow and accommodation rationing systems that had been ins-tituted to solve the problem.

'For instance,' he said, 'a young lady like yourself working, let's say, as a doctor or engineer, would not be occupying alone an apartment so spacious.'

She smiled hesitantly. 'As a matter of fact I share the flat.' She wasn't sure whether it was the right thing to say.

'With another model?' I asked.

'No.' She hesitated and looked at Pushkin. 'With my boy-friend, actually.'

'I see.' Pushkin put her at her ease, lifting his hands and gesturing enquiringly around the flat as if she were keeping him locked in a cupboard.

She laughed: 'Oh, he's just slipped out for a moment to get some wine.' She looked at an old railway clock hanging at hip-height beside the fireplace. 'Should we be off?'

'No, no hurry, Miss Broadley,' Pushkin reassured her. 'We mustn't arrive while my colleagues are at dinner.'

'Then another drink?' she suggested.

We both accepted and she jumped up, glad to be moving about again. For the second time today I felt bad about my cover story. She seemed a pleasant, ordinary girl blessed with a somewhat unusual prettiness. She didn't deserve what was going to happen next.

She had topped up our drinks and was just adding ice and fresh tonic to her own when I heard the outer door open. A man, whistling no particular tune, approached the flat door. It opened and a man of about 32, with sandy hair and a long, thin face stopped in the doorway. He was carrying a brown paper bag, from which the red foil tops of two or three wine bottles protruded.

'Still here?' he said to the girl. She jumped up again. 'Darling, this is Mr Kirkup and Mr Pushkin.'

He smiled at me and turned towards Pushkin for the first time. He recognised him immediately. His jaw snapped open, his pale green eyes fixed on Pushkin's face. I don't really blame him for being scared. Some curtain had fallen across the affability. Still holding the bag of wine bottles, Sugden trembled.

The girl moved next to him. 'What is it, darling?' she said anxiously. 'Do you know each other?'

Pushkin moved across to the door and closed it. Watched by Sugden and the girl he came back and slowly eased the bag from Sugden's arms and pointed to a chair.

If his aim was menace Hitchcock could not have directed him better. The girl was too frightened to talk. From time to time she shot appealing glances at me. Sugden dropped back into the chair Pushkin had indicated, while I stepped across and took the girl's hand. 'Just sit over here,' I said, leading her to the far corner of the room. She opened her mouth to ask a question but I shook my head. She looked once quickly towards Sugden but he was watching Pushkin like a paralysed rabbit. Her lips began to tremble but she clamped her hand hard over her mouth and sat down.

Pushkin lifted his chair to position it between Sugden and the door and looked at me. I moved across to stand over Sugden. His eyes left Pushkin and turned to look up at me.

'You will know my friend,' I began slowly. 'He stood in a couple of times for a colleague of his you used to meet regularly to sell reports on your students to.'

Sugden's mouth hardly moved. But a faint whispered 'Yes' was emitted. I have seldom seen a man more terrified.

'That colleague you used to meet is now dead. Did you know that?'

His head moved a half millimetre in the direction of a nod.

'On your last regular meeting with my friend's colleague you sold him a list of the Red Banner leadership for four thousand pounds.'

'Robin! . .' the girl exploded in a dismayed sob from the far corner of the room. I glanced across, but could not make out her face in the shadows. Only her shimmering legs protruded from the darkness.

'I'm going to ask you some questions about that list,' I resumed very slowly. 'I doubt if it's necessary to threaten you . . .'

He looked across at Pushkin and shook his head.

'Where did the list come from, Sugden?'

He fumbled in his pocket. 'Can I smoke?'

'Just tell us where the list came from.'

He dragged out his cigarettes and tremblingly pulled one out of the packet.

'I was in a student meeting one night. I . . . I can't remember what it was about. Yes, I know – it was a talk-in on Vietnam from the fall of Saigon to the present. The speaker was Vietnamese – a member of the old South Vietnamese Peoples Liberation Movement. He had operated from Saigon even under President Thieu. Guerilla warfare in the last month. Afterwards we had questions. I asked quite a lot myself –' he bared his teeth as he sucked in smoke from his cigarette and glanced over towards the girl – 'I always asked a lot of questions because it established my views with the students.'

'You mean they talked more freely to you afterwards because they knew your views were on the same lines as their own?'

'Yes.'

There was a rustle from the girl's dress in the corner of the room and she stepped forward with her glass. Ignoring us, she dropped on her knees before the leather trunk and began pouring herself a drink. She was sniffling miserably.

Sugden half-swivelled in his seat towards her. Pushkin's voice hissed out telling him to continue.

'There were a lot of people at the meeting. Not just students and . . . it was a hall with a licensed beer bar . . . and afterwards we all had a drink. At some point, I can't quite remember now how it happened, but I started talking to someone. I remember I was very careful because he didn't particularly look like a student. I mean he was older, for one thing. About my age. And I thought he might have been police. You know, Special Branch. Well, after a drink or two he suggested we went across the road where they sold something more than beer and I said okay.'

'You went across to a pub?'

'Yes. The Bird in Hand. It's just next to the North Western.'

'Go on.'

'Well, we had quite a lot there, I suppose. I know we talked a long time –'

'What about?'

'Mostly the Vietnamese lecture at first. But after a while we started talking about the situation here at home. He asked me my views about it –'

'And what were they?' the girl shrieked suddenly. 'What were you willing to tell a complete stranger that you'd never told me? That you were selling information to the Russians?'

I stepped across and took her by the shoulders. 'You're going to have to keep out of this,' I said as gently as possible. 'Your turn comes later. For the moment sit down and be quiet.'

She sat back in the shadows again, her drink in her hand.

'All right, Sugden. He asked you what you thought of the situation here at home. What did you tell him?'

'I told him I believed in Socialism as the only way out of the mess we're in.'

'And . . .?'

'He agreed. He asked me what I thought of the social anarchy groups like Red Banner. And I told him I thought what they were doing could put the real revolution back twenty years.'

'What did he say to that?'

'He really agreed with that. He said that unless they were stopped the whole of Europe would go Fascist – that the Action committees would take over. Then he said that he knew something about the social anarchists. He became sort of very confidential and started saying he knew quite a bit about them, as a matter of fact. Especially Red Banner.'

'How did you react to that?'

'I was a bit scared, to tell you the truth. I still didn't know for certain who he was. And he was such a strange guy . . .'

'We'll come to that in a minute. So he said he knew something about Red Banner?'

'Yes. Then he asked me if I had information would I know what to do with it. Who to give it to.' He lit another cigarette from the first one and stubbed out the butt. 'By this time I was really scared. That question – did I know who to give information to – you know it seemed as if he knew about my meetings with the Soviet Embassy. So I was really wary of him. Then suddenly he produced this list. "I've a dozen names here," he said. "All top

Red Banner men. In the right quarters it could be worth a bit." '

'Did he suggest how much?'

'No. He didn't dwell on it. Really just planted the idea, I suppose. Then he shoved the list into my top pocket and finished his drink and left.'

'Have you seen him since?'

'No; I asked around among the students but nobody seemed to know him.'

'So what did you do next?'

He hunched his shoulders and stared at the floor. 'I didn't know what to do. I thought it may have been a put-up job. You know, by Special Branch. So for a few days I didn't do anything.'

'But all that time the list was burning a hole in your pocket. Because your friend had planted the idea that it was worth something.'

'I was short of money. Lately, you know, I don't earn as much as Sue. I thought if I didn't get hold of some money . . .'

'Don't you dare blame your dirty work on me,' she said from the shadows.

'I'm sorry, darling . . .' he turned again towards her.

Pushkin leaned forward. 'Mr Sugden . . .'

Sugden's head jerked round.

'Mr Sugden, why do you think we are here tonight?'

I didn't really understand at first why Pushkin was asking the question. Then it occurred to me he was right. Sugden's whole fearful attitude was based on something more concrete than Pushkin's power of menace. I had assumed it was related to the fact that Tchaikovsky was dead. Or that Sugden had used the money to change flats and get out from under the Russians.

'Well, Mr Sugden?' Pushkin persisted.

Sugden gave him his trapped rabbit look. 'For the money,' he whispered.

'And why should we expect to recover the money? We know how a good capitalist should behave. A word of honour. A fair deal. Well . . .?'

'I didn't know there was anything wrong with the list at first. That's the truth.'

'What was wrong with the list, Sugden?' He swivelled his head towards me. As long as he was convinced Pushkin knew, he had no choice but to explain to me.

'It was . . . phoney. The names on that list were just ordinary left-wingers. They had nothing to do with Red Banner.'

I looked at Pushkin. His mouth turned down with grim satisfaction.

'And how did you discover this?' I asked Sugden.

He looked for a moment as if he were going to be sick. He
was torn between fear of Pushkin and shame at the revelations to
the girl. Fear of Pushkin proved stronger.

'I knew some of the names on the list,' he said at length. 'One
of them in particular.'

'So you sold the list – then tipped them all off!'

He nearly fell out of his chair with shock and fright. 'God, no,'
he spluttered, and dropped his third cigarette. 'Oh God, no, I
didn't do that, I promise.' He looked imploringly to Pushkin. 'I
didn't tell a soul about the list.'

Pushkin walked over and poured a scotch for himself and one
for me. 'Do you believe him?' he asked, handing me the drink.

I let Sugden wait for my answer. He had craned his neck round
and was looking from Pushkin to me.

'Does it matter whether you believe the little rat?' the girl said
suddenly. 'The boy he was talking about, the one he knew *in
particular* was one of his students. That's why John Pepper was
phoning you in such a state, wasn't it? Nothing to do with work?'

Sugden closed his eyes, refusing to look at her. She looked down
at him with loathing then turned back to us. 'I thought his aunt
had given him some money to avoid death duties. I didn't
realise he was selling his friends to people like you.'

I had to admit the girl had spirit. She began to pour herself
another drink. 'Do you mind?' she said heavily to Pushkin. 'After
all you do seem to have paid for it.'

'Be a guest of the Soviet Embassy,' he said. I could see from
his change of manner that he liked her too.

'Well, Mr Hart, what do you think of this *stilyagi*, this scum?
Is he telling us the truth?'

'I promise you . . .' Sugden began again, but Pushkin silenced
him with a gesture of his hand. I turned on him. 'All right,
Sugden, you had a friend, a student who was on the list, and you
were pretty certain that he at least wasn't connected with Red
Banner. But what made you so sure the others weren't either?
You couldn't have known all the names in Amsterdam or Paris
or Milan.'

For a man who'd not had a finger laid on him he looked
utterly whipped. He cringed. 'I knew all the names from the
first moment I looked at the list.' Saliva bubbled uncontrolled
over his lower lip. 'For my reports each month I had to keep up

with everything on the left-wing student scene. The names on the list I recognised as delegates to an extra-parliamentary action conference in Leipzig last summer. I'd taken a note of them myself at the time. When John Pepper came back he'd told me how they were all scared that the social anarchists would ruin the chances for the militant Left – you know, create a back-lash.'

I sat back heavily in one of the wickerwork chairs. In some crucial area Sugden wasn't telling the whole story. As he would have us believe it he had been picked out of a meeting almost at random and handed a list. But that made no sense at all unless the man in the pub had *known* Sugden was in contact with the Soviet Embassy, which is where he obviously intended the list to go. Otherwise he would have chosen a meeting of the Young Conservatives to hand it over. But who knew Sugden was in touch with the Russians? Tchaikovsky himself – and Pushkin of course. No one else. Unless . . .

I jumped to my feet. 'You lying little bastard,' I said. 'You'd met the man who gave you the list before, hadn't you?' I stabbed a finger at him. 'You'd been blown, by Special Branch, hadn't you, Sugden?'

Like the features of a melting wax dummy his face began to collapse.

'There was nothing I could do.' he wailed into his hands.

Pushkin ambled forward. He took a handful of Sugden's jacket and jerked him into an upright sitting position. Again I was astonished at the menace implicit in Pushkin's movements. 'How long ago, Mr Sugden. When?'

Fear controlled Sugden's face. 'About four months ago,' he said. 'They'd been following me to my meetings with the Embassy. After that they told me what to write in my reports.' Self-pity overwhelmed him. 'Don't you see? I was trapped . . .'

Pushkin saw and didn't care.

'The man who gave you the list – was he your regular contact with Special Branch?'

Sugden nodded. 'I met him every month just before my . . . my other meetings.'

'And he threatened you'd be arrested if you didn't co-operate?'

He shook his head vigorously. 'No, by that time I think I'd have welcomed it. No, he made it very clear what would happen. He said if I . . . if I told anybody he'd personally take pleasure in crippling me for life. And he would have done it too.' He looked appealingly at Pushkin. 'He was a great big blond guy.

Scarred. South African . . .'

Dyson.

We left the flat at Parsons Green with a bagful of treasury notes – £2500, which was all that was left of Sugden's blood-money. Sugden himself, drained white by his interview with us, now had to face the girl. As we closed the door behind us we heard the crash of shattering glass as she began.

In the taxi neither of us talked very much. I suppose we were both engrossed in the effort to absorb what we had learned. And perhaps there was, too, the thought on both sides that our paths could not run in parallel for ever.

At Lawrence Street we parted with a handshake, and Pushkin took the taxi on to wrestle with his loyalties in the gloomy rooms of Kensington Palace Gardens.

Chapter 21

I rapped at the Judas window of the Gay Night Owl and it flew aside as if on a spring. 'Yes, love?' The doorman didn't recognise me from my last visit.

'Guest of Mr Stevens,' I said.

The languid polo-necked doorman opened the door. He frowned. 'Mr Stevens is with a friend. I hope he'll be pleased to see another one.'

I walked through the first room with the long bar into the restaurant beyond. Stevens was sitting at his corner table. His friend was Andrew, the Scottish guitarist. They both looked up as my shadow fell across the table.

Stevens gestured to a seat: 'Thomas, how good to see you. You know Andrew?'

I nodded to Andrew, who looked at me with pursed lips and half-closed eyes.

'Andrew's frightfully talented with the guitar. Aren't you, Andrew?'

The boy's wide rubber mouth operated a turn-on, turn-off smile.

'Are we going to get a chance to hear Andrew play?' I asked

Stevens as if we were humouring a three-year-old.

'There, Andrew,' Stevens withdrew his chubby hand from its position high on the boy's thigh, 'a request.'

The boy pushed his head forward to within inches of Stevens and again produced the smile, rapid as a camera shutter.

'Doesn't he like playing?' I asked Stevens.

'It's his life, Thomas.' His tone rebuked me.

'Now run along and play for us, Andrew, and don't be tetchy.'

The boy dragged himself up, heavy-limbed and sullen-faced, refusing to look at Stevens who patted his tight jeans as he bent to pick up his guitar. To me he directed a toss of the head, redolent of Glaswegian Spanish pride, and hurled himself into a furious flamenco on the apron stage.

I looked across at Stevens. He smiled. 'Of course he's a dreadful little tart really. But don't be too superior, Thomas – I've seen you dance attendance on the most mindless doxies just for the enormity of their mammaries.' He took his eyes off the boy and poured me a glass of wine. 'When I saw Mansfield, this morning,' he said slowly, 'he was congratulating himself on having got you into hospital.'

'On a voluntary commitment signature,' I nodded.

'But you decided not to go through with it?'

'I decided to delay my arrival for a few hours. There was something I had to follow up first.'

He made a small distressed, impatient gesture. 'Please, Thomas . . .'

'You don't want to hear about it?'

'No. I want you to collect your bag and deliver yourself at the hospital gates. I'll even forgo a night of bliss in the arms of fair Caledonia to drive you there, but I will *not* continue to discuss the matter, Thomas.'

'It was Dyson who had the list delivered to the Russians. I found that out tonight.'

'Another confession, Thomas? Look, since I last saw you Mansfield gave me your report to read. I don't want to hurt you, Thomas – but I'm bound to agree with almost everything in it. Just at the moment you're a danger to others – and at least equally to yourself.'

'That's behind me now. I've accepted the report. I know what happened in New York. *And* why. What I'm asking you to do is to help me go over the facts. Precisely because I see the possibility of error – not as a paranoid now but as a normal man. It's in the nature of this lousy job – even when you are completely sane and sober.'

' "This lousy job" is the one you've spent six months trying to get back.'

'No longer. Once this whole business is over I wouldn't come back in if they offered me the job of Director.'

He lifted his eyebrows.

'It's true,' I said. 'Not sour grapes. I know someone has to do the job, but I've done it for long enough. Far too long in fact, because it's crippled me. If I take it easy in the next year or two I may even have a chance of recovery.'

He swirled the wine in his glass.

'You see, I've realised that I don't have the mettle for the job. For a dozen years the Department tried to bend me into shape. In the event they bent so hard I snapped. What I'm doing now is putting the pieces together. Then I leave this life for good.'

He shook his head slowly. 'You think you're cured? You'll only be cured when you're able to give up trying. Now don't think me hard, will you, but my plan from now is to spend the rest of the evening and as much of the night as possible thinking about that boy's truly remarkable endowments. In the game of life, Thomas, Andrew was generously equipped to bat.'

I stood up and threaded my way through the red-clothed tables towards the door, pursued by twanging discordancies as the boy triumphantly flung his knuckles at the guitar strings.

The *Daily Telegraph* keeps one of the best newspaper libraries in the world. And in Roger Slade, head of the night staff, undoubtedly one of the most knowledgeable newspaper librarians who ever lived. Twenty years marking and cutting each day's papers, sorting and filing the cuttings, allied to a superb memory, make him unique in Fleet Street. Senator Jackson? If he can't immediately tell you how he voted on the Grand Canyon (Pollution) Bill he can certainly tell you how to find out inside five minutes. The proportion of votes for Lecanuet in that first French Presidential against De Gaulle? Look under France, Election, Presidential, or Lecanuet, Personal for September 1968. Red Banner? . . . it was well past one o'clock and we were standing between the ranks of green filing cabinets on the first floor of the *Telegraph* building . . . Red Banner? Yes, a big new section for that – under Accidents, Bombings, Red Banner. He flicked through the files and withdrew three or four thick paper envelopes.

I took the envelopes, each one stuffed with cuttings, and carried them across to a table in the far corner of the room as Roger left on the trail of yet more information for one of his night sub-editors.

I took the neatly packed wads of cuttings, each secured by an elastic band, from the first folder. The date stamp on the earliest cutting was just over a year old, and under a typical *Telegraph* headline gave an account of a bomb incident in Clapham. What was described by the police as a 'bomb factory' had exploded in a basement of a house killing a man and girl. Neither had been identified at the time of writing. But a black-bordered card had been received the next morning – I was on to the second cutting now – inviting reporters of the national newspapers to the funeral. It was signed 'Red Banner'.

I turned over the next cutting dated a couple of weeks later. It was a London *Times* report of a letter it had received setting out the aims of the Red Banner organisation. The precise objectives of the group didn't seem worthy of too much examination – they were mostly familiar social anarchist claims for the de-industrialisation of society and the re-organisation of the State as interdependent communities – a convincing basis, I thought, for a return to tribal warfare. But the *Times* report did carry the first indication that Red Banner was more than an English phenomenon. Apparently *Le Monde*, *Die Welt* and the *Corriere della Sera* had all received similar statements the day before, posted in France, Germany and Italy respectively.

The next series of cuttings all covered one single bombing incident. A tube train between Lancaster Gate and Marble Arch had exploded, killing fourteen people. In some ways even more macabre were the descriptions of panic-stricken survivors struggling in the dark. From the number of clippings devoted to the bombing and the size of the headlines the incident had obviously made a tremendous impact on the imagination of readers. I had been in New York at the time, but I could recall the coverage American papers had accorded the outrage. After two days of silence a man had phoned Associated Press and, claiming to speak on behalf of Red Banner, had described the Lancaster Gate tragedy as only the first step in a massive extension of the war against capitalism.

Red Banner was now very definitely on the map, although there were plenty of signs that splinter groups and other social anarchist organisations resented its rapidly increasing claims to 'credit'.

The number of hooded and anonymous young men found dead on strips of wasteland throughout the country seemed to rise dramatically. Claims and counter-claims for responsibility surrounded every murder. All that could be said with any certainty was that Red Banner (many of the young dead were claimed to be members) had rapidly become the object of the bitter envy and hatred of its fellow terrorist groups.

From the cuttings now the precise development of Red Banner activities became very difficult to trace. So many calls threatening bombs and claiming Red Banner responsibility were put through to the Press Association that it was impossible to relate them to specific incidents, or indeed distinguish between their claims and those of the seven or eight other groups operating in England.

By the time I returned from New York Red Banner had, nevertheless, firmly established its presence and stature in both English and European terrorism.

From this point on I was able to move through the wads of cuttings more rapidly, and the pattern that emerged was the same throughout. The violent hostility of the other groups to Red Banner clearly derived from its habit of claiming other groups' atrocities for its own in what appeared to be an attempt to establish some sort of hegemony and leadership over them.

As I read the cuttings it began to seem to me that only the freighter hi-jack and the slaughter at the Four Square Disco in Leicester Square could, beyond all shadow of doubt, be established as the responsibility of Red Banner alone.

I packed the wads of cuttings back in their envelopes and took them over to Roger.

'Any luck?' he asked, chewing on his supper – a vast beef sandwich from the canteen upstairs.

'I'm not entirely sure. I find the whole Red Banner set-up confusing. I only now realise how unlike their rivals they are.'

'Same methods,' he said, finishing the middle of the sandwich with one final bite and tossing the crusts down on the grease-proof paper it had been wrapped in.

'But they're pushing for the headlines all the time,' I said, borrowing a sip of his coffee.

'Aren't the others?'

'Yes, the others too. But my impression is they cultivate smaller gardens. Red Banner's different – the whole of Europe's their backyard.' I lit a cigarette while he took a query from a messenger and rapidly produced the appropriate file of cuttings. He came back and signed the file out of the book.

The kernel of an idea was beginning to form in my mind. I had to admit that on the face of it it was crazy. But it did have the virtue of making part-sense of the Dyson – Sugden – Red Banner story. And possibly even of the Dyson – freighter – Red Banner relationship. But for confirmation I had to find out from General Deedes who exactly had given him the first information about the hi-jacking of the *François Villon*.

Chapter 22

A quarter of a mile away from the General's house I became aware of dark blue Land-Rovers guarding the intersections. I continued towards the turn-off I wanted but it was no surprise to me to see that the street was blocked by a pole fence manned by blue-capped Action England troopers. I stopped at the barricade and got out of the Lancia. The days had passed so quickly since I was picked up on Chelsea Embankment that it had not registered that the massive Alert of the various Action committees was planned for only two days' time.

As I walked towards the guards I could see down the barred road to where a long line of blue trucks and Land-Rovers were parked outside the General's house. From almost every vehicle long aerials bent and swayed, and the air crackled with radio transmissions. I stopped in front of one of the barrier guards.

'I would like to see Major-General Sir Richard Deedes immediately, please.'

'Press, sir?'

'No; this is extremely important business connected with your organisation.'

'Can I have your name, sir? You do appreciate that this is a very busy time for the General.'

'Yes, I realise that. But if you could stress the importance of my seeing him – better still . . .' I searched my pockets for a pen, 'I'll write him a note.'

The guard gave me a notebook and I wrote a brief note telling the General that it was of the utmost importance he saw me. Deliberately I gave no indication of what it was about.

I walked back to the Lancia and lit a cigarette while I waited for the guard to return. I leaned on the car bonnet listening to the radios, the shouted orders and the revving motorbikes, and it was easy for me to close my eyes and ignore the chill fenland winds and be transported back nearly twenty years to an SAS laager in the mountains of Trucial and Oman. There it had been a strange sort of war with myself, a subaltern of twenty, leader of a troop of red-bereted brigands who fought with turbaned brigands from the hills for the same primordial reason – a stark love of fighting itself. Every month or so we subalterns would be required to lecture our troops on the political rôle of the SAS in the Trucial and Oman States – but all the explanations in the world weren't worth a pint of cold beer to my squadron. At home the Left Wing called us 'mercenaries' but we thought of ourselves as volunteers doing what we were doing for comradeship and excitement and the sense of self-importance that comes from carrying a gun. That's dangerous enough – but we weren't ideologues like the men in blue caps who looked ready to stake life on the chances of their being right. Your life, of course.

The guard returned. 'Would you like to come this way, sir?' he said, with a new deference in his tone. I nodded and followed him along the road to the house.

The front door was wide open despite the chill November weather, and men in dark para-military garb were clattering in and out. A guard at the door asked me to wait and a second guard clattered inside. In a moment or two he emerged with a man of about 30 with that sleek well-fed look of a general's aide. In Etonian accents he asked me to follow him. We went along the narrow passage and descended into the rubber plants and bougainvillaea of the conservatory. He opened the green-shaded glass door, and I saw that the lawn was covered by a huge marquee.

'You can see why we need a tactical headquarters when we really get going,' he said with an apologetic smile. Nodding to the patrolling guards he swept aside the canvas sheeting that hung in the doorway and motioned me to enter. The heat and din inside was considerable. About a dozen girls worked on typewriters, another dozen men at least operated field telephone handsets. The Etonian lifted a nostril in amused distaste.

'Never mind, come the day . . .' I said. He wasn't sure if I was joking. He composed his face and stepped across to the rear section of the tent which had been partitioned off with timber and hardboard. He rapped on the unpainted hardboard door and entered, leaving me alone. I looked back into the main part of the tent. Near me a young man was speaking into the telephone.

'Sussex,' he said, 'this is Central TAC HQ. We've received and passed your petrol requisition.' He paused and smiled proudly. 'Quick? Of course it's quick. That's what we're here for. You can take this as your authority to start issuing from stores. Written authorisation follows.' He pressed down the rest and gave the handle three rapid turns. 'Get me Reading, please,' he said into the receiver. He was very young and aware of my presence just behind him. 'Oh Reading, this is Deputy MOT Central TAC. Give me your MOT please.'

The trouble is, war is fun.

I turned away as the hardboard door opened. 'The General will see you, Mr Hart,' the ADC said, and I walked past him into Deedes's office.

Hardboard had been laid across the grass of what had once been Virginia's lawn. A large oak desk had been carried in from the house and about twenty folding hire-chairs had been arranged in front of it for briefings. Maps studded with fluorescent buttons linked by coloured tapes covered the canvas walls. The General stood examining one of them, hands behind his back. He was wearing dark trousers and a dark sweater, with the collars of a pale buff shirt showing at the neck. He contrived to make this unexceptionally civilian garb look military.

'What can I do for you, Hart?' he asked, turning away from his maps. 'I can give you ten minutes.' He waved his arm towards the front row of hire-chairs and crossed to sit behind his desk.

Looking up at me he said, 'I'm pleased to see you've sorted out your problems with the police. What was the trouble?'

'Mistaken identity,' I said shortly.

'I'm very glad to hear it,' he said coldly. He was visibly remembering our last meeting.

'Anyway,' I closed the subject, 'that's all over now.'

I sat down on one chair with my arm along the back of the next.

'Your note mentioned a matter of importance,' he said.

'Yes. I want to put to you a very wild idea, General.'

'Really, Hart, I've no time for wild ideas.'

'Listen to it, General. I think you might find it surprisingly interesting.'

I took his silence for assent.

'For almost a year,' I went on, 'we've been hearing about the Red Banner group. For every bombing in Dortmund or Doncaster, Toulouse or Turin we get claims from this or that social anarchist gang – with Red Banner always among them claiming

171

the so-called "credit".'

'It's perfectly obvious all these groups are struggling among themselves for leadership,' he said impatiently.

'Since this very wild idea hit me, which was only last night,' I went on, 'I've been doing some serious homework on Red Banner. What would you say were its most spectacular actions to date, General?'

His foot was tapping under the desk. 'Obviously the hi-jacking of the *François Villon*. And that appalling Leicester Square outrage.'

'The Four Square Disco?'

'Yes.'

'I'm going to suggest to you, General, that these were the *only* actions for which Red Banner was responsible.'

'Nonsense. There have been a hundred incidents.'

'I'm going on to suggest, General, that in the terms we have normally considered the problem, Red Banner simply does not exist at all.'

'You've taken leave of your senses, man,' he said.

'I'll be frank with you, General. After the last few days I'm not a hundred per cent sure. But I don't think so. You see I now know who hi-jacked the freighter.'

He sat up in his chair and placed both large palms flat on the desk in front of him. In the body-language of generals I assumed this was an interrogative.

'The *François Villon* was hi-jacked by a mercenary thug named Dyson.'

'Working for Red Banner, you mean?'

I took out a Gauloise and lit it. 'General,' I said slowly, 'how could he have been working for Red Banner if there was no Red Banner to work for?'

He picked up a ruler and beat the desk like a kettle-drum. 'Let's accept the hypothesis for a moment,' he said after a pause. 'If there *is* no Red Banner, why did this man Dyson hi-jack the freighter at all?'

I waved him down. 'Let me throw another fact into the middle. Shortly before the hi-jack this same thug Dyson arranged for a fake list of Red Banner leaders to reach the authorities.'

'You mean they weren't Red Banner leaders?'

'Not one of them.'

He frowned and started drumming with the ruler again.

'I find it interesting, General, that you haven't asked what all this has to do with you.'

He stopped drumming. 'Simply because it's an interesting thesis anyway,' he said.

I looked at my watch. 'My ten minutes is nearly up.'

He waved the idea aside as no longer being of particular importance. Suddenly his time was at my disposal. 'If you're right about Dyson,' he said thoughtfully, 'what would his motives have been?'

'Exactly the same as the motive for claiming Red Banner participation in dozens of bombings all the way across Europe. The motives were to inflate the importance of Red Banner – to give it body and menace. To create an international terrorist organisation out of the fears of the British man in the street.'

'But why?'

I put my cigarette out on the hardboard floor. 'I don't know, General,' I said. 'Do you?'

He abandoned the ruler and began to drum with his fingers. The normal person drums from the little finger to the index. The General, I noticed, drummed in the reverse order, from the index down to the little finger. A psychiatrist had once told me the significance – but it's since escaped me.

'What you're saying, Hart,' the General stopped his aberrated drumming and fixed his eyes upon me, 'what you're saying is that organisations like Action England are likely to benefit from public alarm at terrorist groups like Red Banner.'

'I'm saying a whole lot of people could benefit. Action England certainly – Aktion Deutschland, Actione Italia, Action France . . .'

'I come back to my original question,' he said briskly now. 'Why should this "mercenary thug", as you describe him, be concerned to forward the aims of the European Action committees?'

I lit another cigarette and blew a stream of smoke tumbling and billowing under the bright central light. 'Before this afternoon, General – had you ever heard of, or met, Dyson?'

He straightened his legs and lifted himself out of his seat in one single movement. 'By God, Hart, you'll live to regret that insinuation. No, Dyson is not a member of Action England, nor, as far as I am aware, of any Action committee in Europe. I am disgusted by the suggestion that the hi-jacking of the *François Villon*, not to mention the Leicester Square incident, was carried out to advance our interests.' He quietened down with effort. 'I would like you to withdraw that allegation,' he said deliberately.

'I can withdraw it if you can answer me one question, General.'

'And that is?'

173

'When you hired me to investigate the freighter incident you had received information – including the captain's name – from someone who clearly already knew most of the details. I'll withdraw the suggestion if you tell me who it was.'

He looked at me squarely. Chopping the words for emphasis, he said: 'I can assure you it was not this man Dyson.'

I sat back in the chair and shook my head. 'Not good enough, General.'

'I am giving you my solemn word of honour,' he said harshly, 'my word of honour that it was *not* Dyson, that I had never heard of Dyson until you mentioned him and that my informant is an honest, respectable member of society. My word of honour, Hart. I am bound by an earlier promise not to divulge his name.'

There was no point in prolonging the interview. Did I believe him? I don't know. The restoration of confidence at the discovery from Sugden that Dyson *was* involved in Red Banner in some way wasn't enough to expunge New York, the doctors' document and some of those flawed reports I had sent from America.

We faced each other silently for a moment until the General leaned forward and pressed a bell on the desk.

The Etonian ADC entered and I rose heavily.

'Goodbye, Hart.' The General extended a hand across the desk. I didn't feel like shaking it. I nodded to him and turned to follow the aide.

We came out from the bright lights of the tent into the grey November afternoon and crossed towards the door of the conservatory. As the ADC reached for the handle it was opened by von Arnitz. Behind him stood a small, neat figure I recognised from the Central Hall meeting as Marshal Fausto Amarotti of Actione Italia.

'Peter,' von Arnitz addressed the aide and affected not to recognise me. 'Is General Deedes free yet?'

The Etonian stepped aside. 'I'm sure he is, sir. Will you come with me?' As the tall German and much smaller Italian moved towards the canvas door of the marquee, the General's ADC smiled an apology. 'See yourself out, old boy,' he whispered.

I went through the conservatory and into the house. Dark-sweatered young men bustled past me with sheaves of papers in their hands. I stopped one of them. 'Is Lady Deedes upstairs?'

He was young enough to react favourably to my brusque manner. 'No, sir, I believe she's out. You could confirm that with Miss Cavendish. That's her office, there.'

I thanked him and knocked on the door he had indicated. The

gentle tones of the General's secretary bade me come in.

Miss Cavendish's room was the eye of the administrative hurricane swirling around her. She was taking tea.

'Mr Hart, isn't it?' she said. 'Do come in.'

I closed the door after me. The office was quite large, perfectly ordered and comfortably furnished with mahogany tables and chintz sofas. A fire burnt in the grate. After the frenetic activity outside it seemed warm and relaxed.

'It's bedlam out there,' I said. 'I don't know how you stand it.'

'I don't try to, Mr Hart. That's my secret. Would you like tea?'

I thanked her, and at her invitation sat opposite her beside the fire. She poured tea from an elegant Victorian teapot, indicated the milk and sugar and proferred biscuits. 'I find these young men so intense,' she said àpropos of nothing as far as I could see. 'When I was young the boys were all so gay.'

I agreed they certainly took themselves pretty seriously out there.

'Yes, you see I was a WAAF plotter at Biggin Hill. I used to move the boys about the sky, bring them down for refuelling, scramble twenty minutes later to meet the next fleet of bandits, but they always remained so cheerful. And in the mess at night, of course, you can't imagine the high jinks we all got up to.'

'You never know, Miss Cavendish, perhaps I can.'

'You're flattering an ageing lady,' she said, pleased. 'But don't forget I was twenty-three in nineteen-thirty-nine. I was considered quite a beauty, if I may say so. And all those young men . . . all those young men . . .' Her voice trailed off. She looked into her teacup. It was a long silence.

'What happened to him, Miss Cavendish?' I asked at length. 'Was he killed?'

She shook her head. 'He was married with a wife and family in New Zealand. I felt so sorry for them, and so guilty for myself.'

'He went back after the war?'

'No. They needed fighter-pilot instructors back in New Zealand. I persuaded him to apply just as the Battle of Britain was ending, late nineteen-forty-one, it must have been.'

'And you've never seen him since?'

'Oh, yes,' she looked up out of her teacup and smiled brightly. 'He's been over twice. He was President or Treasurer or something of the South Island Farmers' Union. We had two weeks together – once in about nineteen-fifty, once five or six years later.'

'And now?'

'And now he's dead. He died last year. I heard purely by

175

chance, so I wrote to New Zealand for all the newspapers. They carried a little piece on him, you know. He was quite important in his way. That's how I learnt he wasn't married.'

'You mean he was divorced?'

'No. Not married. Never had been. The gayest of bachelors. And there was silly old me, sitting here in England, waiting all my life for the gayest of bachelors.'

There was nothing I could say. She smiled. 'Your own fault, Mr Hart, for having such a sympathetic face. Believe it or not I don't accost strangers in the street and tell them my story. More tea?'

She poured me tea and considered. 'You've come to ask me where you can find Virginia Deedes, haven't you?'

'Did you read that in the tealeaves?' I asked her.

'No. I'll confess I watched you both from an upstairs window the first day you came here. I'll also confess that I was walking along the backs at King's the second time you came here. Cambridge, you should know, Mr Hart, is a very, very small town.'

I put my cup on the tray. 'So are you going to tell me where she is this afternoon?' I asked. 'Or does that too much divide your loyalties?'

'I have no loyalty to General Deedes,' she said sharply. 'I've worked for him ever since he retired. In all that time I doubt if he's ever recognised me as a human being.'

She meant, of course, as a woman.

'Do you know the cinema in Arts Passage?' she asked, standing to stack the teacups.

'Yes – just off the Market Place.'

'She's gone there to get out of the way of all this' – she gestured to the passing footsteps outside the room. 'If you hurry you should catch her as the film ends.'

I dropped off the car in the Pembroke Fellows' car park, and as the early evening closed in I walked along King's Parade and through St Edward's Passage to the Market Place. The stall-holders were beginning to close up and go home, but there were still cheerful paraffin lamps hanging over the second-hand bookstalls and I was almost tempted to stop and browse.

The Arts Cinema was showing *Les Enfants du Paradis* for perhaps the 300th time. I checked the hours and found I had little more than ten minutes to wait.

It was getting colder and colder. It was early in November for snow, but it was that sort of weather, cold beneath a heavy sky. I stamped up and down Arts Passage and watched the first customers begin to trickle out of the cinema: an undergraduate and a moon-faced Swedish girl . . . two Irishmen who looked as if they had gone in to sleep off the dead afternoon hours when the pubs closed . . . and then a trickle of heavily-coated anonymous figures . . .

I almost missed Virginia. She had continued on up Arts Passage towards Magdalene Street, and I had to run to catch up the dark head bobbing among the crowd.

I took her arm and half-turned her towards me.

'Remember me?' I said.

She stopped, delightfully astonished. 'Very well. I remember you very well indeed, Mr Tom Hart.'

'Did you wonder why I didn't contact you?' I asked her. We were walking across the Market Place.

'No,' she said. 'I saw your photograph in the press, of course. And the piece about you having . . .'

'. . . been eliminated from police enquiries?'

She nodded. 'So it's all cleared up now, is it? The misunderstandings?'

'I think the misunderstandings are clearing up, yes.'

She side-glanced at me and smiled. 'It must be the habit of a lifetime. Some day you must tell me the whole story without any evasions whatsoever.'

We entered the long lounge of the Rose and Crown. It had once been the coaching yard of the inn. Now it was roofed with glass and decorated with potted palms. An ancient waiter approached. I ordered a bottle of Chablis and she nodded her agreement. I looked at the wine list and found a very promising Thorin 1964.

We sat close together in low, Edwardian basket-weave chairs with worn mahogany arms. While the waiter uncorked the wine I watched her slim fingers and immaculate red nails drum the deep, brown woodwork of the chair. She drummed, I'm happy to say, in the normal direction – little finger to index. She also wore a superb sapphire ring that sparkled on her finger against the dark warmth of the mahogany. Girls have told me I'm fixated on ladies' hands, and it may be true. At one time I had hopes to raise it to the status of a fetish, but I never quite made it. Now I'm older I accept the loss gracefully and can resign myself to an ordinary male appreciation of a good-looking hand with a socking great sapphire on the ring finger.

The ancient waiter poured a little wine into my glass and I sniffed and sipped it before giving it the *imprimatur*. He then filled Virginia's glass and mine and placed the bottle in an ice-bucket. It was all done without undue deference but with a consciousness that good wine benefits from a touch of ceremony. He was slightly surprised therefore when I ordered a second bottle, hardly having passed judgment on the first.

'I've been to see the General,' I told her. 'Miss Cavendish gave me tea and a brief glimpse of a very sad life. I think she's very fond of you.'

'Yes, I think she is. I find it very difficult because I do know how she regards my husband.'

'She thinks you're wasting your life on him. Just as she wasted her life on her New Zealand fighter pilot.'

'She told you that?' She was shocked.

'No. But I think that's the basis of her feeling for you. She identifies with you.'

'I can't make out, Tom, whether you're a cynic or a hopeless romantic.'

'A hopeless romantic,' I said, thinking of the doctors' report. 'But I'm getting over it.'

She looked at me as she drank her wine. I remembered that when we met that day for lunch in the Blue Boar it had taken a couple of bottles of wine to relax us both. This time I was willing to wait.

'What have you been doing since the bridge on the Serpentine?' I wanted to remind her of the moment. She wanted to be reminded. For a second or two she paused. 'The usual things since then. Richard's been overwhelmed with work and visitors to the house. I've tried to keep out of it as much as I could. I'd only be in the way otherwise.'

'And when it's all over?'

'The Alert, you mean?'

'Yes. When the Alert's all over what then?'

'You mean, what will Richard do? I've no idea what his plans are . . .'

I shook my head. 'No, I wasn't asking about his plans. I meant when the Alert's all over will there be more time for you?'

'I'm sure he would spare as much time as I wanted,' she said stiffly. She drank some wine and immediately drank some more.

'Are you sure you aren't going to be a grass widow to Action England for as long as it lasts?'

'I've told you how I feel about my husband. I'd prefer not to

178

talk about this any more.'

'All right. Let's talk about you. And about me.'

She sighed. 'I've told you about that too,' she said.

For a moment we both sat drinking wine. Two or three of the inn guests drifted into the lounge for drinks before dinner. A sun-tanned American couple caught my eye and I focused my interest on them for a few moments. He was tall, probably over six foot, and she very little shorter. He wore a conservative hounds-tooth check sports jacket and had those aristocratic good looks that fourth and fifth generations of New Englanders seem so often to acquire whatever their family's social origins in Somerset or County Clare or the Glaswegian slums. She had a splendid showgirl's figure, with a long slender back, long legs and a well-rounded bust. They sat down opposite us and ordered Martinis. I could have told them that the old waiter would have been more at home mixing a Molotov cocktail but I held my peace.

Virginia thought I was looking only at the girl. 'She's beautiful,' she said.

I didn't deny it. She looked at me. 'May I have some more wine?'

'Of course.' I reached for the bottle but the old waiter material-ised at my right hand and took the Chablis from the ice-bucket. He poured the two final glasses from the second bottle.

'When we last met,' I said slowly, 'you told me that since you were married there had been other men. Two or three. Discreetly, I believe you said.'

'Yes . . .'

'Tell me,' I turned my face away from the long-legged Ameri-can girl.

'The first one was a young officer on my husband's staff. We were in the Far East during the Indonesian confrontation. Richard was away a great deal and I was in Singapore. One day this young officer turned up with orders to collect some personal things of Richard's and take them over to him, when his week's leave was completed. I'd known him before, of course, but not very well.'

'How did it happen?'

She wanted to shock me. She shrugged. 'He arrived at the house, I offered him a drink and he stayed . . . and stayed until his leave was up.'

'That doesn't sound the soul of discretion. You must have had servants in the house.'

'Which I hired.'

'And if necessary fired.'

'It proved not to be necessary. He returned to my husband's staff and neither of us mentioned that week again. As a matter of fact, about three months later he married the daughter of one of the senior Air officers.'

'And you were at the wedding?'

'Naturally Richard and I were both invited.'

I signalled the waiter to bring us another bottle of wine. 'And number two?' I asked her.

' "Number two", as you put it, was in Germany. Very brief.'

'Another member of your husband's staff?'

'No. As a matter of fact he was German. We were marooned in a hunting lodge by a sudden snowfall.'

The waiter poured the wine and she looked at me sharply. 'What are you smiling at?'

'A hunting lodge,' I said. 'It wasn't by chance old loyal Hans von Arnitz that you were snowed in with?'

She blushed. 'I'm stupid to talk about it,' she said angrily. 'I've had too much wine. Let's stop.'

'All right – but just tell me this. Was the last one the same?'

'The same? In what way?'

'Was he also tied by some bond of loyalty or rank to your husband?'

She really hesitated. 'Yes,' she said finally. 'Yes, I suppose he was.'

'A trio of substitute bed-fellows.'

'Please don't moralise, Tom. I don't know why I've told you all this.'

'You told me because you enjoy telling me,' I said. 'And because you're trying to set out the rules.'

'You know very well that I don't believe the rules would apply to you.'

I touched her smooth, nyloned knee. 'But you're willing to take the risk?'

'You know I want to.'

'Then do it.'

She reached out and held my hand. 'Tomorrow, Wednesday,' she said quickly. 'But I have to be back by Friday morning at the latest.'

My mouth was dry. 'Will you come to London?'

She thought for a moment. 'My aunt, the one with the flat in Chester Square, she also has a cottage on the river.'

'Where is she now?'

'In Scotland, visiting her son.'

'And you have the keys?'

She opened her bag. 'Cranfield Cottage, River Walk, near Taplow.' She detached a key from her key ring. 'In case you get there first,' she said and placed the key, like a token, in the palm of my hand.

Chapter 23

I'm not really sure now when I first became vaguely alarmed. Somewhere in Hertfordshire, I think, around Boreham Wood, bells had begun to tinkle faintly in my head. The headlights of the car behind me seemed to remain persistently in place whether I accelerated to 65 or dropped back to 40 miles an hour. By Hendon Broadway I was pretty sure I had company, but I reminded myself that this was one of the principal roads into Central London from Cambridge and the north, and it was hardly a cause for surprise or alarm if another driver chose the same route.

At Finchley Road the traffic thickened a little and I had no way of knowing which, if any, other car was trying to stay close to mine. I memorised several makes and numbers and drove on towards Baker Street. At the turn-off for the Shepherd's Bush flyover I was followed round by an old Ford and an acid yellow Volvo. Both seemed to be carrying several passengers.

I put my foot on the accelerator and soon left the ancient Ford some distance behind. In the driving mirror I saw the Volvo pull out past the Ford into the fast lane and come up behind me at speed. Signalling left, I transferred through the central to the slow lane and let the Volvo sweep on past.

The Ford was some way back now and the red tail lights of the Volvo were obscured by other fast traffic. So far so good.

I took the South London slip-road off the flyover and turned down towards Chelsea. At the Shepherd's Bush roundabout I stopped to see the Volvo killing time, circling the central grass mound with no intention of using any of the exit roads. That confirmed it for me. I was not prepared to believe the driver was a Swedish tourist unfamiliar with the English system of roundabouts. I let him pass again and came out quickly about twenty feet behind him. His problem now was not to be forced to pass an exit road which I then took.

He solved the problem decisively by braking hard. I wrenched the wheel right, and to a cacophony of truck horns blasting in my ear I drove for the Holland Road exit.

Frankly, I'm not the best driver in the world. My physical reactions are, if anything, below average. In my lifetime, I may have backed my masculine identity into some difficult corners, and even blind alleys, but I have never associated it with my ability to drive a car. This is fortunate for what remains of my mental health because, as I said, I don't drive particularly well.

The Volvo driver was a Fittipaldi by comparison. I turned right at Hammersmith Road, sped down to the Broadway and did two full circles of the block before heading south again down Fulham Palace Road. Fittipaldi was about 50 feet behind me.

It was getting late now, and the traffic was thin on the roads. I had left Cambridge after dinner with Virginia at about 11.30. Glancing at my dashboard clock I saw it was now gone 1. 30.

A little more traffic might have been an advantage, but from New King's Road onwards I knew the side-streets well and I had already worked out a rough plan to evade the Volvo.

I took it very gently down New King's Road, past the Eel Brook Common and the bend which signifies the beginning of King's Road proper. I could guess that in the Volvo they were themselves probably uncertain of when and how to strike. The occasional blue police patrol car crossing our front or nosing from a side-street didn't make their problem any easier.

Ideally of course they would have followed at a distance until I arrived home – in this case Jazz's flat – and then got me there. But I had no intention of allowing them to choose the ground.

At the Edith Grove intersection I stopped on the green. The Volvo pulled to the kerb about 50 or 60 feet behind me. I sat with my foot poised, watching the light through amber to red. As it changed I accelerated inches past the headlamps of a huge truck and braked. As I flung open the door and ran across the road I could see the Volvo waiting for a chance to press through the traffic that was crossing its front.

I ran for the towering, brick Council flats at World's End. With their courtyards and their bleak, split-level piazzas they were a mugger's dream environment. And at the moment they promised escape to me too.

As I ran I could hear behind me the footsteps of three, perhaps even four men and I was vividly reminded of that night in

Honfleur. In fact I was prepared to take the similarities considerably further – I would have bet a lot of money on Dyson being one of my pursuers.

I emerged on to Cheyne Walk at about where Seaton Street used to be before the vandal officialdom of the Royal Borough of Chelsea and Kensington demolished it, and ran along the Embankment towards the bridge, looking back over my shoulder every few steps.

They were comfortably far behind. Two men, neither of whom I recognised at this distance, came running on to Cheyne Walk. But only two. I was still wondering what had happened to the others when I saw the acid yellow Volvo drawing to the kerb about a hundred yards in front of me. Two men were getting out. One of them was Dyson.

This was not the time for analysis. 'Information . . . assessment . . . conclusion' could wait for a more suitable occasion. At the moment I was more impressed by the fact that traffic on the river road was sparse, that I had two men behind me and another two in front, and that any single one of them could be carrying a silenced pistol. I ran straight across the road, vaulted the stone embankment, and landed on the hump of sand below among a flurry of beating swans' wings.

Staying tight under the lee of the embankment wall I ran for the cover of Battersea Bridge. At the two old, bleached hulks of the Chelsea Yacht Club I left the line of the embankment and splashed through the mud to put them between me and anyone firing from the road. I was only a hundred yards now from the bridge and making good speed across the shallow, watery mud when I saw Dyson at St Thomas More's mulberry tree vault the iron fence and start down the steps to the level of the river.

He fired as I passed him. If you're the target of even a silenced pistol you hear the sharp crack as the bullet breaks the sound barrier above your head. The second bullet hit the mud somewhere in front of me at a flat angle and ricocheted away with a thwack and whine across the river. I stumbled forward, splashing muddy water up into my face. My fingertips in the mud steadied me as I recovered my balance and a third shot cracked the air high above my head.

The first span of the bridge was now looming across my front. I could have run straight on under it but Dyson was only 30 or 40 yards behind me with a pistol, and the other three men up on the embankment could pick me off as soon as I emerged from under the bridge's protecting span.

As a boy I'd played down here during the school holidays, telling my father I was off to tea with fat Algie Porter-Smith but instead seeking out the company of the World's End kids who were always engaged on a project to sail to Putney in a rotting dinghy or salvage a rusting outboard motor from the mud. It was they who had first introduced me to the mysteries of the steel-ribbed construction of Battersea Bridge. But that was 25 years ago when I was a slender-bodied twelve-year-old boy. Whether I could still do it remained to be seen.

The street lights on the bridge above me cast a deep shadow as I ran under the span. The moment I stopped I could hear Dyson behind me crunching across the muddy gravel. Ahead two men dropped from the embankment and began to run towards me.

I looked up into the curving grey steel spans of the bridge. By reaching up I could grip the lowest girder. With more effort than I remembered from the past I swung myself up on top of the girder and, standing, ran along it until the cambered steel-work closed down from above me. The spans of the bridge, I remembered, were sectioned into steel compartments, each of which was connected by a small porthole. It was through these portholes, tearing aside the wire mesh designed to stop nesting pigeons, that, as boys, we made our way across the span, traffic rumbling on the bridge above us, towards the first massive stone bastion.

Behind and about twenty feet below me I could hear the voices of Dyson and his men. I tore aside the wire mesh on the first porthole and pushed my head into the darkness. With a struggling movement I managed to get my shoulders through. Dragging and clawing at the great steel nuts inside the first compartment I heaved my hips and legs after me. Another few inches round the waist and I would undoubtedly have stuck.

In the total blackness of the compartment I scrambled on my hands and knees across the sharply-cambered floor and felt for the next porthole. The wire mesh tore at my fingers as I pulled it aside, and as I dragged myself through my outstretched hands slid on my own blood across the sloping steelwork.

Somebody had mounted into the underneath of the bridge behind me. The echoed curses and grunts as he tried to negotiate the black unknown gave me some satisfaction. They clearly assumed I was intending to cross the bridge this way and drop down on the mud on the Battersea side of the river. On the pavement above my head I heard the running footsteps of two, perhaps three men, as they crossed to the Battersea bank.

In fact I had no intention of going all the way across. At the end of the span the last compartment gives on to a small, low doorway set in the stone support. Below it the brown water swirls past the stonework. It is exactly one-third of the way across the bridge.

I stepped from the last steel girder, in what was for a twelve-year-old a death-defying leap, into the low opening in the stonework. The echoing clatter of my pursuer cut immediately to a deep damp silence.

I could no longer remember the shape of the stone passageways and chambers that like ancient mineworkings honeycombed the inside of the bastion. But I thumbed my lighter and the dark smell of the river and the weeping stone walls in the flickering light brought back vividly the excitement of first exploring these Victorian chambers. I headed forward confidently now, passing through the main chamber until I saw what I was looking for, the iron ladder leading up to the vaulted stone roof.

I climbed the ten or dozen steps of the ladder, hunched my shoulder against the steep manhole above, and heaved gently. The cold night air cut through the wet, warm air around my head. At pavement level I peered across the bridge towards Battersea.

A late-night bus rumbled across the bridge towards me, huge and alarming, when seen from ground level. When it passed I saw that two men were stationed on the far side of the bridge, each watching the mud below.

I eased up the steel cover and scrambled out on to the bridge. Dropping it gently into place I walked briskly back across the span towards the Chelsea bank. Glancing over the parapet I could see that Dyson's fourth man was awaiting him at the water's edge.

I was careful not to run, although relief from tension made me want to expend some more energy. Instead I walked quickly past Corby Hall, past Chelsea Old Church and headed for the King's Head and Eight Bells. There I turned left and made for Jazz's flat.

Letting myself in I thought longingly of a very large whisky. I stepped across the hall hearing the squelch of my shoes for the first time, and entered the sitting room. There on the drinks table in front of me was a large bottle of duty-free whisky, a jumbo of duty-free gin and a bottle of cognac. Jazz was back.

'What in God's name have you been doing to yourself?' she said from behind me.

I turned. She stood in the bedroom doorway completely naked. She was a very shapely and very blonde lady. At the thought of all her Japanese friend had been getting this last week something around chest level lurched inside me.

'Welcome home,' I said – because I couldn't think of anything else to disguise just how pleased I was to see her.

'Are you in trouble, Tom?' she said anxiously, still completely unselfconscious about her nakedness.

'Not yet,' I said.

She looked down at herself and smiled. Then turned into the bedroom for a housecoat.

'Duty-free cognac?' I called to her through the open door.

'Help yourself,' she said. 'I'll start with coffee.' She went into the kitchen and put the coffee on while I poured myself a very large brandy. Then I carried it through to the kitchen.

'I suppose you know roughly what you look like?' She stared at my soaked trousers. As I sipped the cognac I could feel the gritty mud between my lips and the glass.

'I can probably guess,' I said, ineffectually brushing wet pigeon feathers from my leather jacket.

I leaned forward to kiss her welcome home, but she turned her lips away so that I brushed her cheek only.

'Stevens rang me in Munich,' she said. 'He told me you had agreed to go to hospital for a month.'

'Did he also tell you about the doctors' report on New York?'

'In the longest long-distance phone call in my life. My Japanese friend began to get very jealous.'

I didn't much want to hear about her Japanese friend.

'Are you ready to sit down and listen, Jazz?' I asked her.

'When I've got my coffee. Want some?'

I nodded and walked back into the sitting room. I turned on the heating and supplemented it with an electric fire before collapsing on to the sofa.

Jazz came into the room with her coffee. For a moment she stood looking at me – coolly, I thought. Then she sat down in one of the armchairs opposite me. 'Munich's a fantastic place,' she said.

'Even now?'

'More so, if anything. There's a *Götterdämmerung* feeling about the whole city.'

'*Götterdämmerung?*'

'I imagine it's like Berlin before Hitler took over – night clubs, restaurants booming, the brothels with queues outside.'

'And the unemployment centres?'

'Queues there, too. But things are still better than they are here. They're about a year behind us in everybody's opinion.'

'They'll catch up.'

'Maybe.' She drank her coffee. 'I had quite a time. I ran into Ragnar while I was there.'

Ragnar was a German-Swedish businessman who had once taken Jazz on a trip to Acapulco. I had met him briefly once, a tall, heavy-shouldered man in his mid-30s, polite and intelligent, a buyer of modern paintings. He and Jazz had a lot in common.

'I'm surprised you're back so soon. You didn't manage to ditch the Japanese for Ragnar?'

She looked up slowly at me, pursing her lips and shaking her head.

'No,' she said 'You know I don't do things like that, Tom.' She got up and poured herself a brandy. 'I could have done that for you,' I offered.

She shrugged and brought the drink back to her chair. Something had happened to her while she was in Munich, I felt sure of that.

She sat down. 'Stevens was really pleased about the way things were working out for you.' Then, after a pause, 'What went wrong?'

I looked down at my clothes. 'You mean all this?'

I couldn't quite understand the look on her face – maybe it was pity. She shook her head suddenly, impatiently. 'No, I don't want to know. I shouldn't have asked.' She was shaking.

Of course what had happened to her in Munich was not the Japanese, or even perhaps Ragnar – it was that all-time record phone call from Stevens. I suppose the doctors' report had pulled the rug from under our relationship. I felt sad – then almost immediately very angry.

'I'm bloody right about Dyson, Jazz,' I said. 'I was right about him in France and I was right about him tonight when he and a few friends tried to pick me up on my way back from Cambridge.'

'Cambridge?'

'I went to see General Deedes. He's in it up to his neck, Jazz.'

She jerked upright, looking suddenly pale and shocked. 'General Deedes?'

'Yes, Major-General Sir Richard Deedes, VC.'

She pursed her lips. I could see the explosion coming. 'For God's sake, Tom! Can't you see what you're doing to yourself?'

'I can see what everybody else is doing to me.'

'Including the General's wife?'

'Don't be crazy. I haven't told her what I think. In any case, I wasn't a hundred per cent sure about him until Dyson intercepted me on the way back. It must have been the General who contacted him just after I left.'

She dropped her head. 'I'm sorry, Tom. I don't understand the way you think.'

'Then let me explain, Jazz.'

'No. Stevens said if you went into hospital everything would be sorted out.'

'I thought so too, for a few hours. But it wouldn't have resolved anything. I'm sure I'm right this time, Jazz.'

Her hair flew as she shook her head wildly. 'I can't stand it, Tom. I can't stand seeing you do this to yourself. You fancy his wife so you suspect the General. It's just so bloody obvious.'

'And if I told you I don't fancy his wife?'

'Then I wouldn't believe you. Unless you've already had it off with her and found she's into troilism with teddy bears.'

I stood up. 'Can I get myself a cup of coffee?' I asked her.

Suddenly she smiled. 'You look terrible,' she said. 'Why don't you take a shower? I'll make the coffee. If I twist your arm will you have cognac to go with it?'

I said I would and took myself into the shower. I threw off my jacket and peeled off the warm dampness of my clothes. Under the hissing hot jets I thought about Virginia Deedes.

I dried myself and brushed my hair and put on the robe Jazz handed me. As I came into the sitting room she was pouring the brandy. I put my arms round her and kissed the very pale blonde hairs on the back of her bent neck.

'Your coffee's on the table,' she said, moving out of range of my hands. Then she turned and thrust the drink towards me.

I took it and padded barefoot to the sofa. I wasn't used to being refused by Jazz.

She had made herself some more coffee while I was in the shower, and for a moment she stood in the middle of the room holding the cup and saucer high, sipping the coffee cautiously then grimacing to herself as the heat burnt her mouth. She lowered the cup and looked at me frowning. 'Tom,' she came over and sat next to me on the sofa, 'Tom, you can still put everything right.' She was more than asking me: she was imploring me.

I stretched out and held her hand. She didn't pull away this time. But I knew she would as soon as I spoke.

'Tomorrow, Tom,' she said softly, 'let me drive you over to the hospital. Take a lot of books and get a private room. If we can't afford it we'll charge the Department. They'll pay.'

I began to say something, but she shook her head.

'No, just listen. You don't need to have treatment. Just rest and read, and I promise I'll come in and see you every day. And at the end of the month this whole thing will have passed. Stevens says that Mansfield will be on to Red Banner by then.'

'He'll be lucky,' I said. 'How can he get on to Red Banner if it doesn't exist?'

She looked at me, baffled.

'It's a front title, Jazz. Its function is to act as *agent provocateur* for Deedes's Action committee.'

She jerked her hand away from mine. Her eyes were fixed on the carpet. 'You won't go tomorrow?' she said.

'No, Jazz. Not now. I can't.'

'What will you do?'

'Tomorrow?'

She nodded miserably.

I thought of the cottage at Taplow. 'I'll be away tomorrow.'

She turned with that woman's intuition. 'How long for?'

I shrugged. 'Back the next day.'

She nodded. Could she possibly know?

'I'll go to bed, then,' she stood up. 'You'll be all right here?'

'Yuh. I'll be fine.'

She went towards the bedroom door. Somehow I felt I had to tell her. 'I'm going to Taplow,' I said. 'Virginia's aunt has a cottage there.'

She turned at the door. 'Taplow? On the river. Yes . . .' she thought for a moment. 'Sounds nice . . .'

'Jazz, let me tell you . . .'

'About the General's wife.'

'Yes. I want to.'

She wrinkled her nose. 'No thanks, Tom. Some secrets should be kept.'

'Not this one.'

'Perhaps. Is this why you decided not to go into the hospital?'

'No. It happened later. I only arranged it this evening.'

'Too bad. I knew I should have come back earlier.'

'I didn't expect to see you back so soon anyway. What really happened – apart from your meeting with Ragnar?'

She recrossed the room and picked up the two coffee cups. 'What really happened, Tom, was that I got an awful feeling that I'd left you in the lurch.' She took the cups into the kitchen.

I heard the rattle as she set them down on the steel sink and she reappeared. 'Stevens thought it was the only thing for us to do – both of us, him and me. He thought it was the only way to get you to see . . .'

'Sense?'

'If you like.' She leaned against the doorway biting her lip. 'There wasn't any Japanese, Tom,' she said after a moment.

'You just upped and went to Munich?'

'I phoned Ragnar and asked him if I could come.'

I finished my brandy and looked towards the bottle. She nodded. As I walked across to fill my glass she said, 'Ragnar sent his best wishes.'

It seemed a strange thing to say.

'I'd better let you get some rest,' I said. 'You've probably been having a pretty tiring week.'

'Ragnar met me at the airport and took me out to his house in Rosenheim. Then he left for Rome on business. But even if he'd been there it would have made no difference.' She tumbled out the words, one sentence after another.

'No difference?'

'No.' She walked towards the bedroom door. 'Because,' she said deliberately, 'I am off Germans.'

'Why is that?'

She shrugged. 'If you're interested, I'm off South Americans as well.'

'South Americans?' I didn't know she even knew any South Americans.

'I am also,' she went on with equal deliberation, 'off Indonesians, Turks, Afghans, Kuwaitis, Americans . . .'

What the hell was she talking about?

'. . . Greeks, Persians, Canadians and even Japanese.'

'What about Englishmen?' I said slowly.

She nodded vigorously. There were tears in her eyes. 'Englishmen, too,' she said, trying to smile. 'Except one. And he just doesn't want to know.'

I stood watching her. She was shaking. 'I'm sorry, Tom,' she said. 'I shouldn't have embarrassed you like that. My family have always said I could do with a little more of the stiff upper lip. But it seemed an important enough thing to say not to have to stand on too much ceremony.' She opened the bedroom door. 'Very bad of me. But I wanted you to know before you went down to Taplow tomorrow.'

I tried to get across the room towards her but she wasn't having any of that. She shook her head and I stopped, still this side of the armchair.

'Jazz,' I began, 'Jazz, I don't want to sleep on the sofa tonight. Let's both . . .'

Again she shook her head. 'You'd wear yourself out for tomorrow. That wouldn't be fair.' She managed to say it without a trace of bitchiness.

'I've got to go tomorrow, Jazz. It's something I've got to do.'

'Shame,' she said. She smiled. ' 'Night, Tom.'

She closed the door behind her and I turned back to the sofa and lay down, resting my head against the rolled arm. For an intolerable time I could hear the sounds of her muffled crying from the other room. But there was nothing I could do about it – I knew I couldn't possibly tell her what I planned to do tomorrow.

Chapter 24

Jazz was already up when I awoke. She had put on a paint-smudged smock and very carefully done her hair and arranged her make-up to reduce the redness that still lingered round the eyes. As I stumbled into the kitchen she was sitting at the table eating bacon and eggs and reading the *Guardian*. She looked up and smiled. 'Breakfast? Toast, bacon and eggs? And I've got kidneys and sausages in the fridge. Like those too?'

Normally I eat a big breakfast, which was why Jazz had been out shopping for kidneys and sausages. This morning I would have preferred just toast and coffee, but I didn't feel I could disappoint her. Again.

As she cooked I took up the *Guardian* from her side of the kitchen table. The whole of the front page was devoted to the General's Alert tomorrow. The promised scale of the operation had the Government in a panic. Whereas the last Alert had been kept under wraps until the last moment this one had been given maximum publicity. And when the General claimed there would be a turn-out of nearly a million men nobody in the country was disposed to disbelieve him.

In Parliament the Government's Left Wing had naturally enough demanded that the Alert be banned, but the certainty was that the Cabinet had known that there was little chance of making a ban effective if the General decided to go ahead. And everybody in the country knew he would. When I thought back over the last few weeks it was astounding how quickly the Action England movement had grown. Six months ago the General was universally sneered at as a political dinosaur whose ideas and organisation were unlikely to attract more than the right-wing lunatic fringe. The first Alert had changed all that. It was not only an open and successful challenge to the Government's authority; it had also revealed how deep was the malaise in England and how wide-spread the frustration of its people at the inability of the democratic process to reflect anything more than the demands of the minority of left-wing activists in the country. As soon as decisions are no longer made by the ballot box, the General had said, they will inevitably be made by the gun. And who could deny the truth of that? The trouble was, he only applied the thesis to the totalitarians of the Left.

And while England tossed feverishly on its sick bed the rest of Europe gathered watching. In some way that most Europeans recognised, what happened to England in the next days or weeks would happen to their own countries in the next months or years. We had seen the process inexorably at work since the first crises of 1976. While Britain, as it still was, floundered, the rest of Europe trembled on the brink of economic disaster. Then the Italian crisis was followed by crises in France, Sweden and Holland until even the mighty economic strength of the German Republic began to totter under inflation and unemployment and a labour force desperate to save something, as individuals at least, from their massive and disciplined efforts of the post-war years. Nevertheless, by an irony of history, many now thought that German democracy might yet save Europe. But they had their social anarchists too – and von Arnitz's Aktion Deutschland was known to be flexing its muscles to challenge the Government with an Alert.

Was it just my own mental unbalance that ascribed to me some part in these vast events? After Jazz had finally quietened last night, I had stayed awake smoking and drinking coffee and going over the thing step by careful step. And I was still sure I was right. And if I was right there seemed only one course of action.

I finished my breakfast with effort and sat smoking over coffee, looking at Jazz. At about eleven o'clock I got myself dressed. From the bathroom I could hear that Jazz had turned on the radio while she tidied the flat and did the washing up. The music stations had closed down, and like a General Election continuous broadcasts were coming from every county in the country, describing the build-up to tomorrow's Alert. As I shaved I heard a reporter at Leicester announce that special trains would be bringing the local contingent to London. From Plymouth there was a report of a convoy of over 80 trucks, all painted blue, bringing the West Country squads up to the capital. In Lancashire road blocks were already appearing, and their contingent was motoring down under their own escort to arrive in London late tonight. It was an English version of the march on Rome.

The General's stated objective was two-fold – first to demonstrate local strength – by means of command posts and movement control throughout the country – and, second, at the same time dispatch disciplined contingents from every part of England to parade tomorrow in London. By mid-day he would have thrown down the gauntlet. An enfeebled Government would pick it up – or ignore it – at its peril.

'I'd like to come back,' I told Jazz as she saw me to the door.

She thought for a moment. 'Leave it for a while, Tom, will you?' She laughed. 'To tell you the truth, I've embarrassed myself a bit. Give me a little time to get back on the track.'

'I meant I'd like to come back tomorrow.'

She was hurt. 'No, Tom. Please.' She stopped. 'You can be a cruel bastard, you know,' she said slowly. She made an effort to smile. 'Still, while you're in Taplow screwing the General's wife you're at least not going to be taking off against the General himself. I suppose I should be grateful for that.' She pursed her lips into a whistle of surprise at herself. 'You have a bad effect on me, Tom Hart,' she said. 'I never expected to hear myself thinking that way. Wish me luck with the Irish wolfhounds.'

'I thought you were starting with Pekinese.'

She nodded. 'Small Is Beautiful – but big pays more.'

I stood in the doorway as she drifted inconclusively down the hall. At the sitting room she turned. 'Go on, then – or you'll find yourself caught up in this Alert.'

It was a clear, crisp winter morning with the white sparkle of hoar frost on the grass. As I drove into Taplow a squad of men came marching past me. They were wearing the already familiar blue caps with the long peaks, dark blue sweaters and trousers. Each man carried a shotgun at the trail. A policeman on traffic duty stepped forward to stop them, then hesitated and changed his mind. I couldn't blame him. He'd received no instructions from above; the obvious uniform of Action England had not been declared illegal; the shotgun was a licensed weapon. He shook his head as they passed.

I drove into the town and parked. And now for the first time I noticed something else. Posters featuring the General looking sternly straight at me had gone up overnight. In my hundred-yard walk to a phone box I saw perhaps half a dozen. Underneath his picture was the inscription 'Action Now!'

I entered the phone box and dialled Roger Slade's home number. His wife answered, and told me he had been asked to do an extra shift to cover the build-up of tomorrow's Alert. I thanked her, jiggled the phone rest for a dialling tone, and called the *Daily Telegraph*. The girl on the switchboard put me through to the library.

'The whole building's jumping,' Roger said when he came on the line. He really enjoyed his job. 'I can't remember so much excitement since Hungary and Suez overlapped.'

'How would you like the story of the year, Roger?'

He thought I was joking. 'I'm serious,' I told him. 'You can give it to any reporter you like. Or sell it if you want to. Just as long as you use it.'

He became immediately conspiratorial. 'Does it concern your field of interest the other night?' There was a touch of pedantry in him which made him the ideal newspaper librarian.

'Yes. And tomorrow's Alert,' I told him.

'Hold on,' he said, and I could see him peering over his shoulder, 'I'll go into the office and call you back on the private line.'

It was lunchtime before I finished briefing Roger.

I regained the car and drove out of Taplow down towards the river. Virginia had given me directions, and I found the cottage by the river without any difficulty. I bumped down an unmade-up lane and turned into the short drive of a perfect seventeenth-century cottage with black beams on white stucco, sloping door frames and ivy creeping the height of the brick chimney. In the summer there would be roses and gliding kingfishers from the river on my right, tea in the garden and the rattle of a hand-mower across the lawn. If you're going to have an English country cottage it should look like this.

Her white Mini was parked in the back of the drive. I drew up beside it.

I left my bag in the boot and walked up to the front door. With the key in my pocket I still knocked. There was no answer. I knocked again, louder this time. Taking the key from my pocket I let myself in.

There was no hall. The front door led straight into the main room and a staircase wound up to the floor above. A deep-set brick fireplace dominated the sitting room and a log fire blazed warmth. I turned for the light switch and five or six table lamps leapt to life at my touch. I looked round me – gleaming furniture, silver trays, Chinese carpets – the restrained, mannered taste was almost overpowering. I looked around for a drink. There was no sign of a bottle.

Outside a footstep crunched on the gravel drive and I turned to see Virginia coming towards the front door. She was carrying a brown paper bag in her arms.

I opened the door and stood on the step. She smiled at me over the top of the paper bag. 'How long have you been here?' she asked, handing me the bag. The bottles inside chinked together as I adjusted to the weight.

'Just got here,' I said. 'You should have told me your aunt was a teetotaller.'

'Far from it,' she said. 'But she will only drink sherry, wine and very occasionally brandy. Whisky she thinks is just about acceptable for men. Gin and vodka she regards as irredeemably vulgar.'

I took the whisky and gin from the paper bag and set them on the table. 'Who is this aunt that conveniently leaves you keys to places like this?'

'My father's younger sister. Her husband died last year, and she spends quite a lot of time with her daughter in Canada. She says Vancouver is the only civilised town left in the world.'

She seemed to be a lady of strong opinions. I poured whisky for us both, added a little water and handed her a glass.

She took it with a crisp 'Thank you' and drank. Was she embarrassed? I'm not sure. But I knew damn well I was. Here we were in an idyllic cottage in the middle of a darkening November afternoon . . . was it good form to throw her down on the Chinese rug in front of the fire?

'I hope you haven't had lunch?' she said.

I would have said 'no' if I'd just consumed a whole baron of beef. 'No,' I said. 'What do we have?'

'I got here quite early, in fact,' she was walking towards the kitchen. 'I was hoping you hadn't eaten.'

We walked through a small, well-equipped kitchen into an arched dining alcove. A table was laid for two.

She handed me a bottle of white burgundy to open while she produced salmon pâté and buttered brown bread from the refrigerator.

'I had a terrible feeling, as I put the key in the lock,' I told her as we sat down, 'that I was going to come face-to-face with your aunt. She was about sixty-five, a pale grey twin-set across an ample bosom, a heavy man's watch on her wrist, and thunder written all over her face. Her first words were: "Sampson . . ."'

'Sampson?'

'She was summoning her Rhodesian Ridgeback.'

'I see.'

'And when the drooling beast sprang to her side she demanded to know what exactly I was doing with a key to her cottage.'

'You didn't tell her you'd come to spend a dirty mid-week with her niece, I hope?'

'What else could I say, with the Ridgeback's fangs straining for my vitals?'

'You confessed everything?'

'I told her the whole story. From the beginning.'

She stood up and took the plates into the kitchen. 'I wonder,' she said as she opened the refrigerator again, 'if it'd be the same version as my own.' She put a plate of cold pheasant in front of me and rested her hand on my shoulder. A finger reached out and touched the back of my neck. I turned to look at her staring down at me. Her hazel eyes had a strange, fixed quality. For a long moment she looked at me, her eyes intense in a passive face. Then she put her own plate down on the table.

'I hope you like your pheasant cold,' she said, and began passing me the salad.

'What would your version be?'

'That I'm a lot more interested in you than you are in me.

I shook my head.

'No protestations, Tom,' she said. 'I know the risks I'm taking.' She didn't.

We finished lunch and cleared it up together. It was about 3.30.

'Let's take a walk,' I suggested, 'before it gets completely dark. Or are you too well-known in the area to be seen out walking with me?'

She hesitated. I think she would have preferred to stay in front of the fire but she had decided to let me set the pace.

'How would you like to go on the river?' she asked. 'My aunt keeps a small boat. We could take it up to Cookham.'

I said I liked the idea, and she went upstairs to change into something warmer than the dress she was wearing.

I sat before the fire drinking good black coffee and listened to her movements above, trying to analyse what I felt about her. I was already, of course, feeling an intense anticipatory guilt. Guilt from which I found it impossible to unravel strands of lust, as I thought of her now naked in the room above me. Guilt intertwined with the deep satisfaction of knowing I was doing the right thing. Because, for all my life of lust and gluttony, I am an unshakable Puritan at heart. A Godless believer in justification by faith.

It was almost dark by the time we untied the boat and I helped her down from the creaking wooden jetty. The outboard motor started at the first string-pull, and the little dinghy nosed its way through the still water and towards the centre of the river in the direction of Cookham. With the rising beech forests on our right we sat with the rudder arm between us, and enjoyed the chill white river mist that floated round the dinghy insulating us from the dim winking lights of houses on the bank or the distant chink of shunting railway engines.

It was hard to believe that all out there beyond the enveloping river mist across the wooded slopes and the hawthorn thickets an army of blue-capped men were preparing for tomorrow's Alert. She sat in close to me as the lights of Cookham dispelled the mist and we glided towards the bank. She had spoken very little on the way here, and once or twice half-turned to fix me with that disconcerting look.

'You're so much not as I imagined you to be,' she said as we walked towards the King's Head. 'I thought of you as accessible to me, I suppose, and now I find some core elusive and remote.'

We entered the low bar and stood ordering drinks. It was only a few minutes after opening time and the bar was empty.

'May I ask you one question – just once? I won't return to it, I promise.'

'Of course.' We sat down with our drinks in the far corner of the room. 'What was the question?'

She thought for a moment and then said very deliberately: 'Did you really want to come to the cottage with me? Or were you just performing in a way that you'd come to expect of yourself? An available woman is automatically an opportunity to be taken, perhaps.'

197

'Isn't that what you'd prefer? A plain uncomplicated sexuality? Wouldn't that make things simpler for you?'

'I know it would, of course. But I'm not sure any longer whether I'd find it enough.' She stopped and looked at me. 'In some way I don't quite understand, Tom, I'm aware of being afraid of you.'

I took her hand and held it tight. 'Have you ever felt afraid of your husband? In the same way?'

'Of course not. The demands he makes on me are ones I understand. Social demands, mostly.'

I shook my head. 'No, it's much more than that. Your loyalty to him makes you very protective, defensive even.'

She looked sceptical. 'Loyalty to Richard seems to be an odd thing to be talking about when we're about to spend the night together.'

'Not at all,' I said. 'You've always made it pretty clear that, from your point of view, fidelity was never part of the deal. You're not going to tell me that your conscience will give you trouble afterwards?'

'I don't think about afterwards.'

We both sat listening in some part of our minds to the sound of men's voices outside, then the door was pushed open and seven or eight young men entered the bar. They were all dressed in dark blue sweaters and trousers. One or two of them carried or wore the long-peaked blue cap.

They were already fairly drunk, their faces flushed, their voices loud. They began to talk with the young, white-coated barman about the Alert the next day. Their assignment was to cover the Taplow-Hedsor Road, stop and examine cars and ensure the maintenance of communications.

The barman asked what they were maintaining communications against.

'Left-wing sabotage operations,' the young leader of the group told him. 'We've been warned that there could be an attempt to cut phone wires and even electricity supplies in the area.'

'Bollocks,' the young barman said incisively.

'What the hell do you know about it?' the other man said. His friends went silent and looked on, nodding agreement. 'We've already picked up a couple of pretty strange beardies wandering around.'

'And then what do you do with them?' the barman asked, outraged.

'We send them off to Maidenhead TAC HQ for questioning.'

'Bloody marvellous' – the barman was really angry now. 'What authority have you got to stop people and cart them off for questioning? None at all.'

'Listen, friend,' the blue-cap leaned across the bar. 'This country is going to the dogs.'

'Right,' said the barman. 'Dead right.'

'I told you to listen, friend,' the other man was menacing now, conscious of the support of the others behind him. 'If some of us choose to fight for what we believe is right that's only because people like you haven't stood up to be counted in the past.'

'We've got a government, we've got a police force and we've got an army. We don't need you. That's the way I look at it.' He turned to pick up a glass from behind the bar but the blue-cap leaned across and grabbed the shoulder of his white coat. 'They had all those things when Scotland went independent,' he said. 'And now look what's happening with a new Russian delegation arriving in Edinburgh every day.'

'If that's what the people of Scotland want it's okay by me.' The barman twisted his shoulder free. 'Now just keep your hands off me, please, or I'll have to ask you and your friends to leave.'

'Did you hear that?' the blue-cap laughed, looking at his friends. He turned back to the barman. 'You're too big for your boots, friend,' he said. 'You're lucky I don't decide to send you on a little trip to Maidenhead.' He pushed his glass forward. 'Now just draw us off seven pints before I change my mind.'

The incident, small as it was, nevertheless had an impact on Virginia. I knew she was thinking about the General, and that this was probably the first time she had ever had any contact with the practice of Action England. I thought again of those movements of the early '70s, run by essentially decent ex-soldier citizens like General Sir Walter Walker or David Stirling. I had thought Major-General Deedes's movement was similar in its aims and style. But I was wrong. Its aims were distinctly dubious – and it had more in common with the para-military street rowdies of the inter-war years.

I took her arm. 'Let's go,' I said.

She nodded quickly.

'There are a lot more pubs in Cookham,' I said as we stood outside in the cold air.

'Tom.' She came very close and slipped both her hands around my waist. 'I'd like to go back now. Would you?'

'You don't want to run into any more bully-boys.'

'I just want to go back, Tom.'

'Let's find the boat then.' I unclasped her hands and led her back down to the stone jetty. The mist on the river lay at a thickness of about six feet, improbably white in the moonlight like the icing on a cake. I started the engine and set the nose of the little dinghy deep into the mist.

It was very much thicker now that night had fallen, and two or three times we were completely lost, forced to nose into a narrow creek to check our whereabouts against a remembered cypress tree or a desolate boat-shed. Once, even, in a moment of hilarity, we found that we had changed direction entirely and had been chugging back upriver towards Cookham.

It was after half past eight before we tied up again and made our way up the lane towards the cottage. I used my key to let us in, and while Virginia went upstairs I built up the fire and opened a bottle of her aunt's Richebourg.

I was sitting and drinking soft velvety wine by the light of the fire when she came down again. She was bare-legged, and, I could easily guess, naked beneath a short dark-red towelling robe. I glanced down at my watch. It was a little before nine o'clock.

She crossed the room behind the sofa and in the small gilt-framed mirror beside the fireplace I could see her take up her glass of wine and turn to look at me. She stood for a few moments sipping the wine, until I turned on the sofa and held out a hand to her. Unsmiling she set her glass aside and crossed the room to sit on the back of the sofa. Along the length of her thigh the red robe fell open.

'I don't like gentlemen,' she said, looking down at me. 'I don't like considerate lovers.' Something in her expression disturbed me – the set of her beautiful mouth or the fixed intensity of her eyes. I was kneeling on the sofa now, pulling off my shirt and trousers.

'I like selfish men,' she said, and lifted her legs to slide over the back of the sofa and down beside me.

From the depths of her isolation she reached out and took my erection, pulling me towards her as she lay back. As I moved my hand across the curve of her thigh she was breathing heavily, her nostrils flaring with each sharp exhalation. The black pinpoints of her pupils still held me with that disturbing intensity. Moving my hand forward through the warm soft down to an even warmer liquid softness I penetrated her with my fingers. The depth of her breathing lifted her breasts clear of the robe. In the hall a clock unhurriedly struck nine.

I came down beside her leaning forward to kiss her, but her

mouth was tense and unresponsive.

'Now,' she said. 'Now!'

And she slid beneath me with a sigh that became a gasp as I found my way inside her. Then, as I began to thrust, her body was instantaneously racked with a series of shuddering orgasms.

'For Christ's sake,' she screamed. 'For Christ's sake . . .'

I looked down at her head rolling from side to side, her closed eyes and flared nostrils and I knew she didn't need me. She was there in her own eternity, sobbing and threshing, alone out there on her own heath.

I ejaculated. And only then as I gradually began to lose my hardness did she begin to fade back to consciousness. Her eyes opened and her breathing quietened. The long fingers which had been locked around the back of my neck slipped round to touch my face. She wouldn't have known a considerate lover from Attila the Hun.

I knew she was ashamed of her performance, and I wanted to tell her it wasn't half as shameful as my own. But she wouldn't have understood that yet, and she padded barefoot to the drinks table, her robe loose around her shoulders, and poured us both more wine.

She came back and lay down beside me on the wide sofa. I balanced the wine on my chest and lit a cigarette. The fire threw deep shadows across the beamed ceiling, the sap hissed in the wood and the sweetness of woodsmoke filled the room.

Virginia leaned on one elbow, occasionally sipping her wine, her light brown eyes searching my face for reassurance. It was half past nine – how could I possibly give her any?

She heard the car first, and lifted her head to the sweep of headlights across the darkened room.

'Tom, that was a car.' It was more frowning curiosity than alarm that showed on her face. She got up, wrapped the robe around her shoulders, and went to the window. 'It's stopped in the lane.' She turned her head towards me but I stayed on the sofa. 'Tom, what do you think?'

'Could be a couple less lucky than we are. No aunt with a vacant cottage when they want it.'

She turned away from the window and came to sit on the back of the sofa, trailing her red-nailed, sapphire-ringed fingers in my groin. 'Of course,' she said. 'It hadn't occurred to me.'

Then outside a car door slammed and men's voices could be heard in the lane.

She was frightened now. 'Tom, they're coming here,' she said, regaining the window. I got up and slipped my trousers on as the footsteps approached across the gravel of the drive. At the door they stopped and the brass knocker shook the door-frame.

Virginia stood rigid in the shadows by the window. 'Don't . . .' she shook her head, 'don't answer it.'

I moved towards the door and stopped a foot or two short. From outside there was the crackle of crushed twigs and a figure appeared at the window. In dark outline the man strained forward to look into the firelit room. But Virginia had drawn back into the shadow and I was beyond his direct line of sight. He rapped on the window with a coin. 'Anyone at home?' he shouted.

She was suffering badly. I could see that the palms of her hands were pressed against her cheeks. She was probably too frightened to be crying.

'Give the front door another try,' one of the voices said. 'They're probably upstairs.'

The knocking this time seemed to shake the whole framework of the house. Then a voice outside called peremptorily: 'Lady Deedes. We'd like a word with you.'

She looked at me wild-eyed, trapped like a delicate deer in Richmond Park. 'It must be the police,' she whispered.

She gasped as I stepped forward and opened the door. The cold air cut at my bare chest. Three men stood in a tight clutch round the door.

'Mr Hart?' one of them asked.

'You'd better come in.' I stepped back and the two men entered. Virginia looked stunned with shock. As she pulled her robe about her an electric-blue flash dispelled the shadows. The third man renewed the bulb on his camera and caught her again as she stumbled across to wrench at my arm.

'Who are they, Tom? Who are these men?'

The oldest of the three, balding, perhaps 50, in a black leather trenchcoat, closed the door. 'John Ruggles,' he said, flipping open an identification wallet, 'Central Picture Features. We're reporters, Lady Deedes.'

She covered her eyes. 'Tell them to go, Tom. For God's sake, tell them to go.'

'Have you left your husband for good, Lady Deedes?'

'No, please go.'

'I see. Just bored with this whole Action England business?' Virginia frowned at him, unaware he was setting her up for a direct quote. In the paper tomorrow morning it would come out as, ' "Of course I haven't left my husband for good – I'm just

202

bored by this whole Action England business," said the beautiful Lady Deedes.'

They had enough. I told Virginia to go upstairs and get dressed, and I shepherded Ruggles and the other two towards the door.

'How long have you known Lady Deedes, Mr Hart?'

'Just a matter of weeks.'

'Is she in love with you?'

'I've no reason to think so.'

He looked at me and grinned salaciously. Then cocked his head. 'If you say so, Mr Hart. Is this the first time you've met here?'

'It is.' I pushed Ruggles towards the door. 'All right, that's enough for now.'

'Just one more question.'

'Out,' I said.

He looked at me and sniffed contemptuously. 'Sure,' he said, 'sure.'

I closed the door after them and turned to see Virginia halfway down the stairs. She was wearing trousers and a sweater now, standing motionless watching me. I glanced away from her and walked across to draw the curtains and put on the lights.

She winced at the brightness as the table lamps sprang to life. Her face was ravaged with sex and shock. She came down the stairs slowly and poured herself a glass of whisky. Looking down at it she said softly, shaking her head, 'You knew. You knew they were coming.'

I poured myself a whisky too, and sat in the corner of the sofa. 'Yes,' I said. 'I knew.'

'You not only knew. You arranged for them to come.' She spoke slowly, making statements rather than asking questions. 'You wanted them to find us together.'

I stayed silent. She knew she was right. She drank some whisky, her lips quivering. 'You unspeakable bastard. How much did they pay you?'

'Not a penny.' I thought of Roger Slade, and hoped he'd make something out of it.

'Do you expect me to believe that?' she said, her whole face contorting with contempt.

'Yes. And I think you will believe it. Not tonight perhaps, but very soon.'

'What in God's name are you talking about?'

'I'm talking about your husband. I'm talking about his vile organisation that won't even stop short of the murder of kids to get what it wants.'

'Are you mad?' The question was becoming a theme song from almost everybody I knew.

'No, I don't think I'm mad. I think I've found out the truth about Action England. And about your husband. Sadly, this was the only way I had of doing anything about it.'

She still didn't understand. But the tears were beginning to roll from her brown eyes as we both turned towards the door. A car had come up fast out of the silence outside, braking on squealing tyres. She got to the window and pulled aside the curtain as I heard the car doors slamming.

'Oh God in Heaven. Oh God in Heaven...' she was whispering to herself as she dropped the curtain and turned round. 'You'll kill him,' she said to me: 'Don't you understand? You'll kill him.'

The door burst open and Major-General Deedes stepped in and hurled it closed behind him. His face was white as death itself. He looked at Virginia. Then, without a word, he stepped forward and slapped her hard across the face. As she reeled back he took her arm and dragged her towards the door. Jerking it open he pushed her outside. I crossed the room and stood in the doorway. I was probably in the background of the shot that Ruggles's waiting photographer exploded in the face of the General as he dragged his wife towards their car.

Chapter 25

I watched the scuffle from my position in the doorway. Two men had leapt from the General's car as the camera had flashed in Virginia and her husband's faces. But Ruggles and his team were experienced in getting away with the booty. As the two men advanced on him the photographer tossed the camera to Ruggles, who leapt into his own car. While the two aides tried to drag open the passenger door the photographer rounded the car and climbed into the back seat. With spinning wheels and tyres spurting mud Ruggles's driver accelerated past the General's parked Daimler and the two aides were left to chase it ineffectually for a few yards until its red tail lights disappeared at a bend in the lane.

I closed the door. It was too painful to watch Virginia being bundled into the back of the Daimler. I thought perhaps for a brief moment she had looked back at me, but even if she had it would only have been in baffled contempt.

I put on my shirt and sat hunched over what remained of the fire. Everything had happened exactly according to plan. Roger Slade had done his part well, contacting the agency and briefing them along exactly the lines I had suggested to get the General to arrive at just the right time. But I still felt far from triumphant. About the impact on Virginia of the night's traumas I felt totally wretched. I wasn't happy about the idea of Jazz reading to-morrow's papers, either. Stevens, of course, would probably guess what I was doing; Pushkin too. For the General himself I felt not a shred of sympathy. As I saw it he deserved all I hoped he was going to get.

I leaned forward to poke the fire and I was aware that I had not yet heard the Daimler pull away. A moment later, as I lit a cigarette, I understood why. Footsteps on the drive outside approached the door. I was crazy not to have thought about it before. Of course the General was not the sort of man to let me get away with it.

I was pulling on my socks and shoes as the door opened. The General and his two aides entered the room. I looked the two men over. They were both quite a lot bigger than I had registered them to be outside in the dark.

The General stopped in the middle of the room with the two men slightly behind him.

'Get on your feet,' he said. His hands clasped a non-existent swagger stick behind his back. His lips formed a very thin dark line in his white face. He was only just in control of himself.

I got up, tucking in my shirt as I rounded the sofa.

'You're going to pay for tonight, Hart.' His hands came round to his sides. I noticed his fingers plucking at his trouser seams. 'I should have recognised the scum you are from the beginning.'

'Don't blame yourself, General. You need *some* moral values to recognise moral scum. You just aren't equipped to do it.'

'I'm not here to bandy words with you.' He stepped aside and jerked his head towards the two men. 'Give him the good hiding he deserves.'

I knew I'd have one chance only with each of them. I had already worked my right heel free of my shoe so that, as they came forward, I was able to jerk my foot up and send the shoe flying straight at the face of the first man. It hit him hard and noisily across the bridge of the nose. As they both reacted to the unexpected missile, I stepped left and hit the second man. It was a textbook blow, the extended fingers deep into the solar plexus. With a wheezing gasp of pain he doubled up and I rebalanced for a flat-hand chop along the line of the jawbone of the first man. Self-defence as taught at the Chester-le-Street training school seldom works out according to the book. Because fighting is a messy, unpredictable business, because men vary in strength and speed and ability to absorb a blow, it's not unusual to damage your opponent unnecessarily or fail to incapacitate as you intended. Perhaps the only real chance is with an unwary opponent at the very beginning of a fight. The over-confidence of the General's thugs worked in my favour – both of them now lay sprawled on the ground, one retching as he desperately fought for breath, the other a crumpled silent hump on the carpet. Yet I was fairly sure neither of them was anything more than temporarily hurt.

I recovered my shoe and slipped it on. The General watched me without the least trace of fear for himself. 'I should have remembered,' he said in a cold, flat voice. 'You did of course receive a suitable training for your trade.'

I picked up my coat. 'I'm leaving now, General. But I'm not giving up. Tonight was just the first step. When those newspapers come out tomorrow I'll be interested to see how many loyal adherents you can muster for your Alert.'

His head jerked up.

'But this is just the beginning.' I stepped over the two men and crossed to the door. 'I'll go on until you're where you should be – in a prison for the criminally insane.'

'Hart . . .' his voice cracked out with an authority that stopped me dead. 'Say that again,' he ordered.

'You heard me the first time. And I don't plan to wait around until your friends recover their wind.'

'You intended those reporters to be here. Is that what you're saying?'

I glanced down at the two men. One was stirring, the other was still doubled with pain. I had a minute or two yet. 'You blew it, General, when you put Dyson on to me. That was the final connection. The bridge between Action England and Red Banner. For people like you the means always justify the ends. But your sort never sees straight, General. What always happens is that the means destroy the ends. And you end up as a grubby murderous bastard like the people you set out to oppose.'

He was standing ramrod stiff. 'Wait,' he said, as I reached for the door. 'You seduced my wife in order to discredit me. Is that what you're saying?'

I pulled open the door. 'Goodbye, General,' I said. I couldn't take the idea of being in the same room with him a moment longer.

He must have been wearing the holster high on his hip. Certainly the first indication I had that he was carrying a gun was when it was pointing straight at me.

'Come back and close the door,' he said quietly. At fifteen feet I had no choice. I pulled the door to, and turned towards him.

He pulled up the edge of his sweater and put the gun away. 'I have never seen or heard of this man Dyson in my life,' he said very deliberately. 'I told you that yesterday in Cambridge. It remains true.'

He walked to the drinks table and poured a very small whisky into a tumbler. Then he added water, still not looking at me. The two men on the floor were climbing painfully on to their knees. He drank a little whisky and, as they hauled themselves up, said crisply: 'Wait outside for me. I want to talk to Hart alone.'

They both gave me wary glances as they moved past me. I opened the door for them and they stumbled out into the dark.

'Close the door,' he said. I hesitated, then did so.

'Did you hear what I said?' he asked after a moment.

'About Dyson?'

He nodded.

'Yes, I heard. But I don't believe it.'

'I think you do. I think you're beginning to have doubts.'

I took out a cigarette and lit it. Doubts? No . . . I didn't have doubts. He must have told Dyson I was on my way back from Cambridge. I had to believe that. All I had done to Virginia was predicated on that fact.

'Dyson hi-jacked the freighter,' I said. 'Dyson gave you the details so that you could arrange the farce of me confirming them and then announce it to the press. Credit to your Action committee and evidence that Red Banner is growing in strength. At the same time Dyson supplies a fake list of the Red Banner leadership to my former department and tips off the names on the list that they are in danger of arrest. Object – to inflate Red Banner into an international organisation.

'And the bigger and more sinister Red Banner looks the more need there is for an organisation like yours to take over. There are a hell of a lot of people in every country who'd give a lot to see the trains run on time.'

He was thinking hard, I could see that. 'Why,' he asked slowly, 'should I create Red Banner when there are already several other terrorist groups in existence?'

'Because Red Banner, as a fiction, can be manoeuvred as you will. I've no doubt that it's very much part of your plans for tomorrow. Perhaps a massive explosion of the stolen gelignite. Something big enough and bloody enough to create a popular demand for a leader who can act against the terrorists. And of course you will be there – in Parliament Square with thousands of your blue-caps. And thousands of others will be controlling traffic movement and communications throughout the country. Tomorrow's your day, isn't it, General? Tomorrow, with the aid of Red Banner, is the day of the *Putsch* – the day you, by popular demand, turf out the legal government and take over yourself.'

I stopped talking. He poured another whisky and to my surprise handed it to me. 'You really believe that's the plan, do you?'

'I believe that's part of it. I believe that once England goes the other Action groups in Europe will have an example and an inspiration. Who takes the road next – Italy with Signor Amarotti – or Germany with von Arnitz and Aktion Deutschland? Don't tell me you haven't got a programme.'

He sat down in an upright, hard-backed chair with the same small whisky held in both huge hands. From time to time he glanced up at me, then down again at the whisky in the glass. 'I understand you've recently been sick,' he said. 'Indeed that that was the reason you were dismissed from the Service.'

That hurt. But I had to learn to accept it. 'That's roughly true,' I said. 'Very roughly.'

He nodded to himself. 'What makes you think you're able to evaluate this situation accurately? Isn't it conceivable that you're simply compounding former errors?'

He knew a lot about me. 'No, General,' I said. 'If Red Banner didn't exist it would have had to have been invented. You did exactly that. And publicised it with the deaths of sixty youngsters in Leicester Square.'

He nodded, again more to himself than in agreement. Suddenly he looked an utterly spent man. As if he'd removed his dentures for the night and his cheeks had collapsed. The angry pallor of a few minutes ago was replaced by a haggard, grey look. With the back of his big-knuckled hand he wiped tears from his eyes. He took a drink of the whisky but obviously not because he enjoyed it. 'I think you're only wrong about one thing,' he said.

'For the rest . . .' he lifted his shoulders helplessly and again rubbed at his face. 'For the rest . . . yes.'

I was terrified. I knew he wasn't play-acting. 'Which one thing?' I said. 'Which one thing have I got wrong?'

He raised his head. 'I will swear to you on my wife's life,' he said. 'I will swear to you that I do not know this man Dyson.'

I felt an immediate coldness in the room. My thumb squeaked on the glass I was holding. I didn't think I could survive another blow like New York. I couldn't survive knowing what I'd done to Virginia if the General wasn't guilty.

My mind raced to put the pieces together. 'Dyson was waiting for me when I left Cambridge yesterday. You must have told him I'd been to see you. How else could he have known? After I left you phoned him.'

He shook his head.

'You told *someone*!' I said, desperately.

'Yes. Yes, I made a telephone call. I called the head of our political committee.'

As he spoke it all seemed to leap into place. 'You were the front figure? The man they were going to get rid of the moment Action England had taken over. You were dispensable.'

His head dropped. 'They always say that Generals make naïve politicians, don't they?'

So I was right. And wrong, disastrously wrong, all at the same time. My head was swimming – if the General was the figurehead, who was to be the power behind the throne? And then, suddenly, the whole network of connections appeared to make sense. 'The head of your political committee – it's Mansfield, isn't it?'

He shook his head. 'No, it's someone that's been with us from the beginning. No one you know – it's a man named Stevens.'

Chapter 26

The General sat on his upright chair, the tumbler of whisky untouched in his hand. The last two hours had shattered too many of his dreams.

I remembered Virginia telling me he had been an exceptionally efficient soldier, and I was very prepared to believe it. I had seen the way he had produced an organisation out of Action England in less than a year. But it was an organisation ripe for exploitation by a ruthless, devious mind like Stevens's. Yet standing, watching the General in that cottage room, I was aware that I was as shocked as he was.

I had made another desperate miscalculation. Action England may have been an unsavoury organisation, but General Deedes was certainly not the cold-blooded killer I had imagined. And although he and Virginia were to suffer in a good cause it still wasn't quite the cause I had persuaded myself it was.

'This man Stevens,' he said. 'You know him well?'

I leaned my back against the wall. 'Yes. I know him very well. At least, I thought I did.'

'He was marvellously helpful in the early days.' The General's eyes searched restlessly among the shadows in the corner of the room, as if to find there some answer to the obliquity of men. 'He joined immediately I made that first announcement. He drove down that same day to Cambridge to see me. Obviously he'd been thinking along the same lines. Indeed, I recall he said at the time he'd been waiting for some rallying point, some figurehead. Yes, "figurehead". That was the word he used.' The General glanced at me for a moment, then back again to search the shadows. 'I couldn't have done it all without him. He drafted all the policy statements, all my speeches. He seemed to be so sure-footed politically. Of course I knew he worked for the Government. I assume now he worked for the Intelligence Services, as you did.'

'He was Assessment and Evaluation Controller,' I told him. 'Raw information was "processed", as they say, in his Department.'

The General nodded. 'Yes, he was clearly in the know about so many things. He suggested you were the man to investigate the hi-jack, of course.'

'It seemed a good choice,' I said. 'If I accidently stumbled on a little too much information I could easily be branded as unbalanced.'

He nodded, but he was no longer interested in the detail of Stevens's betrayal. He sat there with his chin lifted, his pale eyes quite blank now. The hands holding the whisky glass sagged a little like an old man dozing off. But it was the only movement in his otherwise immobile body.

I crossed to him and took his drink from his hand. 'You should go and talk to your wife, General. She needs you at this moment.'

He looked at me without bitterness and shook his head despairingly.

'I'm responsible, Hart. In the end I'm responsible for everything Red Banner has done.'

I found it greatly to his credit that he was more immediately concerned with that than he was with his wife's infidelity. He stood up and started towards the door. 'I can't thank you,' he said. 'Although I know I should.' He opened the door and walked, stiff-legged, like a drunk, down the drive towards the waiting Daimler.

I sat smoking behind the wheel in the deserted High Street at Taplow and watched the passing car slow and pull into the kerb in front of me.

The lights cut and the stocky figure of Pushkin climbed out. Meticulously he locked the door and, with his rolling gait, approached my car. Opening the passenger door, he got in beside me.

'Good evening, Mr Hart,' he said, raising his hand in a Roman salute. He shifted his bulk round to face me.

'I appreciate your coming,' I said.

'And I for my part greatly appreciate your asking me.' There was a curious old-world courtesy about this citizen of the world's greatest Soviet State. 'You anticipate trouble?'

'How much trouble I'm not sure. But my guess is that Dyson, at least, will be there. Possibly one or two of his friends.'

'And you believe it is possible that Stevens or Dyson was responsible for the death of Sergei Sergeivitch?'

'Let's see what answers we get there,' I said. 'I've come to the conclusion that I'm not that good with the crystal ball.'

I explained the metaphor to him as we drove down into Maidenhead. Just short of Boulter's Lock I pulled in to the side and glanced at Pushkin. He had pulled his enormous silenced pistol from inside his top-coat. Working the action he watched the heavy bullet nose into the breach, then he checked the safety catch with his thumb and, satisfied, slipped the huge weapon back inside his coat. 'Are you armed, Mr Hart?' he asked.

'Only with this.' I reached past him into the glove compartment, and took out a lead-loaded strap. He frowned. I let its weight swing against his leg, and he understood.

'Perhaps we should go then, Mr Hart.'

I buttoned the strap into the arm of my leather jacket, and we got out of the car. Stevens's cottage was about two or three hundred yards further down the road. In the darkness we walked

211

along the verge towards it.

At the telephone box I stopped. Pushkin continued on towards the low, dark outline of the cottage. I entered the box and dialled Stevens's number. As it began to ring I counted off eleven seconds on my watch and replaced the receiver. He would be sitting in his white silk pyjamas on the side of the bed, his feet fumbling into his bedroom slippers. A minute or two perhaps to find a dressing-gown and to assure Dyson it was only Hart phoning from God knows where, and the cottage door would open. From my position by the phone box I saw the lights go on in the cottage and the rotund figure of Stevens emerge. Hands deep in his dressing-gown pockets, hair ruffled from sleep, he slopped in his black chamois slippers towards the phone box. He was shivering in the cold November night air as he pulled open the door of the phone box and stepped inside.

I let him wait a minute or two, mostly to give Pushkin enough time, but also because I enjoyed watching him smooth down his hair and preen himself in the little mirror above the phone. He grimaced a few times at the finished result, then lifted his head to smoothe away the folds of extra chin. Then he looked at the phone petulantly. It was high time it began to ring again.

I stepped out of the ditch and jerked open the phone box door. As he turned round I grabbed a handful of his fat jowl and dragged him out of the box. He tripped in his chamois slippers, lost one in the ditch and rolled on the grass verge. I knelt down beside him. He was breathing heavily. 'Thomas,' he said. 'For God's sake, what are you playing at? . .'

'We're going back to the house and you're going to tell me exactly where that gelignite is hidden.'

'Gelignite? I'm more concerned at the moment about my slipper. Do you realise they're Gucci? Asprey's charge a fortune for them. Now it must have fallen somewhere down here . . .'

I took him by the shoulder of his robe and hauled him to his feet. 'Stop the play-acting,' I said, and pushed him in the direction of the cottage.

'I don't know what all this is about,' he protested reasonably convincingly. 'But you read your report. You're in no condition to evaluate a problem, Thomas. You're sick. Accept the fact, for God's sake.'

We were nearing the front gate of the cottage. A Jensen was parked on the stone slab forecourt. Stevens's Bentley was no doubt in the garage.

'Visitors?' I asked him.

'No. I'm changing cars,' he lied. 'I'm test-driving this one for a week or two.'

He let himself in the front door, and I followed close behind him, principally to watch his face. His mouth dropped open as he looked baffled at Dyson who was at 45 degrees to the wall, his weight on the palms of his hands, one ankle hooked over a chair leg in the favoured Voronezh heron stance. Then Stevens's eyes swivelled across the room to where Pushkin was sitting in an armchair with his monstrous pistol in his hand. He didn't look in the least amiable now.

'Do you need this jackal alive, Mr Hart?' Pushkin asked as I closed the door behind me.

'Dyson? No, not really.' I felt the shock-wave run through Dyson's body.

'Then be warned, Mr Dyson.' He got up and placed the pistol barrel against Dyson's thigh. 'If you cause the very least trouble I will bite off your leg.'

The colour left Dyson's battered cheeks. He didn't need telling that Pushkin's .45 would do no less.

I looked at Stevens and jerked my head towards the bedroom. He glanced quickly at Dyson and hurried in. I followed him and closed the door behind us. As he walked across the room I reached out my foot and tripped him so that he went down heavily face first and rolled startled on to his back. I knew he couldn't bear physical indignity, and this was the quickest way I knew to insert a barrier between our old relationship and the present. He lay on his back breathing heavily, waiting for my next move.

I took my loaded strap from inside my sleeve and watched him flinch. 'I'm going to use it,' I said. 'You know that, don't you?'

He looked at me through narrowed eyes.

'It won't even be difficult for me. Now get up.'

He scrambled to his feet.

'We're going to talk about the gelignite,' I said slowly. 'Every time I even half-think you're being evasive you know what to expect.'

'You're a sadist,' he said, and sat heavily on the corner of the bed watching the strap.

'Don't feel at liberty to provoke me, Stevens. The gelignite – where is it?'

He had already made up his mind to talk – probably from the moment I had tripped him.

'It's in a motor barge,' he said flatly. 'Moored at Westminster Pier.'

'Guarded?'

'By three of Dyson's people.'

'Detonators?'

'Yes, it's been heavily wired and booby-trapped.'

'Is there a wiring plan?'

'No. It was deliberately haphazard. Apparently that's the best way to ensure . . .' he paused, '. . . effectiveness.'

'You mean the best way of ensuring it blows up in the face of a bomb disposal squad.'

Birdlike, he pecked the air. 'Yes.'

We were making progress. 'Where was it to be detonated?'

For the first time he hesitated, fractionally. 'Westminster Bridge,' he said.

'When?'

'Nine o'clock tomorrow morning.' When the busloads of commuters would be travelling in to work. An explosion big enough to rip the bridge apart, probably big enough to tear down part of the Houses of Parliament, Old Scotland Yard and even the Air Ministry building. An explosion big enough to enflame the thousands of blue-caps, marching on Parliament Square for the mid-day rally, to trample aside the police barriers outside ministry buildings alongside Whitehall. An explosion big enough to sweep the General into Downing Street itself. And, with the General, his political committee chairman, Stevens. How long, I wondered, would the General have lasted, once Stevens got his hands on the police and security forces in the country?

'One last thing,' I told Stevens, 'Mr Puskhin seems to have got it into his head that you might have been responsible for his friend Tchaikovsky's death.'

Stevens got to his feet. 'No. That isn't true. Thomas, whatever you now think about me, that isn't true.'

He knew that if he couldn't convince me (or rather Pushkin) of that he wouldn't live the night through. 'As soon as we were sure that Sugden had passed the list to Soviet Military Intelligence, to Tchaikovsky in fact, we made sure that KGB also knew of the existence of the list.'

'You knew that KGB wouldn't approve of handing it over to Mansfield.'

'We wanted them to warn the names on the list. When Mansfield discovered that KGB were helping Red Banner it would give the list more authenticity.'

214

'But Mansfield never was convinced that KGB had tipped off Red Banner,' I said.

Stevens nodded anxiously. 'Because by then, unfortunately, he had decided it was you.'

'All right,' I said, 'so why was Tchaikovsky killed?'

'Don't you see?' In his desperate anxiety to convince me that he wasn't responsible, Stevens gestured almost angrily. 'Don't you see? The KGB believed the list was genuine. They believed Tchaikovsky's contact would supply another copy of the list on demand. But the KGB didn't know who the contact was. There was only one point at which they could break the chain of information – Tchaikovsky.'

'And the KGB contact you used?' I already knew the answer. Koloniev was the hardest of hard-liners in the Soviet Embassy in London. To go to anyone else would have been madness.

Stevens nodded. 'Koloniev, of course.'

I walked to the door. 'Well, maybe you didn't actually draw the string round Tchaikovsky's neck. But you sure as hell pushed his head into the noose. I'm afraid you're just going to have to take your chances with Mr Pushkin.' I opened the bedroom door. Dyson was still against the wall. Pushkin was seated in the armchair opposite.

'I think you should go and have a word with Stevens,' I said to him. 'He's got a story to tell you. You'll have to make up your own mind what you think.'

Pushkin nodded soberly and got up. Handing me the gun he walked into the other room.

I crossed to the phone. 'What did Stevens promise you out of all this?' I asked Dyson as I lifted the receiver. 'Chief of the new English Secret Police?'

Dyson didn't answer. I couldn't blame him for not being in a talkative mood.

I dialled Mansfield's number and when his irritated voice answered told him who was calling.

'For Christ's sake, Hart,' he exploded, 'I've got better things to do than to talk to you. I have to be up in two hours' time because of this bloody Alert.'

'There won't be an Alert,' I said. 'Or at least it won't be exactly as planned. Get someone to get the first edition of this morning's papers. Then ring me back. I'm at Stevens's number.'

I put the phone down and went over and poured myself a drink.

Pushkin was still in the other room with Stevens when Mansfield rang back fifteen minutes later.

'Jesus Christ, Hart,' he said, 'why didn't you say the General had shot himself?'

It was like a dreadful blow to my chest. The nausea swept over me. I could hear Mansfield's voice yelling my name. I could hear the cottage door opening and Dyson's running footsteps and the Jensen starting and crashing through the wooden fence on to the road. It didn't seem to matter.

'Hart,' Mansfield said, as the objects in the pampered room swung back into focus, 'I want the sordid story from the very beginning . . .'

I was putting the phone down as Pushkin came out of the bedroom. He glanced enquiringly towards the wall where Dyson had been propped. I shrugged. 'He'll be picked up,' I said.

Pushkin took the gun I handed him. 'In that case,' he said deliberately, 'we might as well go.'

I glanced briefly at the closed bedroom door and nodded.

The cold air was piercing after the warmth of the cottage. We walked along the dark road towards the car, his heavy shoulders brushing mine at each alternate step.

Chapter 27

They hung around in small bewildered groups, oddly pathetic in their long-peaked blue caps, reading newspapers and listening to transistor radios. On every street corner in Central London they stood gazing aimlessly at the passing traffic like a vast semi-uniformed army of the unemployed.

In the side-streets blue-painted jeeps and lorries parked with unused banners strapped to their sides and the drivers gathered by their vehicles drinking from hip flasks and wondering when they should start for home.

Outside London some road blocks had been lifted when the first news came through, when the leader was seen as a ludicrous cuckolded figure in front-page pictures under headlines that proclaimed: 'Action General storms wife's love-nest.' Then, as later editions carried the news of the General's suicide, his followers began to drift steadily from their posts. Along the roads to London trampled posters and abandoned blue caps lay in the gutters like the detritus of a retreating army.

In midstream it was dark and cold and the spray burst in fine droplets over the tug's bow as we stood watching the lights of Gravesend and Tilbury fall back behind us. The river was opening out now as we passed through Lower Hope Reach into Sea Reach, watching the motor barge with its mass of red warning lights leading our convoy on out towards the open sea.

I stood beside Pushkin in the bow of one of the following tugs, and looked across at the silent river banks from which everybody but the police had been evacuated.

The decision had been taken, after the first inspection, to move the motor barge downriver to open sea. The main detonator had been removed shortly after Special Branch men under Mansfield's control had surrounded the barge in the early hours of the morning and arrested Dyson's men aboard. But the complexity of the secondary detonators offered no real chance of defusing the barge before moving it. And now, manned by two crewmen, a Lieutenant-Commander and Petty Officer of the Royal Naval Bomb Disposal Unit, it chugged on past Shoeburyness towards the open sea.

Leaving Allhallows on the Kent bank behind us it was apparent that the motor barge was pulling away as our own tug's speed slackened until we hove-to. Out here with the sea-birds shrieking round us and sea-tides slapping hard against our sides I began to think of Virginia.

I had tried to see her this afternoon. After a long debriefing session with Mansfield I had driven to Cambridge to find the town, the headquarters of the movement, full of young people in dark sweaters and trousers. But the blue caps and the military gaiters had been thrown away and the ex-soldiers of Action England sat on low walls or jostled and bumped each other along the narrow pavements like disconsolate tourists.

Only outside the General's house was the sense of apathy disputed by a loyal palace guard which kept the press at bay. I was far from anxious to show my face, even less to announce my name to this remnant of the General's followers. Backing the car up quickly I had driven to the nearest phone box.

I suppose I tried for over half an hour dialling and redialling before I got through. Miss Cavendish announced the number.

'Miss Cavendish,' I said quickly, 'this is Tom Hart. Is Lady Deedes there?'

I don't think she knew anything more than the bare newspaper story: that Virginia and I had gone to the cottage together, that the General had found out, and that the press had been there when he had burst in upon us. Humiliated by the whole affair, he had committed suicide. I could tell by her voice that, if she wasn't exactly on my side, she wasn't really against me either.

'Lady Deedes has been in her room all day. I could tell her you're on the line.'

'Do that please, Miss Cavendish. Tell her I desperately want to speak to her.'

'I will. It's been a dreadful day, Mr Hart. Thank God for the men outside; these reporters stop at nothing to interview her.'

'Just tell her I must speak to her, Miss Cavendish.'

'Of course. Just hold the line.'

I stood in the phone box as the minutes ticked past. Twice I fed more coins into the slot. Then I heard the phone being picked up.

'Virginia? . .' I said into the receiver.

There was a moment's silence and again I heard the same sounds of the phone being picked up. Miss Cavendish's voice came on the line and I realised Virginia must be listening on the extension.

'Mr Hart,' Miss Cavendish said carefully, 'I have a message from Lady Deedes. She wanted me to repeat it to you word for word. She says she has no wish to speak to you and – ' her voice faltered a little, ' . . . and will you please not try to contact her again.'

'Put the phone down, Miss Cavendish – I've got the message.' The phone went down but the extension remained open. 'Virginia, I said, 'I won't waste time by saying sorry. But when you begin to pull out of this nightmare for God's sake remember that men aren't just tailors' dummies marked "security", "authority" or "rampant sex", with the price tag neatly filled in underneath. Any loving connection is a messy, confused and sometimes painful business – there's nothing neat and compartmented about it. I'd like to see you find a flesh and blood man, Virginia, and I'd like to see you throw your whole self at him.'

The phone clicked dead. Which is perhaps what the homily deserved. We talk to ourselves through others.

The motor barge with its bright warning lights was about a mile away now and the two crewmen were riding the sea waves towards us in a Zodiac rubber dinghy. Pushkin watched as they were picked up by one of the tugs in the convoy. As the two men clambered over the side of the tug we both looked towards the red-lit motor barge wallowing crewless in the North Sea waves about a mile ahead of us.

It was intensely cold now and flurries of snow swept across the deck of the tug and died in the black water.

After a few moments a Tannoy crackled and a brisk naval voice said: 'Approximately twenty seconds, Gentlemen.'

I lit a cigarette in my cupped hands, turning out of the wind, and saw that Mansfield had joined us in the bow. He had a white polo-neck sweater and reefer jacket and managed to look as if he'd never left the Navy.

'Ten seconds, Gentlemen,' the Tannoy voice said.

Pushkin rubbed his chin, looked across at Mansfield, staring like a self-conscious bulldog out at sea, and smiled.

'Eight seconds,' the voice floated across the water. I caught Pushkin's eye, and in a brief nod he transmitted the acute sense of satisfaction we both felt that somehow we had avoided another Kreshchatik or Leicester Square.

'Five . . . Four . . . Three . . . Two . . . One . . .'

A whole area of sea in front of me seemed to glow like a gigantic light bulb. I gripped the wet iron rail in front of me and braced myself against the splitting double crack that seemed to shatter the air above my head. Then the vast light bulb burst in an ejaculation of orange flame and a low, sinister rumble moved out in a half-circle around us. Flames chased mad patterns around the sky and shrunk fast into the sea. As the deep rumble died away I was aware of the splash of falling debris into the water somewhere in the darkness ahead of us.

Mansfield lit his pipe. 'Take three months' leave, Tom,' he said. 'Be in my office February the fifteenth at ten o'clock. I'll be waiting for you.' He had, of course, grown up on American musicals – but then so had I.

'I wouldn't work for you,' I said, 'if I never play sax again.'

The tug dropped us at Tower Pier. Mansfield tramped off into the darkness with a growled goodnight, and Pushkin and I walked back towards our cars.

Across an ocean of time and place and ideology he jerked his thumb at the silhouetted outline of the Tower of London behind us.

My throat contracted. 'Perhaps,' I said, and he climbed into his car and pulled away.

On a day of snow squalls and biting wind we buried Stevens in the graveyard of Cookham's Norman church. Mansfield stood stiffly in a black overcoat with a velvet collar beside Jazz and myself. We seemed to be the only mourners. Then, as we climbed into our cars, I looked back at a strange hollow thudding. A boy was hurling clods of clay ferociously into the open grave. It was Andrew.

Pushkin I never saw again, nor expected to. Perhaps I heard from him, I'm not really sure. At all events I did receive anonymously a newspaper cutting through the post that spring. It was from the *Herald Tribune* and reported an incident in England. A Russian Embassy military attaché, General L. Koloniev, had been killed in a motorway car crash. The driver of the car, a Mr I. V. Lerontov, a cultural attaché at the Embassy, had miraculously escaped unharmed.

Virginia, nobody in Europe could escape hearing about. It was the biggest wedding of the year, with every detail of last year's events dredged up and re-exposed. It took place in Bavaria, of course, and the new Countess von Arnitz was on record as saying how happy she was that this year's economic conditions in Europe had done so much to reduce the fears and tensions of the past.

That spring I published extracts from a new translation of Turgenev. After careful prompting, the University of Florence decided to offer me a professorship in Russian literature.

The young Italians had never seen anything quite like Jazz. When we strolled across the Ponte Vecchio with my arm round her shoulders or sat for breakfast each morning at Alberto's on the Via Venti Settembre she would respond to their admiration with a total and open delight. Through her eyes and the eyes of Florence I began to see another world.

FRANCIS DURBRIDGE

TIM FRAZER GETS THE MESSAGE

For the city dweller thirsting for a breath of country air, St Bride's guest house, resting in the finest countryside in Wales, was the perfect choice. But for Tim Frazer, the idyllic scenery held a sinister and mysterious message – and one that he was determined to unravel.

Miss Thackery, a British Intelligence agent, had been brutally murdered, and her body dumped in a nearby wood. And among the local people Tim questioned there were one or two who seemed to know rather more about her death than they were letting on . . .

'Francis Durbridge is the original magical mystery man . . . right in the Simenon class'

Sunday Telegraph

CORONET BOOKS

VIRGIL SCOTT & DOMINIC KOSKI

WALK IN

WALK IN — Agency jargon for a volunteer defector of high rank and with key information.

One hot September, Colonel Li, the Chinese Air Attache in Washington, walks in seeking political asylum. He carries vitally important information, but in the new volatile world of international espionage, his chances of survival are slim at best.

First the Agency has been discredited, then the President is faced with cancellation of the crucial visit from the Chinese Premier. The Chinese want Colonel Li dead, so does a high-ranking defector loose in America. Somehow the Agency must keep their walk in alive, in a desperate race to the finish . . .

'A compulsive novel, far and away the most revealing thriller I've read for a long time'
Edinburgh Evening News

CORONET BOOKS

PETER ISRAEL

THE STIFF UPPER LIP

It says Public Relations on the card, but make no mistake —
B. F. Cage is a private eye, California style.

Hard-hitting investigator B. F. Cage was no ordinary
bodyguard. But at six feet seven inches tall, and every inch
packed with muscle, Roscoe Hadley was no ordinary body.
France's number one basketball star, Hadley was a man
with a following. And the following just happened to
include the Mafia.

League-fixing, drugs-running — these days the Mob were
into sporting ventures in a big way. Cage had to keep
ahead of the game. And whatever the game was, it sure the
hell wasn't cricket . . .

CORONET BOOKS

ALSO AVAILABLE IN CORONET

PETER ISRAEL

☐ 24265 5 The French Kiss   95p
☐ 24266 3 The Stiff Upper Lip   95p

WILLIAM McILVANNEY

☐ 23670 1 Laidlaw   85p

FRANCIS DURBRIDGE

☐ 21302 7 A Game of Murder   60p
☐ 22704 4 The Passenger   75p
☐ 25238 3 Tim Frazer Gets The Message   95p

DALLAS BARNES

☐ 24865 3 Badge Of Honour   95p
☐ 21826 6 Yesterday is Dead   95p
☐ 22333 2 See The Woman   95p

VIRGIL SCOTT & DOMINIC KOSKI

☐ 25063 1 Walk In   £1.10

All these books are available at your local bookshop or newsagent, or can be ordered direct from the publisher. Just tick the titles you want and fill in the form below.

Prices and availability subject to change without notice.

CORONET BOOKS, P.O. Box 11, Falmouth, Cornwall.
Please send cheque or postal order, and allow the following for postage and packing:

U.K. – One book 25p plus 10p per copy for each additional book ordered, up to a maximum of £1.05.

B.F.P.O. and **Eire** – 25p for the first book plus 10p per copy for the next 8 books, thereafter 5p per book.

OTHER OVERSEAS CUSTOMERS – 40p for the first book and 12p per copy for each additional book.

Name ....

Address ....

....